T0063182

Invasive Species Part Two

HAUL AWAY TO NANTUCKET

Darlene and Logan Pollock

Order this book online at www.trafford.com
or email orders@trafford.com

Most Trafford titles are also available at major online book retailers.

© Copyright 2014 Darlene and Logan Pollock.
All rights reserved. No part of this publication may be reproduced, stored in a retrieval
system, or transmitted, in any form or by any means, electronic, mechanical, photocopying,
recording, or otherwise, without the written prior permission of the author.

Printed in the United States of America.

ISBN: 978-1-4907-3788-1 (sc)
ISBN: 978-1-4907-3790-4 (hc)
ISBN: 978-1-4907-3789-8 (e)

Library of Congress Control Number: 2014909888

Because of the dynamic nature of the Internet, any web addresses or links contained in
this book may have changed since publication and may no longer be valid. The views
expressed in this work are solely those of the author and do not necessarily reflect the
views of the publisher, and the publisher hereby disclaims any responsibility for them.

Any people depicted in stock imagery provided by Thinkstock are models,
and such images are being used for illustrative purposes only.
Certain stock imagery © Thinkstock.

Trafford rev. 06/02/2014

 www.trafford.com

North America & international
toll-free: 1 888 232 4444 (USA & Canada)
fax: 812 355 4082

FOREWORD

Alexander Bay, New York

It was a cold and cloudy morning in the middle of September. It was barely light when a twenty foot boat could be seen moving slowly up the river. It was an older, flat bottomed, wooden boat of local construction. Its latest coat of paint was gray. A man in a wetsuit tied off to the number two anchor buoy when they stopped. If anybody had been looking that way that early in the morning, they would have seen two men helping each other get into scuba gear. When they had their gear on, they both did a backward roll-off into the cold but still water. After twenty minutes, air bubbles ceased coming to the surface.

An hour and a half after the divers went into the water, a worried wife called the sheriff's department and reported that her husband, a part time diver for that department, had failed to call her after his dive. A half hour later a Sheriff's boat found the gray boat tied to the anchor buoy. By noon there were four boats there but it wasn't until four thirty before they brought up the bodies of the divers.

Invasive Species- Part Two

CHAPTER 1
THIS GREAT BIG WORLD

Larry and Cynthia got to the Tropical Breeze promptly at 1800. A thin black man in a suit greeted them.

"Table for two?"

"We should be meeting a man here. His name is Joe Cole."

"Mister Cole hasn't arrived yet. Would you like to wait at the bar?" he asked.

"Take us to his table, please," Larry requested.

"Certainly sir, right this way."

When they got to the table, the host pulled out the chair for Cynthia.

"Would you like something from the bar?" he asked.

"Trust me on this one, sweetie. We'll both have the Citrus blast," Larry requested.

"Two house specials, very good sir. Kitty will be here shortly," he said.

"Very good," Larry replied then the host bowed and walked away.

"I was afraid they would ask for ID," Cynthia said quietly.

"I joined when I was seventeen and nobody has ever refused me," Larry said.

He took Cindy's hands in his.

"Is there anything I shouldn't ask Mister Cole when he gets here?"

"Other than his favorite position with Misses M, I can't think of anything," Larry quipped.

"Mental note: stay away from Navy guys," Cindy said as she slapped him gently on the cheek.

"I'm the best there is, Baby," Larry said.

"Hence the mental note."

"It was a good dive. You have some stuff worth hanging on to. I know this island on the windward side. We were always finding coins, pieces of glass, stuff like that, all the time. Next time we got a couple weeks, I wanted to check it out. Whadda'ya' think?"

"Sounds like a real Gilhooley. Are you bringing Mister Cole along?"

"What's a Gilhooley without ole Joe?"

"You said he was married twice?"

"He married Bonnie seven years ago. He married Sunny about two and a half years ago. I think my reception hangovers lasted longer than his marriages."

"That's mean,' Cindy said.

"That's fact," Larry countered.

"That's forbidden ground?'

'Tramp all over it as much as you like. It's just not very entertaining," Larry opined.

"It must have been rough."

"An old friend named Buddy Varner had a Chinese wife named Me-Me. They swore out a restraining order against Joe. They had only known Sunny for a month. So much for old friends of twenty years."

A young black woman with her hair tied up, approached, carrying a drink tray. They both looked up at her.

"Two house specials", she said as she set the tray down and set the drinks in front of them. "Mister Cole took the liberty of ordering grouper in brandy sauce. He will be here shortly," she said.

"I hope you like grouper," Larry said.

"It sounds great," Cindy replied.

"Let me know if you want anything else."

"Will do," Larry said.

They tasted their drinks for a few minutes.

"I have heard quite a bit of talk about you two and Misses M."

"Before or after the blow-up?" Larry asked as though he wasn't interested.

"I've probably heard just about every conceivable story about what went on underwater, on the water, behind bedroom doors. The tabloids just went nuts with it."

'I told you everything. I'm only responsible for two out of the five killings," Larry said.

"They make you out as the triggerman for Misses M. Whore master to quite a few more women than Little Karen and Jackie Dunlap."

"I don't know how they came out with that. I'm not the kiss and tell type. I was only there for five days. Who do they think I am, Superman?' he asked rhetorically.

"Perhaps. There was talk going around that those divers you killed were after something on the bottom, so they had to get you and Joe outta' the way. A Month ago two guys tried diving in the same location in scuba gear and they both died. The coroner said that they were overcome by nitrogen narcosis and became confused," Cindy said.

"Obviously they weren't thinking. It would take experienced technical divers to work at that depth. You can't get careless, ever."

"How do you think Mrs. M escaped the federal net? She walked while the other casino owners went to jail," Cindy observed.

"See the congressman she had with her? She knows who to sleep with. Congressional whores don't go down first," Larry stated.

He saw Cindy turn her head.

"Hello people. I hope you haven't waited too long."

"Cindy was just catching me up on some of our acquaintances in Alexander Bay," Larry said.

"That's old hat. I was trying to talk Larry into having you two visiting me at my new place in the Virgin Islands." Joe said as he sat down.

"No virgins with you around," Larry quipped.

"That's crude. Sorry, I can't hit an old navy buddy, Cindy," Joe apologized.

Cindy looked at him.

"It's a bungalow. It has two large bedrooms, eight and a half acres and four hundred feet beachfront. There's plenty of room to do anything."

"You must have robbed a bank," Larry quipped.

"I made a tidy sum when I sold my charter boat and the business. You gotta' see this place!" Joe exclaimed untruthfully.

"It sounds like your marriages. We had better see it before it's gone," Larry joked.

"We'd love to see it," Cindy said.

"Who's watching it while you're here?' Larry asked.

"The housekeeper of the former owners is staying there. She is absolutely trustworthy. I call her every day,' Joe said.

"I wanna' check out some bottom in the windward islands," Larry said.

"Just clearing the paperwork will take six months," Joe said.

"We'll wait until next time. We'll be careful so nobody will think we're looking for anything in particular."

"You're killing me here! I'm offering you paradise and you piss it away. Cindy, how did an intelligent girl like you ever get hooked up with this goofball?"

"I told her my marriage lasted 33 years," Larry said.

'I pitied poor Darla every moment of it," Joe sighed ruefully.

"He pities Mrs. M," Larry quipped.

'She's okay. Enjoying the sun and the fun in Costa Rica," Joe said then he took a drink. "The rumor was that you and her were going up the river big time,' Cindy said.

"We were in security detention for our own protection for a short while. Things will eventually work themselves out in Alexander bay. I wouldn't be surprised if Melissa returns after a while."

"How about Larry's protection?" Cindy asked.

"The rest of the world needs protected from Larry," Joe quipped.

"Cindy was telling me that two guys tried to dive at the SUV location and came up dead," Larry informed him.

"I haven't heard anything about that," Joe said.

"The price of carelessness is death," Cindy said.

"It certainly is," Joe said adding-'That's why I have become a careful man. I let Larry do the wet work."

"Your buddy was always one to show up after the dirty work was done. Agent Smith told me that he was the one to put the handcuffs on her."

"He tell you anything else?" Joe asked.

"She made only one very brief call to Jackie, telling her, in code, to get the Seminole outta' there."

'Yeah, Jackie got clean away. Melissa didn't want the feds tearing her airplane to hell and gone," Joey said.

"Nice aircraft, I can't blame her," Larry said as the waitress showed up with the fish. She left their entrees and took their glasses.

"This is good," Cindy said after a minute.

"When they say brandy sauce, they ain't kiddin'," Larry said.

"You don't get anything like this in Alexander bay," Cindy remarked.

"We were over in Washington, installing this underwater pipeline and Larry killed these halibut for the cook."

Cynthia looked at him.

"Those halibut are big flat fish that swim on the bottom. When we moved around we kicked up the sand and exposed these little crabs which the halibut liked, so they stayed around us divers. The cook said that we could get some nice fish if we speared a couple so the next time I was down I took out my knife and stabbed a couple and brought them up. After that the halibut never came back and I felt bad about it," Larry explained.

"Good old Larry. You can kill two hundred people and think nothing about it. What a humanitarian," Joe joked.

"Halibut never had occasion to piss me off."

"Good thing," Joe said adding-"Remember that ROTC instructor giving that presentation paper at Kent State."

"I liked that presentation. It turned out to be quite enjoyable."

Cindy looked at them quizzically.

"An Arab tried to get in his face," Joe said.

"Usually when they get to the Q&A, I'm ready to leave. The camel jockey started in with the usual shit and the general tells him that we don't cow tow to nobody and fuck his Mohammed then they're rolling around on the floor. We all just watched it. Unusual style for a presentation, but who am I to complain?"

"I remember you hit those four guys and the admiral blew it off."

"I clobbered the three troublemakers and told the fourth guy that my hand was sore."

'You shouldn't do that, nutsy. You remember what happened to Patton."

'I hit enlisted men all the time'

"And what did it get you?' he asked rhetorically.

"A sore hand," Larry shot back.

"I gotta' keep you outta' trouble."

"A neighbor of Scott Peterson is gonna' keep me outta' trouble? Not likely.

Now that you're landed gentry, you'll need a source of income. You ever think about that, Kee-mo-sabi?"

"No, I only think about women," Joe quipped.

"You'll never see her again. Get over it. Move on," Larry said.

'There's a lot of fish in the sea and I'm close to the sea."

"You're also overworking the clichés here," Larry observed.

"Joe, Larry told me that your marriages weren't any great success. I would hate to see you lose your house."

Joe just looked at her.

"She means lose it before we ever see it," Larry said.

"It's in the bag this time. It's in my name only. I'm getting one of those Prenups next time," Joe declared.

"Oh Honeybear, cover your ears! I can't let you hear such foul language," Larry said.

"I hear ya', chief."

"So, I have the gear. You show us where to dive. What's a couple more days in your completely wasted life?' Larry asked.

"We'll have to leave tomorrow," Joe said.

"We're secured for sea, old buddy. Paradise Islands Airways at 0900. Bring anything you want to bring."

"I only got fins and snorkel," Joe said.

"Great, I have a jacket type BCD that will work," Larry informed him.

"Cindy, you gotta' keep him on his medication," Joe quipped.

"I'm giving you a break here, in spite of the fact that you screwed up in the Turks."

"Oh no, I'm paying the airfare here," Joe insisted.

"Alright, I'll prepay and you can pay me back."

"So helpful! Like the guy that straps them into the electric chair," Joe quipped.

"Sweet deal," Cindy said.

Larry turned to her and they locked their lips together.

"MMM mmmm MMM," Larry said as they kissed.

"You're so ornery," Cindy said happily.

"Thank God you haven't seen the things I've seen," Joe said.

After they were done eating, Cindy excused herself and they stood up as she left the table.

"Thousand Island girls! I can't believe it. You gotta' give it up, Old Buddy," Joe said after they sat down.

"It's the only thing I have now," Larry said.

"Look, old guys like us smell bad to young women. It's something in their endocrine system. Honest to God, it keeps older guys from getting the girls."

"Thank God for deodorant and toothpaste," Larry said.

"Even now, do you know how much of the world doesn't have those?" Joe asked rhetorically.

"As surfers say, I'm riding this wave all the way in."

"It's Dumpsville for you. Crash and burn. Don't waste another day on this," Joe insisted.

"Even if it's just one more day, it's still an enjoyable day in the finite number of days left for me."

"Man, you never learn!"

"I have learned. I'm not planning twenty years ahead. Twenty years ago, I couldn't have seen this. I don't wake up in the morning worrying about king and country or taking care of my family. It went down hard for you because it was your whole life. If Cindy leaves, life goes on. This is just a vacation."

"It's not 'if', it's 'when'!" Joe exclaimed.

"Speaking of 'when', how about St. Lucia?"

"I'll have to get back to you on that. I'll get the paperwork done, but I'm not sure about the wet work."

"Fair enough," Larry said.

"Man, I don't understand you."

"It's simple, I'm not gonna' be a miserable old man who sits around drinking beer and muttering about how I got fucked around by life."

"I got the philosophy, Nietzsche," Joe said as Cindy approached.

"What's the discussion?" Cindy asked as they stood up.

"We were talking about future salvage operations in your neck of the woods," Larry lied.

"Well count me out. I'm happy diving here," Cindy said.

They saw Kitty coming.

"I got it...The rest is for you," Joe said as he handed the check holder, with the money, to Kitty.

"Thank you," she said as she took it from him.

After supper, Larry and Cindy returned to their motel room. Cindy turned on the TV to catch the news while Larry made a phone call to the airport. After he was done purchasing the tickets, he sat next to Cindy and put his arm around her.

"What if you get me, you booger?" Cindy asked.

"What do you think about red and white carnations?" Larry asked.

Cindy looked at him puzzled.

"That was the fourth question I asked Darla."

"What were the first three?"

"Democrat or Republican? Do you ride a horse? What is your hat size?"

"What did she answer?"

"Republican. When I was Younger. I have no idea." Larry said.

"You were a fun guy back in those days," she quipped.

"She got two right and she liked the spirit of the fourth question."

"What was that about carnations?"

"For our wedding reception," Larry replied.

"You two just couldn't stop," she remarked.

"Not at that age."

They kissed again and Larry pushed her gently down onto the couch.

"I would have said 'Independent'," Cynthia said softly.

"Oh, you have ruined the mood, Baby."

"For you, is that possible?" she asked softly.

"I always guarantee success," Larry said as he pinned her down with his weight.

The sun shining through the partly opened curtain woke him up. Larry was glad they hit the sack early. He stretched and looked at the clock. The sun was shining on the display so all he could see was that it was six something. He rolled over and saw Cindy's bare back so he began to rub it gently. She sighed softly after a minute.

"You bad," she said.

"I'm the one with the bite. People are gonna' think I don't feed you," Larry joked.

"I'm the one that will get the big, fat belly."

"When Darla was showing, I liked to walk with her. People would look at us. I know they were thinking-'Ha ha, he got her'. That made me feel good," Larry said.

"You're a sick puppy," Cindy said as she rolled over and faced him.

"People change," Larry said as he slid his arm under her neck then he held her for a while. He tried to close his eyes and take a little cat nap. He was certainly enjoying himself, he thought.

Later they got up and showered and packed their things and checked out. It was just past eight when they got to the airfield. Larry bought a locker and put the treasure they found and their spare luggage in it. A commuter plane was towed out onto the runway. Since they hadn't left the country, the baggage check was easy enough. They waited in the loading area until Joe showed up.

"I was afraid you took the boat," Larry said.

"Such a worry wart."

"I'll stop worrying when we get to St. Thomas."

"That's a long trip. What's the deal with Gooney Bird airlines?"

"We get there alive or we get our money back," Larry quipped.

"What if we die of old age?"

"That detour around Cuba eats up an hour and a half so we stop in Puerto Rico," Larry said.

"I know some nice women in Puerto Rico."

"None of them dive and none of them have any money," Larry said.

"Nobody's perfect."

"We don't need any doubtful people like that hanging around," Larry said.

"Darn, no fun this trip," Joe said, adding in Yoda style- 'A bad feeling about this I have."

They watched while the luggage was loaded onto the airplane then a ladder was pushed up to the door and they boarded. There were only twenty passengers for the thirty two seats on the plane. Cindy and Larry tried to sleep as much as they could until the plane landed in Puerto Rico. They had about an hour layover while the plane was refueled and serviced. They were having coffee on the terrace when Larry heard the familiar moan of twin engines on the approach glide. The aircraft flew nearly overhead so the only thing Larry could see was the lines of a Seminole.

"That looks like a Seminole," he said.

"You can see those things anywhere," Joe remarked.

"Yes, I suppose so," Larry said as he watched it touch down a ways past the tower. He could swear there was something familiar about the style of flying. He remembered Jackie saying that she flies the Seminole like wearing a suit. When the plane turned off onto the taxiway, Larry could tell by the tail that it was a Seminole but it was too far away to see the numbers. He decided not to worry about it. Melissa and /or Jackie could have business here after all.

"According to this, it's only another hour and ten minutes to St.Thomas," Cindy said while looking at the schedule.

"Good, I hope the weather holds," Larry said.

"No rain checks. Dive or go home," Joe stated.

"I'll get everything ready when we arrive then we'll get out early tomorrow," Larry said.

"That sounds good," Joe said.

"We'll do some beachcombing."

"Does it look that promising?" Cindy asked.

"I always found something interesting and the water is clear, so the photography is great."

"I hope this isn't a crowded place."

"It never has been," Larry replied.

"We're starting into the tourist season," Joe pointed out.

"So we're guests of yours. What can they say?"

"Let's see-He's too old for her. They start out awful early in the morning. They aren't here for the nightlife," Joe answered.

"So we're atypical tourists. You can tell the locals that we're on our honeymoon," Larry said then he kissed Cindy again.

"We better shove off here, Olson," Joe said then they stood up.

They started walking toward the airport gate.

"Who is Olson," Cindy asked.

"Another one of our more colorful comrades in arms," Larry said.

"Don't worry. You'll never meet him," Joe assured her.

They got on the same airplane and took the same seats that they had before. They regaled each other with stories until the plane landed at the Cyril E. King airport. Since it was a U. S. territory, there was no inspection by customs. When they landed, the air was warm, the sun was shining and there was a nice breeze. An airport van took them and their luggage to Joe's house. Joe insisted on carrying Cindy's bags. A woman who looked half black and about fifty years old opened the door for them.

"Miriam, these are my friends, Cynthia Morrow and Larry Mayer," Joe said.

"Welcome. Mister Joe say you are old friends."

"Yes, we have been friends a long time," Larry said.

"Your room is in the back. On the right, past the bathroom," Joe said, adding-"It smells like supper is ready."

"Near ready, boss," Miriam said.

"Carry on. I'll get these two settled in," Joe said.

After supper, Joe took them to a local dance club. They listened to the music of an American band rock band, Mister Show. None of Joe's buddies showed up, so they left after an hour.

CHAPTER TWO
-CAN THIS BE TRUE?

THE NEXT DAY

While they were at the gas station, a small, white Mercedes sedan pulled up on the other side of the pump. A short Latin fellow who looked somewhat older than them got out and went into the store.

"That's Luis Valero. You remember him from the Dominican Republic?" Joe said before Larry could ask.

"Oh yeah," Larry acknowledged.

"I see him around sometimes."

"What's his gig? Still the CIA?"

"Who knows? Nothing going on here. Maybe he's retired."

Larry just looked at him and said nothing.

"You know how it is. You take most of the shit to the grave with you," Joe said.

Larry had a natural dislike for CIA agents. Their job is to get somebody to sell out their country. Their credibility is zero. A diver must have absolute and complete faith and trust in his comrades. Their philosophy in the CIA is totally different. How could you trust somebody who is looking for people to betray their friends or their country. Larry had no use at all for those kinds of people.

The man came out of the store and began walking toward them while looking at them all the time.

"Senor Cole, it is nice seeing you again. I think I must know this man," he said while smiling at Larry and extending his hand.

"He is Larry Mayer. You met him in the Dominican Republic, I believe."

"Senor Mayer! Yes, of course. I believe I saw you in Grenada as well," he said as they shook hands.

"Yes, I was there," Larry said while trying to look happy.

"You are no longer in the Navy?" he asked.

"A medical problem forced me to retire."

"That is too bad. Our country should mourn the loss, No?"

"It was a good thing while it lasted."

"You are still diving, yes?"

"Just for fun now. Joe invited me here for that reason."

"Excellent. I would be honored to have two fine gentlemen like you for my guests. Could you visit me this afternoon?"

"I have a young lady with me," Larry said.

"Bring her along, of course. I have a large yard. Over a hundred yards long. We shoot our guns there all the time."

"Larry can never resist an invitation to bust some caps," Joe said.

"Good, any time after two o'clock so you can meet my family. You know where it is?" Luis said.

"Yes, we'll be there," Joe said.

"Good, see you later," Luis said then he got in his car.

They watched him drive away.

"Beware of 'spooks' bearing gifts," Larry said.

"We don't call them 'spooks' anymore. Don't you remember all that fuss about Valerie Plame. It hurts their god damn feelings."

"They get paid to get over it."

"Everybody knows Luis. He is well liked here," Joe said.

"Doubtless he knows how to find out everything about us."

When they got home, they had a lunch of Clam chowder.

"Miriam makes the best Clam Chowder," Joe said.

"She looks happy. I guess she really enjoys her work," Larry said.

"She enjoys a little joke. Islanders believe that if a man and woman eat Clam chowder together then the woman will get pregnant."

"I doubt if that has anything to do with it," Cynthia said, smiling.

"A guy named Luis has invited the three of us to visit him this afternoon. Me and Larry have known him in past operations. It should be a real hoot."

"A Navy guy?"

"CIA, a spook," Larry replied.

"That means covert operations I take it," Cindy said.

"That could mean anything from a nice guy to a fuckhead that I wouldn't mind stomping," Larry replied.

"He's okay. Married and has children. You'll love meeting them," Joe assured her.

"How old is his wife?" she asked.

"Twenty nine or thirty, I suppose."

"Hmm, it certainly sounds interesting," Cindy remarked.

After lunch, they went to the boat shop to get their tanks filled. When they came back, they checked out their gear again then Joe drove them to the other side of the island in his old jeep. Luis' house was white stucco with a red tile roof.

"Another guy with ocean front property," Cindy remarked as they got out of the jeep.

"These jokers might have land mines in the front yard," Larry quipped.

"Not if he has children."

They stayed on the coral rock walkway as Joe led the way. Before they got there the door opened and a Latino woman about thirty years old, looked at them.

"Hello Marita. These are my friends, Cindy Morrow and Larry Mayer," Joe said.

"We are expecting you. You are welcome here," she said.

After they entered, Larry noticed a girl, about seven and a boy, about five, playing on the floor.

"This is Violeta and Manuel," Marita said.

The children looked at them for a moment then went back to playing.

"Humberto and Angela would stand for you," Marita explained.

"Let them play. They are so darling," Cindy said, smiling.

"You have children, yes?"

"No, I am not married," Cindy replied.

"A fine looking young woman like you?" Marita asked as she looked at Larry.

"Don't ask him. He still hasn't figured it out," Joe quipped.

Luis came into the room.

"Welcome my friends."

"Luis, this is Senorita Cynthia Morrow."

"It is a pleasure to meet you, Senorita," Luis said, taking her right hand in his.

"It is my pleasure. You have a good family, senor."

"Thank you. That is very kind."

"Not at all," Cindy replied.

"Marita has some tea on the verandah. Perhaps you would like to join her?"

"You are most kind," Cindy replied then she and Marita left the room.

"Angela will join them. She is very much like her mother. Come, let me show you the back of the house."

Luis took them to his gunroom. There was a young man who was thirteen or fourteen years old, looking at a rifle.

"This is my oldest boy, Humberto. Humberto, this is Larry Mayer. I believe you know Senor Cole.

"Hello Humberto," Larry said as they shook hands.

"Pleased to meet you, Senor Mayer," Humberto said.

"Your father tells me that you are a bench shooter."

"Yes, here are some photographs of me." He pointed out some 8x10 photos of him in the padded jacket and the heavy glove.

"That is very impressive," Larry said as he looked at the plaques and trophies displayed.

"These are my three shot groups that have only two holes," he said proudly as he pointed out eight targets which were framed and hanging on the wall.

"Obviously you are a very accomplished marksman," Larry said.

"Thank you. My father tells me that you are a great warrior. What you say means a lot."

"You're too kind," Larry said, smiling.

"We would be honored if you would shoot with us," Luis invited.

"Unfortunately, we didn't bring our arms," Joe said.

"I have an M14, a .223 sporter and a Springfield, Senors" Luis said.

"Let's go bust some caps then," Joe said.

"Excellent, Humberto has already set up some targets. This is his usual practice time."

Larry took the M14 while Joe carried the bandoleer and magazines. Luis helped Humberto carry his things to their target range. When they got to the firing line, there was a ten knot wind blowing from right to left.

14

Humberto loaded his rifle and put on his padded jacket and glove and got into the offhand position. Larry noted that it took him about ten seconds to get off a shot. It took him nearly three minutes to make three shots.

"All three in number one, black," Luis said.

Luis handed Joe a .22 target rifle that looked like the one that Humberto was using. Joe chambered a round, closed the bolt, put it to his shoulder and fired off a round at the target on the left.

"I did not see a hit, senor," Luis said while looking in the telescope.

"The barrel must be bent," Joe quipped.

"Perhaps the wind," Luis suggested.

Joe loaded another round, aimed and fired.

"The fourth black circle. Nine o'clock," Luis said.

"These bullets don't fly straight. You must be running the cheap stuff on us," Joe said as he loaded a third round.

"Perhaps adjust a little more right," Luis suggested.

Joe fired again.

"No hit, Senor Cole."

"Let's try a pistol target at a hundred yards. Three seconds to lock on and shoot," Joe suggested.

"You couldn't do it in boot camp," Larry joked.

"Think so? How about it, Luis?"

"That is hardly fair. Humberto hasn't done that kind of shooting," Larry protested.

"Humberto is accepting of the challenge," Luis said.

"Best shot round. Best of three," Joe said.

"This is friendly shooting. Let's not get down and dirty here," Larry suggested.

"It is alright, Senor. Humberto is a competitive shooter," Luis said.

Luis changed the sight on the .22 rifle while Joe slipped a magazine into the M14. Joe fired three rounds to check the battle sighting. Larry checked the timer which was normally used for rapid fire pistol shooting.

"Okay, go on the bell. No shooting after the horn." Larry said.

"Any time, Chief," Joe said.

Larry hit the button and the bell rang. Joe got it to his shoulder faster than Larry remembered him ever doing it. He got off his shot with a half second to spare.

"Number four ring," Luis said.

Humberto came to the firing line. He looked at his sights then studied the target for a few moments.

"Alright, senor."

Larry hit the button and the bell rang. Humberto shouldered his rifle and tried to steady it. He didn't look too steady as he got off his shot right before the horn.

"White paper," Larry said, looking in the telescope.

Humberto didn't look too happy.

"Okay, Chief," Joe said as he came over to the timer and handed Larry the M14.

Larry checked the safety and checked to see if a round was chambered. He got into position.

"Any time."

When he heard the bell, he brought the rifle to his shoulder and put his finger into the trigger guard and made contact with the trigger when the sights were on target. His finger was slightly off on the trigger but he squeezed it through anyway. The report and the recoil were similar to his M1.

"Maggie's drawers," Joe quipped.

"Number two ring," Luis said.

"Gimme' that. This sucker knows how to cheat," Joe declared as he took the rifle from Larry.

"I just knows how to shoot," Larry said, adding-"Don't get flustered now."

"You just watch that timer."

"Whenever you're ready," Larry said.

Joe set up a hasty sling. Larry didn't think there was time enough to get settled into a sling in this sort of shooting.

"Ready," Joe said.

Larry hit the timer. Joe brought the rifle up a little slower and shouldered it slightly lower. Using a sling can do that Larry thought as Joe got off the shot right at the buzzer.

"White paper," Luis said after the report died away.

"You gotta' be kidding," Joe declared as he took the rifle off his shoulder.

"Just to the left of number four and two inches below center," Luis informed him.

"This rifle must be stringing them out."

"Yeah, sure, it's always the rifle. Let's let it cool down a minute," Larry said.

"That's a dirty bit of cheating," Joe declared.

"NASCAR rules. If it's not specifically forbidden then you can do it," Larry joked as he fixed the sling.

"It's your outfit, Luis," Joe said

"The two minute rule seems to apply here, Senor," Luis said.

"Just a moment to get this sling fixed," Larry said as he reattached it.

"Time's up, Fosdick," Joe declared.

"Not by a long way," Larry declared as he pulled the sling up tight.

Taking his stance and locking his eyes onto the target, he said-"Ready."

Joe hit the button and the bell sounded. Larry brought the rifle butt to his shoulder and lined the sights onto the target. This time his finger was on the trigger perfectly. The usual report and recoil and the bullet was on its way.

"Number one," Luis said.

"God, he's beating me outta' drinks again," Joe griped.

"This is just for fun," Larry reiterated.

"It is a good thing for me and you, Senor Cole," Luis said.

They went to the targets and discussed the shots as they put up new targets.

"You can expect no mercy from Larry," Joe said as they started walking back.

"To do less than your best is to sacrifice the gift, no?" Luis said.

"That is a good philosophy. I usually don't keep score, but I like a good practice," Larry replied.

"What a bozo," Joe quipped.

"Chief, I understand that your friend Cynthia is from the thousand Islands."

"Yes, she is," Larry replied.

"That is, you would say-coincidence. An old friend has a friend who is a Melissa Macklin from that place. You said you were there in August, no?"

"Yes I was.

"I heard that some men got killed. Does this sound like something you know?"

"We gotta' keep on rocking in a free world," Larry remarked.

"This can be a small world sometimes, no?"

"I suppose so," Larry said as they got back to the firing line.

They shot another round with similar results. Humberto was looking unhappy. Larry showed him how to get his rifle up and locked in as they were taught in boot camp. Even though Larry had won, they shot a third round in which Humberto did better than Joe. They shot tin cans off a post and shot at balls rolled on the ground before returning to Luis' house. When they got the rifles put away, Luis invited them to have a drink on the verandah.

"Cindy and Marita must have gotten lost," Larry quipped.

"Women will stay out until the money is gone, no?"

"That's what they think, anyway," Joe said.

"They show you what they have bought and you must smile to make them think they have done well."

"Joe always had a problem with that," Larry said.

"This young woman is not your wife, chief?"

"No, she is just a friend."

"No one would know that she is not your wife. You told me her name once but I have forgotten."

"Darla," Larry said, knowing that he meant his former wife.

"Oh yes. I always thought that was a very pretty name. You lost her two years ago?"

Larry didn't remember ever telling him that.

"Yes, she had a heart problem."

"That was very unfortunate, no?"

"It was hard to take," Larry said.

"I have to take care of some personal business. See you in a minute," Joe said as he stood up.

"Certainly senor," Luis said.

"You have known Senor Cole for a long time, yes?" Luis asked after a minute.

"Since we both enlisted in '74."

"He was a friend to Senor Jones, your intelligence Chief, no?"

"I don't know anything about that," Larry answered truthfully.

"The treasury agents arrested the men that were keeping art and money hid in Florida. I heard that Senor Cole was shot in that place."

"That can't be true. He was as fit as ever when I saw him several months ago in Alexander Bay."

"That was not our operation, of course, but a friend told me that Joe used all his money to pay his debts."

"Joe having debts! What else is new?" Larry asked rhetorically.

"That could be why he was in the thousand Islands, you think?"

"I never asked him why he was there. After two bad marriages, he seemed anxious to latch onto a well off woman like Misses Macklin."

"Life with Misses Macklin would be an easy life, no?"

"I understand that four guys tried it without too much success."

"With you, she would be a good match, you think?"

"That subject certainly never came up," Larry stated while hiding his surprise.

"I suppose it would be hard to leave your house and your family in Ohio."

"As it is now, yes," Larry replied.

They saw Joe returning.

"What is the topic of conversation?" Joe asked as he sat down.

"The women in Alexander Bay," Larry said.

"Thousand Island girls marry Thousand Island guys. Better luck next time, Charlie."

"Melissa's name came up."

"I'm sticking with the local lovelies. Alexander Bay might as well be on the moon."

"He's being sore headed about it, Luis," Larry quipped.

"We say 'God works in mysterious ways'. That is usually the case, no?"

"Most of the time it is men's mysterious ways and they blame it on God afterward," Larry opined.

They talked for another half hour then Cindy and Marita came out.

"Is there any money left in the bank?" Larry joked.

Cynthia bent over and kissed him.

"Just for that you're not getting your present," she said.

"I thought that was it." Larry joked.

She reached into the bag and pulled out a little white box and handed it to him. Larry took off the lid and looked in.

"I'll be darned. It's just like my great grandfather's," Larry said then he showed the horsehead fob to Joe and Luis.

"That is very beautiful and rare," Luis remarked.

"It is real shell. The bridle is gold," Cindy said.

"I didn't think there was another one in the world," Larry said as he took it out of the box. He attached the short end to his button hole and attached the long end inside his pocket.

"That is very stylish, senor," Luis said, adding-"Please join us here."

"That is very kind of you," Cindy said as Larry and Joe turned the chairs around for them.

Marita poured them an island punch then they sat down.

"How did the shooting go?" Cindy asked.

"We had fun," Larry replied.

"With an M14, I'm afraid that your friend is unbeatable, senorita," Luis added.

"I didn't know you had an M14. I thought you had an M1."

"I used an M14 in the Navy," Larry replied.

"Larry tells me that you are going diving later, senorita."

"Yes, it looks like we have a good place to take some pictures in the lagoon."

"Take care when diving here. Divers have been hit by boats and jet skis here," Luis informed them.

It was just after five o'clock when they arrived back at Joe's house. They put on their wet suits and put their gear into the neighbor's boat. Joe piloted the boat out into the lagoon and anchored it there. Larry helped Cindy with her gear then Joe helped Larry put on his gear. When they got in the water, Larry filmed Cindy exploring the bottom. He filmed the schools of fish and a couple of sea turtles. After an hour of diving and filming, they surfaced next to the boat and removed their masks.

"Here, take this," Larry said, handing him the camera.

"I was starting to think the sharks got ya'," Joe said as he took the camera.

"We didn't see any sharks. The water is so clear here," Cindy remarked.

Larry took off her tank and Joe helped her into the boat. Joe took both tanks from Larry and Larry lifted himself into the boat.

"Until recently, sharks were hunted here. The water is clear of algae and silt. No wrecks around here but the reef diving is great," Joe said.

"Super! Let's do it again tomorrow," Cynthia suggested.

"Anything for my Honeybear," Larry agreed.

In the middle of the night, Larry woke up for no reason he could figure out. There was only one window to the room. A hurricane window, and it as way up by the ceiling. He thought he heard someone moving around outside. After a minute he heard someone talking. The way they would talk and pause led him to believe that they were either talking on a phone or a radio. They talked for nearly fifteen minutes then Larry heard nothing after that. Was somebody keeping Joe's house under surveillance, he wondered.

In the morning he got up before Cynthia and he ran into Joe in the kitchen.

"Did you have company last night, after we went to bed?"

Joe just looked at him quizzically.

"I thought I heard someone talking outside of the back bedroom about 0200."

"Oh, that was probably the neighbor's teenagers. They sneak out at night after their parents are asleep," Joe said.

"I thought they were prowlers. That's a good way to get killed."

Shortly after that Cynthia got a phone call from her sister, informing her that her grandmother had taken a turn for the worse and all family members were being summoned. Larry got them back to Florida before noon and got Cindy on flights to Rochester and Watertown. She got back home by dark. Larry took care of business and his daughter picked up him and their gear the next evening at Akron-Canton.

Chapter Three
–Come Fly with Me

Two Weeks Later-

It was three o'clock in the afternoon when the phone rang in the control room. Larry picked up the phone.

"Control room, Mayer," Larry said.

"I'll be at Andrew Paton in one hour," a woman's voice said then the call was disconnected.

"Okay...sure," Larry said to himself as he hung up the phone. He called his shift supervisor and told him that he would have to leave a few minutes early then he left a sticky note for the guy following him. He checked the pilot plant to make sure that everything was ready for the next shift, then he changed his clothes and left.

When he got to the airfield, he went through the gate that said 'pilots and aircraft owners only' and went to the Flight Control. By the clock he was already late.

"Excuse me, has November-7-4-3-1-Zulu landed yet? I am supposed to meet the pilot," Larry said.

The young man looked at him doubtfully then checked the flight plans.

"Here it is. The pilot checked in at 15:40. ETA at 16:15. They should be checking in again any minute for ApCon."

"Can I wait by the fence?" Larry asked.

"They have a hangar spot. You might as well wait out there."

"Very good, thank you," Larry said then he left the office via the backdoor and walked toward the hangar. He knew from his school days that the nearest hangar was for airfield use and the other one was for rental and visiting aircraft. As he walked by the near hangar he saw two men in dungarees removing the upper cowling from an engine. He waved at them and continued on his way. He decided to wait by the door of the rental hangar and hope that Jackie saw him. After a few minutes he saw a Seminole off to the north, flying west. He knew that she was on the first leg of the pattern that would take her south then east then north then west on the final approach for an upwind landing. Since she was out of sight now, he looked into the hangar to see if it was clear. He heard someone coming behind him so he turned around.

"Are you a pilot?" one of the men in dungarees asked.

"In fact I am, but I'm just here to pick up my friend. She'll be landing soon."

"What kinda' airplane?" he asked.

"A Piper Seminole," Larry replied.

"We were told to be ready to tow one in. They don't allow taxiing in the hangars anymore."

"I see," Larry said.

"I seem to remember you from somewhere," he said.

"Perhaps at Akron Fulton. I haven't been here in a while."

"You were picking up an O-360 engine," he recalled.

"Yes, that was about two years ago."

"You were flying that ultralight with a K300 engine and the engine quit on you. You side-slipped it and brought it down on the runway."

"A tense moment or two there," Larry said matter-of-factly.

"I'll bet it was. I'm Bob Beal," he said, holding out his hand.

"Larry Mayer," he said as they shook hands.

"How long have you been flying?"

"Thirty years, on and off. Sometimes just doing my PPL checkout," Larry replied.

"Well if you need anything, let me know," he offered.

"Thanks," Larry said.

They heard the sound of an aircraft engine on the approach glide so they both looked in that direction.

"Whose airplane is that?" Bob asked.

"Melissa Macklin from Alexander Bay, New York. Jackie Dunlap is flying it."

Larry didn't have the opportunity to ask Jackie if she was alone.

"I guess they don't come this way too often."

"No, not too much," Larry said.

Jackie had the flaps down and put the wheels down and floated it down onto the runway perfectly in spite of the twelve knot wind from the west. She taxied right up to the hangar door and shutdown the engines. Larry walked around to the starboard side and waited for her to fill out her log. She looked up at him and gave the signal to tow. He went to the cargo compartment and opened the door and removed her bags and the towbar. He went around front and Bob took the towbar from him. Jackie stayed in the plane while Bob and the other guy towed it into the hangar and turned it around. After they unhooked and left, Jackie opened the door and came out onto the wing. She looked at him for a moment.

"You don't look any worse for the wear. That was a real rough deal."

"It just happens like that," Larry said as he put out his hand.

She put her flight bag on the wing and jumped into his arms.

"I've been worried about you," Larry said as he held onto her.

"You're like a fucking cigarette. I can't stop craving you," Jackie said in his ear.

"I've never heard it quite that way, but let's go with it," Larry said then he kissed her.

After a minute he set her down.

"Where's your boss?" he asked.

"Albany," she replied.

"She doesn't need the plane?"

"She met some friends and flew up with them. I get the benefits for a couple days."

"That sounds like a sweet deal," Larry said.

"That depends on you."

"I'm determined to return the hospitality shown to me. Shall we go" Larry asked.

He grabbed her flight bag and they began walking toward the Flight Control. On the way they picked up her bags.

"I heard that you ran into some rather inhospitable types," Jackie said.

"Apparently I cleaned them out. Once again, the world is safe."

"But for how long," Jackie quipped.

When they got to Flight Control, Jackie settled accounts then they carried her things out to Larry's car. Larry set her things on the back seat then he held the door for her.

"You want to stop anywhere?" Larry asked as she got in his car.

"Straight to your house," Jackie replied.

"Roger that."

Larry turned left onto 59 and headed west.

"When I heard that you killed two guys in scuba gear like they were flies, I couldn't believe it. I guess that everything I heard about you isn't the half of it."

"Dealing with the criminal justice system was the hard part. I never had to do that in the service. Never had to explain why I killed anybody."

"They were trying to kill you. They are fucking bastards. They had it coming."

"Half of the folks in the system are lawyers. You can't believe how hard it is to deal with those types," Larry said.

"They took your money?"

Larry knew she meant the money that Melissa had paid him.

"Yeah, but they gave me some money for catching the bad guys."

"Our hero!" she joked.

"You can't believe how hard that is sometimes."

"You'll have to show me here soon," Jackie said as she put her hand on his leg.

"All those people in Alexander Bay that hate me. I didn't do anything to anybody there. Kurtz or Altieri killed Tim and I killed them when they came after me."

"People get over it after a while. Melissa never had a problem with you," Jackie assured him.

"I heard that the Feds were going after her property."

"They tried, but it didn't work. Melissa has been paying the bills and keeping things running while she's been gone. I wouldn't be surprised if she stops there for a couple days this time."

"My goodness, she doesn't lack for pluck," Larry remarked.

"Me and her say the same thing about you."

"I don't know if I should ask what else is being said about me."

"Who did you dive with?"

"Cindy Morrow," Larry replied.

"That's keepin' it real. What did she say?"

"She said the scandal rags were making me out as the biggest whoremaster in the state. Hitman for Melissa. Any absurd nonsense they could think of."

"What did the Feds tell you?"

"Agent Smith told me that he was the one to put the cuffs on Melissa. He said that she made only one brief phone call which was apparently to you. She told you in jargon to get the Seminole outta' there. They told me that Les Barry cut down one treasury agent and winged another before they took him out. I'm glad that I was in police custody at the time," Larry explained.

"Melissa will walk. Correction, she already has walked. They're making it look hard on her because they're going after the other owners. Don't breathe a word of this to anybody else," Jackie said.

"I'm staying away from Alexander Bay. I don't know nothing about it," Larry stated.

"Any ideas for supper?"

"I was going La Choy tonight. I have a good Daquiri mix with rum."

"That sounds acceptable. When did Cindy leave?"

"Two weeks ago yesterday. I put her on a plane in Sarasota."

"She was getting bored?"

"She seemed to enjoy the diving but all good things must come to an end."

"You find anything interesting?"

"A few things. I'll show you," Larry said.

"Have you flown any since the summer?"

"No, I haven't."

"I could give you a checkout ride in the Seminole. How would you like that?"

"That sounds great. Have you been doing much flying since the crap hit the fan?"

"Not as much as you would think. Melissa has a friend in Costa Rica who flew her down there in a Lear Jet. I picked her up in Puerto Rico. Other than that I have been up in Belleville most of the time."

"Was that on the seventh of this month?" Larry asked.

"In fact it was."

"I thought I saw the plane landing in Puerto Rico."

"It's amazing, all the times I have run into people I know at airports."

"Too bad we didn't meet-up there. What a hoot that would have been," Larry remarked.

"Yes, I'm sure," Jackie agreed.

By the time they got to Larry's house, it had started to drizzle.

"So much for the flying lesson," Larry said.

"It is supposed to clear up by tomorrow," Jackie said.

"Let's hope," Larry said as he grabbed her bags then they headed for the front door. Larry unlocked the door and allowed Jackie to go in first. When he came in with her luggage, the phone rang.

"It always happens this way," he said as he set her bags down and picked up the phone.

"Hello, Mayer residence," Larry said.

There was no answer.

"Hello," Larry repeated then he put the phone down again. "It must be a wrong number."

"So annoying," Jackie said.

"Let's take your stuff upstairs."

"You live alone here?"

"My daughters stop by sometimes. Usually unannounced, but they know the drill," Larry replied.

After helping Jackie get her luggage upstairs, Jackie had to make some phone calls so Larry came down and started to make supper. He added some rum to the strawberry daiquiri mix and had a halfway decent cocktail which he put in the refrigerator. He was still cooking the rice when Jackie came into the kitchen.

"What's the good news?" Larry asked.

"Melissa said you can fly the Seminole back home."

"That sounds like a long walk back," he quipped as Jackie embraced him from behind.

"You can stay as long as you want. How about for the rest of your life?"

"Thousand Island girls just don't seem to have the staying power."

"After all the adventure and excitement, you still sound like an old married man," Jackie observed.

"That occurred to me. Unfortunately shuffleboard isn't especially popular here," he quipped as he turned around. Jackie laid her head on his chest.

"The dinner smells good."

"I put a jug of Strawberry Daquiri in the refrigerator."

"I can hear your heart," she said.

"I'm glad for that."

"Isn't diving hard on your heart."

"I try not to let it hurt me."

"Two guys died trying to dive where you did."

"Cindy told me. You have to know what you're doing at that depth," Larry said.

"What's to see at that depth anyway?" Jackie asked rhetorically.

"There were beautiful naked women swimming around me all the time."

"What did you do about it?"

"Ignored them. I never fool around with women in the water."

"Not what I hear. Ten years ago, my fiance thought he was gonna' teach me to swim by shoving me into a swimming pool. Another guy pulled me out. I beat the living shit outta' him in front of all those people. Sent him to the hospital. Needless to say that was the end of our relationship."

"Assault with bodily harm doesn't sound like love," Larry quipped.

Jackie just looked at him.

"Be assured, when you told me that you didn't like the water and had no interest in diving, I heard you," Larry said.

"So how about the check-out in twin engines?"

"It could be snowing by then," Larry said as Jackie moved her hands under his shirt.

"What do you suggest?" Jackie asked.

"Get the jug outta' the refrigerator and I'll dish up the chow."

"Such a romantic," she said as she removed her hands from under his shirt.

"Romantic is not being in a hurry, I'm told."

After supper, they sat on the couch and watched some of his movies he had from his time in the Navy. Besides Joe, he pointed out some of the other guys he knew in their operations.

After the movies he took her to his safe. He opened the safe and took out an M3A1 submachine gun and set it on the chair.

"A little toy I picked up in Grenada."

"My father had one like that in Korea," Jackie said.

"The DoD checked the serial number and said it came from Vietnam. President Reagan was kind enough to expedite the transfer for me. Here's the things I found in the Keys. I gave half of the stuff to Cindy Morrow," he said as he handed her a cigar box.

28

"Heavier than I thought," Jackie said as she sat down in the swivel chair.

She opened the box and looked inside.

"Wow, it's all coins and jewelry!" she exclaimed as she looked at it.

"This is a gold chain that must have held something valuable. A chain that size would probably be for a bishop's cross. This stuff is more valuable if it's not cleaned up," Larry said, showing her the chain.

She picked up a silver disk and looked at it.

"That's a Silver Re-al. It was made in 1610. The back side is somewhat corroded but there is still plenty of silver there," Larry said as she looked at it.

"Wow, it's so crude looking."

"Yes, they used musket ball molds and flattened them into the blanks with a hammer. When they got to Spain, the coins would be melted and made into proper money," Larry explained.

"Holy cow, that was ten years before the pilgrims!"

"Yeah, the Spanish and Portugese knew where to find the gold. Take anything you want from there," Larry said.

"Oh, this stuff is too valuable."

"Take the Silver Re-al then. I won't send you home empty handed," Larry insisted.

"That's so sweet of you," she said as she put it in her purse.

Larry put the box back in the safe and showed her some other things then showed her the M3A1.

"The treasury guys took my Raven. I thought they were going to take this."

"My father always called that a grease gun," Jackie said.

"That was a common name for them. I have used it several times and it never failed."

They had another drink before going to bed. They stayed under the quilt and stayed warm enough. Once they got started, Jackie seemed to have no end of energy. After they exhausted themselves, they rested.

"Such gentle hands for such terrible work," Jackie said as she held his hand. "Melissa got a report from the FBI. They emphasized how you were knocked into the cold water by men in scuba gear but still managed to kill both of them in less than two minutes."

"You have to be totally ruthless. All you can think about is attacking and killing or you'll never be any good in that job," Larry explained.

"It sounds like James Bond in Thunderball."

"I told you about Pussy Galore in Goldfinger. I also remember two guys behind us had a difference of opinion on whether they were flying Piper Cherokees or Beechcraft Bonanzas. When they came in to land, the piper logo was obvious."

Jackie held him for a few minutes.

"Cindy Morrow took some stuff with her?"

"Yes, that was our agreement. Everybody who was on the bottom gets an equal share."

"Joe too?"

"Joe didn't dive with us in Florida. I don't know if Melissa knows, but Joe was a mole for the treasury guys," Larry informed her.

"Melissa doesn't say anything about it, but I think she was informing for the FBI. I can't figure it any other way but I say nothing about it."

"Joe says she is good friends of some congressmen."

"They were grabbing people left and right. Just sitting up in Belleville wouldn't have stopped them from getting me," Jackie said.

"Did you check Melissa's bags for anything other than dirty socks," Larry quipped.

"You think that didn't occur to me when I was up there?" Jackie asked rhetorically.

Larry figured that Melissa wouldn't endanger Jackie and her aircraft by smuggling like that.

"Melissa is too good of a friend for that. You can bet your life on that," Larry asserted.

"How about Joe?"

"He pulled the old 'recon by fire' on me. He didn't tell me anything about his setting the trap by doing the salvage job. I don't care how treasury guys do things, navy divers have inviolable rules. You don't hold back information, ever," Larry explained.

In the morning, the sun was shining but it was still in the forties. Larry took Jackie to a restaurant for breakfast then he took her to a shopping center. It wasn't really warm enough to go walking in the park. It was nearly noon when they got home. Jackie made a phone call and found out that Melissa was in Alexander Bay. She told Larry that Melissa wished to see him. Melissa had given the okay for him to fly back with Jackie. Jackie checked the weather on his computer then checked the temperature, wind speed and ceiling at Andrew Paton and at several other airports between there and Alexander Bay.

"If we get off the ground by three, we should make it before dark with no trouble," Jackie said.

"How's the fuel situation?"

"I have arranged for them to gas it when they tow it outta' the hangar."

"I didn't know they do that," Larry said.

"They'll do it for extra money."

Jackie used his computer to fill out a flight plan and sent it to the airport. They went over the cockpit and the pilot's checklist again. When they arrived at the airport, they went directly to flight operations. The guy at the desk called out to the hangar then Jackie and Larry left via the back door. They could see the door being opened and the tractor hooked to the towbar as they got there. Larry helped Jackie onto the wing. It only took a few minutes to tow the Seminole out of the hangar far enough for the gas truck to have access to it. Larry loaded their bags and put the tow bar in the luggage compartment while the hangar crew fueled it. Jackie checked to make sure that it was 100 LL Blue. The fuel tanks are in the nacelles, behind both engines, so it took a few minutes. After the fuel truck pulled away, Jackie went behind the seat and allowed Larry to pass. He sat in the pilot's seat. He checked the door pouch to make sure that the air worthiness inspection and other documents were there. He adjusted the seat for himself then plugged in his headset. He checked the master power switch and the other switches indicated on the check list then they went out and did the walk around inspection together. Since everything was satisfactory, they entered the aircraft again and Jackie informed flight ops that they were starting the engines. Larry set the throttle for both engines by pushing the lever forward about half an inch. He pushed the levers for prop and mixture all the way forward. He pressed the switch for the electric fuel pump then pressed the primer, then the starter button for the left engine. The engine turned over twice then roared to life. Jackie had him set the brakes and they waited a few minutes before starting the right engine in the exact same way. While waiting for the engines to warm-up, Jackie explained that baffles had been installed in the engine for cold weather operation. Jackie had him monitor the cylinder head temperatures. When they exceeded eighty degrees, Larry advanced the throttles simultaneously while holding the brakes. With the throttles advanced to 25 inches and 2500rpm, Larry checked the magnetos, ammeters and the vacuum. After a couple minutes the engines were running great and Larry pulled back on the throttle and mixture.

Jackie went over the steering technique since this plane steered from the front wheel and not the back wheel like a Piper Cub. She called flight ops and they gave her clearance for the runway. Larry engaged the steering, let off the brakes and gave it some gas by pushing the throttle and the prop levers forward simultaneously. The plane rolled smoothly enough and the view was much better than in a Cub. Using the rudder pedals and the brakes, he turned to the right and got it straightened up on the runway and stopped. He disengaged the steering, checked the ailerons and rudder again.

"You're looking good. Check your trim and remember, if everything is right, you don't have to pull it into the air," Jackie reminded him.

Larry looked down between the seats and checked the trim, then the flaps and the fuel switches while he was at it.

"Okay, here goes," Larry said.

He simultaneously advanced the throttle and the fuel mixture. The Seminole began rolling forward faster than he thought. 'It's like a horse. I gotta' keep hold of the reins,' he thought.

"Looking good. Keep on it," Jackie said.

Larry looked down at the airspeed for a second. It was nearly seventy five knots. He fought the urge to pull back on the stick. In a few seconds he felt the wheels leave the ground. He glanced down quickly and saw an air speed of eighty knots. They were five or six feet off the ground so he gave the stick a slight back pressure and the nose came up a little so he eased off and let it climb on its own.

"Retract the gear," Jackie said after a few more seconds.

"Oh, right," Larry said as he pulled up on the little knob shaped like a wheel.

The airplane seemed to fly even better and the trim was superb at keeping pressure off the stick and rudder while climbing. At a thousand feet, Jackie instructed him to do a gentle bank and turn to the left and set his course for Alexander Bay, which he did. Even in a climb, the aircraft handled great and didn't seem to lack power or control at any time. When they reached their cruising altitude, Larry set the throttle and prop for 23inches and 2300 rpm and the mixture for 5500 feet.

"That was pretty smooth," Jackie remarked.

"A little smoother than I thought," Larry replied.

"It doesn't try to challenge you. What you see is what you get."

"It doesn't seem to lack for anything. Always sweet," Larry said.

"Melissa had the instrument flying upgraded. We're visual all the way home though."

"Good thing."

"On this course the wind is nearly behind us and it's not enough to worry about. Lake Erie will stay off to our left then we'll be over Lake Ontario for an hour. Let me know if you have any questions."

"Will do," Larry replied.

Jackie took out her phone and started looking at messages. Larry continued holding altitude and course manually for an hour.

"I just received a text from a woman named Shirley Douglas. She said that you would know her as Shirley Stuart."

"I don't remember any Shirley Stuart," Larry said.

"She was on the LHD-4 Boxer with you in '95. She was a helicopter pilot."

"It was a new ship then. There were a lot of pilots coming and going. I just don't remember her," Larry said after a few moments.

Jackie texted her again.

"She said that you would punish the sailors for calling women by their first name," Jackie said after a minute.

"Yes, that's the way it was. With women it was rank and last name. Just asking a woman for her first name could get you put on report. We wore the name tags anyway so that was a no-brainer."

"Any of those women would think you wanted a date," Jackie quipped.

"No dates in those days. Me and Misses Mayer had an agreement, I stay faithful and she let me live."

"I'll bet a lot of men had that agreement," Jackie said.

Jackie texted her again.

"Hoo wee! You were some kinda' trouble maker. She says that you and Joe flew a Cub to Nantucket Island then the ATC told you to gas it and get. You flew out to the CVN-68 and landed on the flight deck. You would have been court martialed but the admiral was your buddy. That's pretty ballsy," Jackie remarked.

"We were engaged in unorthodox operations. We had to be unorthodox in our training. They were mean to us on Nantucket. They made us pay for the gasoline."

"What did they say to you on the carrier?"

"The skipper was slightly perturbed. The admiral got us dinner with the pilots. We took off from the carrier and were back in Rhode Island before dark. A fun day, all in all," Larry replied.

"Shirley says that she lives on Nantucket. She says that if you're ever there, look her up."

"Roger that. Good, I have a friend on Nantucket now. That should save on hotel costs," Larry said.

They talked about just about everything in the hour and a half it took them to reach Alexander Bay. Larry cut back to twenty inches of manifold pressure on the downwind leg. He turned to the left and to the left again and was heading west on the final approach. He gave it twenty degrees on the flaps and lowered the wheels at eighty knots. The Seminole had an even and predictable sink rate and it settled down onto the runway as gentle as a lamb. He taxied it up to the hangar and parked in front of it. Jackie helped him fill in the log book then they got out and removed their bags from the luggage compartment. Larry saw a white Ford Expedition approaching.

"Melissa sent someone to pick us up," Jackie said.

"Super."

"You don't mind sitting in back with the bags?" she asked.

"No problem," Larry replied.

The sun was setting and it would be dark soon, he observed. The expedition pulled up right beside the Seminole. Jackie opened the right rear door and placed their bags on the seat. Larry went around to the left side and got in. Jackie sat on the front seat.

"Take me to Riverside," Jackie said.

"Okay," the driver replied.

All Larry could see was that he had dark hair. On the way, Jackie explained that she was staying at Melissa's place and that he had a room reserved at Schooner Bay. The driver said absolutely nothing. When they got there, the driver carried Jackie's bags into the guest house for her. Darkness was coming on fast. As the driver came back to the car, Larry could not see his face clearly. He drove to Schooner Bay and parked in front. Larry told him that he would get his own bag as the driver opened his door to get out. Larry grabbed his two gear bags and got out.

"Thanks, take care," Larry said before he closed the door.

The driver said nothing, he just drove away. A really friendly fucker, Larry thought as he entered the hotel. He immediately recognized Gloria and gay Raymond at the front desk. They seemed to be having a deep discussion about something before they looked up.

"Good evening, folks. How are you keeping?" Larry asked.

"Very good, Chief, and how is yourself?" Raymond asked.

"I couldn't be better. I understand that Mrs. M has reserved a room for me."

Both Raymond and Gloria looked at the computer.

"I don't see anything. Someone must have forgotten to pass the word along. How about room 63? It is the same wing that you were in before?"

"That sounds great," Larry said.

"Is your car out front?" Raymond asked.

"No, I flew in," Larry said, smiling.

They both looked puzzled for a moment.

"Oh, very good, I'll have Simon get your bags."

Raymond pressed a button on the phone and a bell rang.

"Simon will be here in a moment. Are you diving this week, Chief?" Raymond asked.

"No plans to. I brought no gear," Larry replied.

They both looked at him again.

"I guess the water is pretty cold," Ray said.

"It's always cold on the bottom."

"There still seems to be a lot of interest in diving now."

"I heard about Mann and Truett. That should keep the curious away," Larry opined.

"That big boat at the municipal pier is a diving vessel. They don't say anything to newspapers or TV but that's what they are," Raymond informed him.

A rather tall, skinny fellow about sixteen or seventeen came to the desk.

"Simon, take Mister Mayer and his bags to sixty three," Raymond ordered.

"Thank you," Larry said.

"Let us know if you need anything."

"Will do and thanks again," Larry said then he followed Simon to his room.

Simon opened the door then gave him the card key.

"I guess you don't need to use the air conditioning. Have a nice stay," Simon said as he set his bags down then he left before Larry could tip him.

Larry set his larger bag on the bed and unzipped it. He had only brought two sets of casual clothes, another pair of shoes and a warmer coat. He took out his tooth paste, electric razor and deodorant then he zipped his bag closed and set it next to the night stand. He looked at the hotel directory then he went to the dining room. A young woman, about thirty years old, was at the stand-up desk. Larry was about to walk by her.

"Good evening. May I help you?" she said.

"Good evening. I am Larry Mayer. I am a guest of Melissa Macklin."

"I received no notice of any special guests."

"Well, don't that beat all. If you had been here a couple months ago, you would know who I am. Why don't you call the front desk. They will tell you who I am," Larry said pleasantly enough.

"That will take some time."

"Unfortunately I'm hungry now and I don't feel like a discussion, so I'll go eat while you figure it out," Larry said then he walked past her.

Larry went to the buffet and got some roast beef, mashed potatoes and vegetables. He went to the table by the south wall that he frequented previously. Before he could sit down he saw the same woman approaching with Otto.

"Otto, how's it going guy," Larry said as he extended his hand.

"Hello, Mr. Mayer. Mrs. M knows you're here?" Otto asked as they shook hands.

"Yes, in fact she let me fly her airplane here. Really rolling out the red carpet. Talk about fine style," Larry replied.

"Sharon is sorry for questioning you. As a friend of Mrs. Macklin please consider this your home."

"Thank you, Otto, and your name is Sharon?"

"Sharon Moore," she replied.

"Very good. I'll tell Melissa that you both have been very helpful."

"If there is anything that you need from the bar just let anybody here know," Otto said.

"Certainly and thank you again."

"You're welcome and good evening," Otto said then they both turned and left.

Larry sat down. Otto sure saved the day for her. She's probably worried about losing her job. She wasn't wearing a ring. She probably doesn't dive either, Larry thought as he ate.

After a few minutes, he saw six guys, still wearing their coats, come in and talk to Sharon for a minute then they went to the buffet. The way they act, they aren't townies, Larry thought. Eventually they all sat at the same table and a waitress brought them their drinks on a tray. They didn't look like hunters. Probably with the salvage outfit that Raymond was talking about, Larry thought as he ate. Sometimes one of them would look over at him. If he had been curious enough, he would have went to their table and introduced himself.

When he had finished eating and was drinking his coffee, two older women stopped at his table.

"Well hello there," Larry said as he stood up and smiled at them.

"You remember us from Wally's Woods?" the taller one asked.

"Yes indeed, Kate Smith and Linda Brandt."

"There's nothing wrong with your memory," Kate said, adding "Are you salvage diving?"

"Nobody has said anything about salvage diving. I guess I'm here for my good looks," Larry quipped.

"You're not popular enough for that. Somebody means business…. uh…good seeing you again," Kate said then they continued on their way.

Larry finished his coffee then he went back to his room. It was too cold and too dark to go anywhere. He did his evening walk by walking around the gym then he returned to his room and turned in early. He figured that if Melissa didn't contact him tomorrow, he would have to contact her. He slept well enough.

Chapter Four
-A Boat On A River

Larry sat on the bench and took in the scenery at the marina. It was too early in the morning for anybody to be moving much. He saw a man in a Viking gear jacket who appeared to be in his mid-thirties, dark hair and about 5'9", coming up the boardwalk then he stopped and looked at him.

"I'm Tony Raymer. You're Larry Mayer, I take it?"

"You take it right. How is it that you know me?"

"My friend, Sy Lampert, pointed you out to me. His father knew you apparently."

"I knew Sid Lampert," Larry acknowledged.

"Sy is a good technical diver. He went down the same place you did but came up short because of equipment problems."

"Just as well, there is nothing there that I know of."

"He is still in town. Could you meet him tonight?"

"I'm not really here to dive," Larry said.

"I'm sure that he would like to meet you," Tony said.

"I'm hanging around Schooner Bay. We might run into each other."

"I'm diving this afternoon."

"Good luck to you," Larry said.

"Okay, thanks," Tony said then he waved and went on his way.

These folks aren't too bright, Larry thought. They're chasing after a ghost in two hundred feet of water. He brought back some decent silver and copper coins and some gold objects while not having to go down more than sixty feet. He could spend the rest of his life recovering treasure in the Caribbean, he thought. He was about to get up and leave when he spotted a familiar figure in the distance. Since she was headed his way, he waited.

"Hi, hi, hi," Larry said as he stood up and smiled at her."

"Oh, hello, I didn't get to meet Jackie last night so I missed you. How have you been?" Melissa asked.

"I couldn't be better. Did Jackie tell you that I did my twin engine checkout by flying in here," Larry quipped.

"She checked with me about it when I was in Albany."

"You're right, it's a great plane," Larry said, smiling.

"Is Mister Cole here?"

"I don't think we'll be seeing Joe here anymore."

"It's a little late to be doing anything except hunting," she said.

"Funny you should mention that. A half dozen people have asked me about diving. I brought no gear whatsoever."

"I'm heading down to the boat. Why don't you come with me?"

"Glad to. Thank you," Larry said and they began to walk together.

"I suppose that Miss Morrow told you that two men had tried to scuba dive where the Expedition was and they died."

"Yes, there are many dangers at that depth. Nitrogen narcosis, oxygen poisoning, gas embolism, to name a few. A diver has to know what they're doing."

"You dived with no ill effects," Melissa observed.

"Yes, I have worked at that depth quite a bit."

"What do you think about those divers dying like that?"

"No reason for them to be down there. If the treasury would just tell people that there is nothing down there, then they might save some lives and save the people here some trouble," Larry opined.

"Of course, nobody here is allowed to make any statement whatsoever about any of it," Melissa informed him.

"Yes, I figured that," Larry said as they went up the gangway.

When they went below, Larry saw Cookie making breakfast.

"I'm having an Omelette. Is that okay for you?"

"Certainly," Larry replied.

Melissa made them a cup of coffee while they waited. Larry looked at the local paper until the eggs were ready. Cookie had prepared toast as well.

"How are the eggs," Melissa asked after a minute.

"Great. With cheese, just the way I like it."

"I heard that you did some diving in the Caribbean," she said.

"Five good days underwater. Costs me a fortune though," Larry winked.

"I heard that Mister Cole did considerably better. He bought himself a place in the Virgin Islands."

"He said he made some money by selling his charter business," Larry lied.

"Good for him. I wonder what all the sudden interest is in diving here. Diving around here is pretty lame, I understand."

"I couldn't agree more," he agreed.

"I'll have to ask around. I heard this guy's name is Sy Lampert."

"Yes, he is Sid Lampert's boy."

Melissa looked at him quizzically.

"Sid was one of the most famous commercial divers on the planet. Always a riot with old Sid. I never met his son," Larry informed her.

"Hmm, that sounds interesting. Would you consider doing any diving if Lampert or another outfit asked you?"

"No, I probably wouldn't consider it."

"It's getting too cold?" she asked.

"No, it's always cold on the bottom. There's just nothing there to make it worthwhile."

"Well, I hope you find something worthwhile to do. A lot of the local folks stay clear of here now. I trust that Miss Morrow told you how things went down here?"

"Yes, I pretty much know who hates me. Not that I gave anyone a reason to hate me," Larry said.

"They can hate you because they went to jail and you didn't."

"I suppose so."

"You can stay as long as you want. Do you think you can stay out of trouble?" Melissa quipped.

"I can't get anything accomplished if I'm staying out of trouble."

"That seems to be the way of things," Melissa agreed.

After breakfast, they parted company and Larry went back to his room. He read and watched TV for a while then he got in his sweats and jogged for a while on the indoor track that went around the pool. After taking a shower and getting dressed again, he decided to take a little walk around the place. As he went past the front desk, Gloria told him that there was a message for him. He read it at the desk. It was an invitation for a chili and cracker lunch with Melissa at one thirty. Larry told her to tell Melissa that he could make it for lunch, then he continued on his way.

At one thirty, Larry met Melissa in the private dining room for dinner.

"I hope the chili is right for you," Melissa said as they sat down.

"I'm sure it will be," Larry said as the waitress brought the drinks.

"Mister Lampert called me. They should be out in the channel by now."

"They only have five hours of daylight as it is," Larry remarked.

"He invited you and I to come out and observe."

"Observe what? Them wasting their time?"

"He told me that they're using Desco lightweight suits and heliox, whatever that means."

"More modern gear than I used last time. Heliox is safer for the longer dives but it doesn't eliminate all the problems," Larry informed her.

He was wondering why Melissa was so interested in other people's activities. Especially when the activity was commercial diving, which was not in her line of business at all. Melissa mentioned that she had some Spanish treasure that her father had acquired from an old sponge diver who was a friend of her father's. For nearly forty years it had been illegal for people to have buillion gold, so her father kept it secretly in a wall safe. Even her mother didn't know about it, Melissa claimed.

After dinner, Melissa and Larry got into her SUV.

"You wanna' check out the divers?" she asked.

"We might as well since we're heading in that direction."

Melissa left the parking lot and headed east. When they came to the first light and stopped, Melissa took out her cell phone and checked her messages.

"Sunshine today and tomorrow," she said as the light changed.

"It can't last long."

When they got to the wooden pier, she parked in the gravel parking lot. Although there were no other vehicles in the lot, there was a large white boat anchored out by the buoy. They must have come from somewhere up or downstream, Larry thought as he got out of the Expedition.

"They'll send a boat over here," Melissa said.

Larry saw a camouflaged john boat turned upside down on the grass. He figured it must belong to a duck hunter. As Melissa took out her phone, he noticed a smaller boat moving away from the large one.

"Not the time of year for boating," Larry remarked.

"They're enthusiastic for sure."

Larry wondered if enthusiastic meant determined, like in determined to find some money. The Feds would never allow them to keep such a thing.

"I hope they have all licenses and permits for salvaging."

"Not our problem," Melissa said.

Larry thought it was strange how things turned out to be their problem.

As the boat approached, Larry could see it was an older Bayliner with a big outboard motor. The boat came in right next to the wooden dock and stopped. A young crewman helped Melissa step into the boat. Larry stepped over their gunnel after her.

"You can sit there," the crewman said.

"Very good," Larry said and they sat down.

The driver reversed the engine and backed away from the pier then steered toward the salvage vessel. He brought the Bayliner right up to the stern and the other crewman threw the bow painter to a younger guy on deck and he secured it to a cleat immediately. The crewman told them to go up the ladder. As Melissa went up the ladder, a younger guy extended his hand and helped her aboard. As Larry stepped onto the deck, he thought he saw a face he recognized.

"I'm Sy Lampert," the man said as he extended his hand.

"Larry Mayer," Larry said as he shook his hand.

"My father talked about you."

"You look like your father in his younger days."

"Everyone says that. I'm glad you came. Tony just went down in a Desco lightweight. We have enough Heliox for an hour on the bottom. Brad and/or Mike standby in scuba, also heliox. We don't have enough to keep one of them in the water. Let me show you."

"Certainly," Larry said.

As they walked forward, Larry could see that their boat was well equipped. Sy took them to the Diving Control Room. Larry could see a topographic plot of the bottom. A red dot showed the location of the diver.

"We got a pretty good outfit. I had a problem with freezing on the equalization side of the check valve. As the gas squeezes through, it becomes even colder. We're very close to freezing here since it's freshwater," he explained.

"Did you try a Maris type valve?" Larry asked as Sy handed him the check valve.

"No, Tony went down with a slightly larger DIN valve."

Sy keyed the microphone.

"How's it going, Tony?"

"I have nearly covered B2. Nothing so far."

"Roger that. Keep us informed."

"Ten-Four."

"He must be a cop," Sy quipped.

A man came in. He was wearing an exposure suit over his wet suit and the insulated hood. It was obvious that he was ready for cold water work.

"This is Mike Schaeffer. Mike, this is Larry Mayer," Sy introduced them.

"I have heard of you," Mike said as they shook hands.

"Melissa, this is Mike. Mike, Melissa."

"Hello Melissa. I have heard a lot about you," Mike said as they shook hands.

"You're really getting the short shrift here, Larry," Sy quipped.

"That's okay. I have always operated on the premise that the fewer people who know me, the better," Larry said while smiling.

He noticed that Mike appeared to be in excellent shape and nice looking. He didn't have his eyes glued on Melissa like the young guy on deck.

"My father would say that the sharks will never know the difference."

"No sharks here. You got enough problems," Larry said.

"I'll get ready. See you at the railing," Mike said then he left.

"Time?" Sy asked.

"Thirty six- twenty," the controller called out.

"Temperature and flow?"

"Right on the mark."

"How much line out?"

"Three hundred six."

"How much in the last five minutes?"

"Just a couple feet."

He keyed the mike.

"How's it going, Tony?"

"Okay. I found an old hubcap in the mud. Nothing new."

"Keep us informed."

"Roger that, out."

"Okay Ed, we're going outside," Sy said.

"Roger that", Ed replied.

"We stayed out here last night. The food stinks and the bunks aren't fit for any normal man," Sy said as they walked aft.

Larry knew that when you're diving, the last thing you need is a sore back or anything else messed up because of a lousy bed.

"Where are you docking?" Larry asked.

"The Municipal Pier."

"Some good park benches there," Larry quipped.

"The boat owner is an old friend, so I have made rooms available to them," Melissa informed him.

"That's very thoughtful."

"Hopefully we'll be done here in a few days," Sy said as they came out on the stern.

Two men were helping Mike with his gear. He had a dual tank arrangement held by a frame, like a heavy pack. This required straps over the shoulders as well as the straps around his waist and chest. Fastening and adjusting the straps resulted in bunching the protective suits which required one of his tenders to constantly correct that tendency. When Mike was satisfied with the job, he directed them to put on his fins while he checked his equipment again. When this was done, his tenders put up the hood of his survival suit and taped it to the insulated hood. He had the full-face type black rubber mask with the twist and lock type regulator. In another minute, they had the mask on him but kept the regulator out. Another man, in his mid-twenties, in similar gear came out of a hatchway and looked at them.

"This is Brad Baker. Brad, this is Melissa Macklin and Larry Mayer," Sy said.

"I assume Larry is the man," Brad quipped.

He had to come around some equipment to get to them.

"I have heard of you, Mister Mayer," he said as they shook hands.

"Larry, please," Larry said, smiling.

"I have heard that you're the only one who has been to the bottom of this God forsaken ditch and lived to tell about it."

"I don't know about that," Larry said.

"I knew Mann and Truett. The two guys who died here," he said.

"How did that shake out? Who was tending them?" Larry asked.

"No one, as far as we know. They told some people they were going out, that's it," Brad replied.

"A lot can go wrong. What was in their tanks?"

"Nobody said. At least nobody has ever admitted they know."

"Police don't like to talk about that."

"Mann was a diver for the sheriff's department," Brad said.

"It figures they're tight lipped about it," Larry surmised.

They heard the phone jingle. Sy picked it up.

"Lampert...His exhaust valve...How close to the stage is he?...No, tell him he's gotta' come up, now!"

Sy took his head from the receiver.

"We're bringing him up. Mike, head down. Brad, go in and keep the lines from tangling up here."

They both waved as the tenders inserted their regulators and twisted them into place. One after the other, they entered the water. Mike went straight down while Brad swam just below the surface and pulled the cable that held the diving stage, further away from the taut lifeline. Sy listened on the phone for a minute.

"He complained of a terrible pain in his chest. Now he doesn't answer."

"It sounds like a gas embolism," Larry said.

"Ed, contact EMS," Sy said into the phone.

"What does that mean?" Melissa asked.

"Anything from bad to real bad," Larry said.

It took only a few minutes to get Tony to the surface. Brad and Mike moved him to the side of the vessel and helped lift him out of the water. The tenders laid him on a matt on the deck. It took a minute for one of them to unscrew the clamp ring and remove his helmet. They could see blood coming from his nose and mouth. Larry knew it was real bad. Tony wasn't moving. He silently prayed for God to be merciful but death was a foregone conclusion. Lampert tried to examine him as the tenders silently removed his gear. Mike and Brad came up the ladder and also watched the proceedings silently.

"I'm not getting anything," Sy said desperately as he tried to feel his neck for a pulse.

By the looks of him, Larry figured that his lungs and his heart had burst. He knew the human body can't take much internal/external pressure difference. There was nothing that anybody could do for him. A deckhand informed them that the EMS boat would be there in less than a minute. Sy and another guy tried to clean the blood off of him and remove his diving suit and coveralls. Even if he was in a hospital operating room right now, it probably wouldn't do any good Larry thought as he looked at his unmoving eyes staring up at the sky.

"He's catholic. Somebody give him the last rites," Sy requested.

When nobody else responded, Larry began in a sure and steady tone-

"The lord is my shepherd, I shall not want.

He maketh me to lie down in green pastures.

He leadeth me beside still waters.

He restoreth my soul.

He leadeth me in the paths of righteousness for his name sake.

Yeah, though I walk through the valley of the shadow of the dead, I will fear no evil for thou art with me.

Thy rod and thy staff, they comfort me.

Thou prepareth a table before me in the presence of mine enemies.

Thou annoinest my head with oil

My cup overfloweth.

Surely goodness and mercy will follow me all the days of my life and I will dwell in the house of the Lord forever."

Larry bent over and made the sign of the cross on his forehead.

"In the name of the father and the son and the holy spirit, through this holy unction, may the Lord pardon thee, whatever sins or faults thou hast committed."

Sy closed his eyes with his fingers.

They could do nothing but look at him until they heard the horn of the EMS boat. The crewmen prepared to direct the boat alongside.

When they got the EMS boat tied up, three men came onboard. Two of them began examining Tony while the other one talked to Sy for a minute. With help, they got him onto their gurney and transferred to the EMS boat.

Only a couple minutes had passed between their arrival and departure. Everyone stood at the railing and watched the boat head toward shore.

"Let's secure this gear. You guys can unsuit for now," Sy said in a low voice.

The tenders began helping Brad and Mike remove their gear. Sy went back inside. He had the unpleasant job of telling the owner and Tony's relatives, what happened. Not a job that anyone could envy, Larry thought as he looked at Melissa.

"As soon as Sy can get away, I'll have him get somebody to take us back."

It seemed as though a lot of the men would be willing to do that, Larry thought. The old 'leave the scene' impulse was there for sure. Mike and Brad came over to them.

"This is gonna' be an unhappy boat for a while," Mike said.

"That's a good bet," Larry said.

"Excuse me. You're the owner of the Schooner Bay Hotel?" Brad asked.

"Yes I am," Melissa replied.

"I should imagine that it's much more comfortable than this boat."

"If it's not, then let me know."

"Excuse me, Misses Macklin, would you like me to take you back to your car," the younger deckhand asked.

"Yes, very good of you," Melissa said.

If you can stop staring holes through her, Larry thought.

This way," he said as they headed astern. The Bayliner was still tied up where they left it. They stepped down onto the stern diving platform and the deckhand held her hand as she stepped over the gunwale. Larry, being an ugly old man, was not offered any assistance. The other deckhand untied the painter and shoved them off with the boat hook while the first deckhand started the engine. He took the long way around the diving boat and wasn't in any hurry to get them ashore. At the pier, Larry held the boat while the deckhand helped her ashore.

"Thank you for your help," Melissa said.

"Anytime," he replied.

Larry stepped onto the pier when the deckhand was back on board. He waved as he pulled away with the boat.

Chapter Five
–Forget Me Not

"That little trip wasn't what I expected," Melissa said as she turned toward her SUV.

"Yeah, they got problems," Larry said as they walked to her car.

Melissa didn't say anything as they drove to her house. She parked in back by the guest house and they got out.

"We're going to the projection room. I take it that you've been there before," she said as she opened the back door.

"Yes, Jackie took me down there last time."

"What did you see?"

"A couple of old movies of you and Jackie flying. Your father and her father, those sorts of things."

"My father liked to make movies with that old Bell and Howell camera. Sometimes I see those movies and I want to cry," Melissa confided as she pulled out her key and opened the door.

"It is good to be able to remember the times when we were happy."

"Did you make movies of your family?" Melissa asked as they entered the room. She turned on the light.

"I have several of my children when they were younger, on eight millimeter film. I haven't transferred them to DVD yet."

He followed Melissa to the rack that held the movies. She pulled out the two uppermost discs.

"Are these the ones," she asked.

Larry figured that Jackie had already told her about it.

"Those look like it."

"Don is in this one. Don was my first husband."

"You looked very happy together."

"He wasn't altogether trustworthy," Melissa said as she put the movies back.

You have to be completely honest, up front and above the board before you can fault others for that, Larry thought. She requested that he move the cabinet, so he did. She knelt down and removed a section of the paneling and handed it to Larry. He didn't watch her as she reached into the wall and turned the knob of the safe. She pulled out a heavy sheet metal box and he helped her lift it up and set it on the table.

"It's been quite a while since I opened this box. None of my Husbands knew about it because my father was still alive," Melissa said as she opened the box.

Larry knew to not look too anxious or excited.

"That's quite a trust you're having in me," Larry remarked as he looked at the contents.

"You showed Jackie your treasure. I'm convinced that you keep your hands off other people's money."

"May I?" Larry asked.

"Certainly."

Larry picked up several gold coins and a jeweled cross. He laid them neatly on the table after he looked at them.

"Definitely mid seventeenth century. Do know know where the sponge diver got these?"

"I don't think my father knew."

"If you knew his name, we could find out where he lived and what part of the coast he normally dived," Larry said as he put the pieces back into the box.

"You think it would be quite a find?" Melissa asked.

"If I knew the area, I could try to research it and find out what ships were lost there. The records are incomplete, of course, but sometimes I get lucky."

Larry helped her put the box back into the safe and he moved the stereo cabinet shelf back into place then they went back upstairs.

"Would you like me to take you back to the hotel?"

"To the library if you would," Larry said.

"Okay, I'll be right out," Melissa said.

Larry went out and got into her SUV and waited for her to come out. It took her longer than he thought it would if she just had to use the bathroom.

"Anything interesting at the library?" Melissa asked as she got in on the driver's side.

"Oh, I was just checking out an incident that happened a couple months ago," Larry quipped.

"I think we ran those rascals out of town. We don't need those type around here," she countered as she started up her SUV.

"Certainly not. Let them stay in New York."

"Misses Kellogg is the librarian. Misses Arnold, her mother, was before her and Misses Coffing, her grandmother was before her," Melissa informed her.

"So she should know the library pretty well."

"I doubt if there is a book there that she doesn't know about. She remembers everything. She will ask people if they had a particular book out a couple months ago. I wouldn't let her know too much about you," she suggested.

"I'll try not to," Larry said.

Melissa let him off right at the front door.

"Hopefully you can join me for supper at six. Sy said he would try to be there."

"Yes, that sounds like fun. Thank you."

"You're welcome. Bye."

"Bye," Larry said, waving.

Larry went into the library and went straight to the desk. A young woman, about twenty years old was there.

"Excuse me. I'm looking for Misses Kellogg."

"She is over there at that shelf."

"Thank you," Larry said.

Misses Kellogg is her mother, he thought as he walked over to the woman who was putting books on the shelves.

"Misses Kellogg?" he asked.

"I suppose Sally told you that already, Mister Mayer"

Larry looked at her, puzzled.

"I met you at Wally's Woods," she said.

"I'm sorry. I met so many people, I'm afraid I forgot."

"Well, don't turn this town upside down and expect me to forget you."

"I'll try to avoid doing that this time. I had a local history question and I've been told that you're the person to ask."

"Go ahead," she said.

"Have you ever heard of any wrecks in the river that are worth salvaging?"

"That's not much of a history question. The Madamoiselle de Loire."

"Can you elaborate?"

"A French brig that is supposed to have sank out there in 1786. Supposedly there was quite a fuss about it but the water was too deep to do anything about recovering its cargo in those days."

"Do you have any archived information about it?"

"We have a Watertown crier from 1922 that says we do and two editions of the Bay Evening Post from 1932 that say we do but I'll be darned if I can find it myself and I have looked until I'm blue in the face."

"So the documents are missing. Can I see the newspapers you mentioned?"

"They microfilmed that stuff so I'll have to get it for you."

"Thank you, I appreciate it," Larry said.

"By the by, we have so much written work about you and your... er-uh 'friends' that it would probably break my back to try to lift it," she said as they walked down a stairway.

"My goodness, don't let that happen."

"I happened to see two federal guys carrying stacks of white binders at Hartleys. I found out it was Navy records about you. I would have liked to look in them."

"It's just boring stories now," Larry said as she took the cover off the reading machine.

"All newspapers have been microfilmed and the originals burned. All other documents are original or Xerox copies when the original are in too bad a shape to read...... Let's see here, Watertown Crier, 1922," she said as she looked at the microfilm index for a minute.

"Oh, somebody circled the number-WC203."

She looked at the stacks of microfilm

"Here it is," she said as she pulled it out, adding-"There's probably nine hundred days here so we'll have to go about two thirds of the way through to reach October twentieth," she said as she spun the wheel as fast as she could.

Larry picked up the index and looked at it.

"I'll find the other two articles for you," she said as she slowed down the cranking on the wheel.

Larry wondered why she minded him looking at the microfilm index but he didn't say anything.

"Here it is, October twentieth. The paper was only six pages in those days," she said, adding-"Here's your article."

"Great," Larry said as she got up from the chair.

Larry sat down and read the article. It was only a half of one column and it didn't say anything that would be useful. It did mention that the library had archived the records about the sinking but Larry already knew that those were missing. It also mentioned a Jonas Barnes who claimed that he knew where the wreck was.

"Did you find anything useful, Mister Mayer," Misses Kellogg said as she put her hands on his shoulders.

"A mister Barnes who claimed that he knows where the wreck is. I'll bet I know where Mister Barnes is," Larry said.

"He was Widow Hope's father. Grace Hope is hopelessly senile now. You shouldn't stoop, it hurts your shoulders," she said. She pushed back on the machine and slid a thick book under the front of it.

"How's that?"she asked.

"That should be much better, thanks," he said.

"I'll put in the next microfilm."

Misses Kellogg ejected the Watertown microfilm and inserted the Bay Evening Post one. Again, she turned the wheel until she came to July 14th.

"There you go, the fourteenth and fifteenth," she said.

"Thank you," Larry said.

"Let me know when you are done."

"Will do," Larry said.

These articles were a little longer. Probably the editor requested a 2000 word format for the space available on the page, Larry thought. In the July 14th edition, a man named Teddy Horne claimed that the given location of the wreck was incorrect. He believed that it was actually nearly a quarter mile west of Wally's Woods. Joshua Barnes disagreed with his belief but he wasn't revealing where he thought it was. In the July 15th edition, they repeated that the only known documents were archived in the library. Since there was a large map of the area on the wall, Larry decided that he would check the location. He was looking at the map when Misses Kellogg came down the steps.

"Don't go blind looking at that," she quipped.

"I don't have the local landmarks memorized yet," Larry countered.

"My mother and father knew Mister Horne. They claimed that my grandfather and he were old prohibition buddies. One night when he was drunk, he told my grandfather that the brig had collided with a schooner in bad weather at night. The crew abandoned the brig when it was off the old pier. The brig was waterlogged but it didn't sink until it nearly reached Wally's Woods. The depth is two hundred feet there. It might as well been on the moon until Mister Siebe and Mister Cousteau came along."

"Suitable gear was available before the First World War," Larry added.

"The story goes that the officers and crew were returning to France on a warship but it exploded and burned. It was lost with all hands and the secret of the Madamoiselle de Loire. I remember that from the missing documents."

"So nobody can say what it was carrying?" Larry asked.

"A lot of people claimed they knew. The story was that after the defeat of the French army at Quebec, treasures belonging to the aristocracy were secreted away in churches. The Madamoiselle was sailing along and picking up the treasures that belonged to people back in France."

"They know this for sure?"

"No one knows anything for sure. All the 'official' documents mentioned nothing about treasure," she said.

"No insurance adjustors in those days," Larry quipped.

"You can bet there was plenty of investigation. Why would there be all that fuss about a lackluster, workaday brig like that?"

"There had to be owners," Larry said.

"In fact there were. Five gentlemen from the Loire region bought it shortly after it was launched. I remember reading about it in an unrelated article in True magazine. Being called a gentleman could be dangerous since the French Revolution was starting. Only one survived. A fellow named Charpenter. He died penniless in England. He claimed he had salvage rights worth tens of thousands of pounds."

"You don't have 'True' I take it?"

"I'm afraid not."

"I would have to find that edition and see if they cited any government or insurance records."

"Quite likely the old rules don't apply to wrecks like that," Misses Kellogg speculated.

"Depending on how much it is worth, the fight could go on for years. I am finished with the microfilm. Thank you kindly."

"No problem. I am glad to help a gentleman such as yourself."

"You're too kind. Take care," Larry said.

"You do the same," Misses Kellogg said.

Larry went upstairs and went out onto the street. He decided to go back to the hotel. He zipped up his coat since there was a moderate wind blowing now. He walked across the town square and came to the main street. Walking on the sidewalk, he was surprised to see and familiar face. She stared at him blankly as they approached and stopped a few feet apart.

"I didn't expect to see you here so soon. Correction, I didn't expect to see you here at all."

"The trip was unexpected for me as well," Larry said.

"Everybody knows about you and Cindy," Karen said with more sadness than anything else.

Larry had thought that the trouble and the arrests in her family would be having a negative effect on her life.

"Much less treasure than people seem to think. We had a good week of diving though."

"Some people were very angry with you. I was, but as people said more things which were untrue, I realized that it was all untrue. You would never have allowed it to happen that way if you knew about it."

"I knew nothing about federal agents or illegal activities. I would have never come here if I had known," Larry said.

"Are you salvage diving here?" she asked.

"I have a sneaking feeling that I'll be asked."

"Good luck with that. I gotta' be going."

"Nice seeing you. Give it time, it will work out," Larry said.

"Sa'right," Karen said then she proceeded past him.

In spite of everything that had happened, Larry did hope that Karen would be able to have a life that she would be happy with. As he walked toward the hotel, he thought it was odd that on his first full day there he was having three meals with Melissa. In August, he was there for seven days and had only one meal with her. It couldn't be his good looks or his magnetic personality he thought as he smiled to himself. Up ahead he saw an old, white pick-up truck pull over to the curb and park. An older man got out and put a quarter in the meter. The man looked at him and hesitated as Larry waved.

"Well, hello sailor. New in town?"

"It sure looks like it," Larry replied as he shook hands with Bruno Koslowski.

"Where's your alter ego?"

"Down in the Virgin Islands. He says to hell with all this snow and cold," Larry quipped.

"That'll get here soon enough. Are you diving for that salvage outfit?"

"No, but I was out there earlier with Melissa. They lost a diver so they came in," Larry said.

"Oh my goodness, that's not good. You heard about Bobby Truett and Warren Mann?"

"Yes, Cindy Morrow told me about them."

"This place is losing its appeal for sport diving, don't you think?" Bruno asked.

"The water is too cold for that. What do people think they were up to?"

"That's the official line. They had no gear to suggest that they were searching for wrecks."

"Well, regardless, that's not the kind of publicity that this place needs," Larry said.

"Hunters don't care about the shenanigans underwater. By next year the tourists and the fishermen will be back. Who else has castles in the middle of the river?"

"Yeah, good point," Larry agreed."

"Nice seeing you again, Larry," Bruno said as he stuck out his hand.

"Yes, take care Bruno," Larry said as they shook hands.

Larry continued down the sidewalk. In his experience, castles had always reeked of death and destruction. These were built as a labor of love for wives, sweethearts and children. When these people wanted a cottage for privacy, they built an impenetrable fortress, Larry thought. When he got to Schooner Bay, he went in by the front entrance. Gloria called to him and handed him a message from Melissa. Before he could read the message, he saw a man approaching him. He didn't remember him from the boat or as any of the locals.

"Herr Mayer, I am Gunnar Vissten. I am the new tender," he said in a thick Nordic accent as he held out his hand.

"Hello, I think Sy Lampert brought the boat in. They lost a diver a couple hours ago," Larry said as they shook hands.

"Oh, that is too bad," Gunnar said.

"If you stay around here you should run into Sy and some of the other guys," Larry suggested.

"Very good. I am happy to work with you," he said.

"Yes, it should be fun. See you later."

"Yes, Herr Mayer," he said as they shook hands again.

Larry hadn't signed onto any diving outfit. Lampert hadn't even asked him while he was on their boat. Vissten sounded Norwegian he thought as he walked to the dining room. When he got there, he saw Melissa talking to a waitress.

"Good evening, Larry. I'm glad you could make it."

"It's always a pleasure, Melissa."

"Sy is supposed to be dining with us. He may be held up because he's dealing with the Tony Raymer affair."

"I'm sure it is complicated. Are we waiting for him?"

"No, we'll start," Melissa said and Larry followed her into the private dining room and she closed the door.

"I took the liberty of ordering porterhouse steak, mashed potatoes and steamed vegetables for you. I hope that suits you."

"That suits me fine," Larry said while wondering if she had talked to Cindy.

"Sy and I both like the local fish. I know that some people find fish tiresome. Are the appetizers okay?"

"They look great," Larry said as he took a bowl of mozzarella sticks and a cup of marinara sauce.

"Jackie told me that you don't like beans or eggplant."

"In fact I don't. Where has Jackie got off to?"

"I sent her to Quebec to pick up a diver," Melissa replied.

"Anybody I know?"

"I don't know who they sent. I don't think that Sy even knows."

"Does Sy seem like a secretive fellow to you?" Larry asked.

"He makes no secret of his admiration for you."

"He didn't mention what they were looking for out there."

"The owner is tight lipped. He doesn't want newspaper reporters or TV camera crews out here," Melissa explained.

Larry thought about Jackie flying out to pick up a diver like she had picked him up. He began to wonder how deeply involved Melissa was with the owner. Gretchen brought in the cart with their entrees, drinks and more coffee. Only Melissa spoke to her while she worked, then she left. Melissa asked him about his steak, so he told her that it was fine. Melissa picked up her glass and looked at it.

"This is a local cocktail called a 'dead man's chest'. That's an old sea chanty isn't it?"

Larry was sure that she was subtlely trying to steer the conversation to diving.

"Dead man's Chest is a dry island. The local history records that Captain Teach left forty eight rebellious crewmen there with a bottle of rum. Two weeks later he returned and picked up the fifteen survivors."

"In the meantime, their grievances had been redressed?" Melissa quipped.

"Except for the shortage of rum."

"They were navy guys after all," Melissa observed.

"Not quite regular navy."

"You sound like an old navy guy."

"Everybody says I sound like an old married man."

"Mister Raymer didn't look or sound like an old married man but he came up with blood coming from his nose and mouth," Melissa pointed out.

"All these fun city aspects of living in Alexander Bay."

"Everything will get back to normal here. This is really a fun place," Melissa said.

Larry thought about what he had told Karen about not knowing about the illegal activities.

"Why don't we cut the crap here. I go back for years with Joe but diver's rules aren't broken for any reason." Larry said as he put down his knife and fork and looked at her.

'I have instructions from federal agents to talk to no one."

"I had a top secret security clearance for twenty years. I know how things work," Larry said.

Melissa looked at him as she took a drink of coffee.

"My father had the casino shares. He and four other guys originally put up the money to build it. All of them were legitimate, of course. He gave me the name and phone number of an FBI guy he knew. A couple years after he died, two of the partners began skimming money. I went to the FBI. They arranged a clear channel for me. They told me to take the money and keep feeding the information to them. I didn't know anything about the treasury guys. You heard about the 2.8 million in my car. I didn't know what those guys would do when they found out that their money was on the bottom of the river. Tim said that he knew where it was but I was to claim that he didn't. I caught on real quick that he was involved in a plan to steal the money while it was underwater. When Joe Cole showed up, I thought he was a guy looking to find a gig here. He told me that he had been a navy diver and experienced in salvage work. My contact told me to get him interested in the expedition. They set it up with the EPA to send me letters to make it look like an ordinary salvage job. Joe told me that he knew a diver who was white on white and wouldn't screw over anybody for any reason. You know the rest."

"I found out after the fact that Joe was broke after his second divorce. He was borrowing money from old navy buddies and trying not to pay alimony. An officer we knew hooked him up with a treasury agent in Florida. He was a mole in an art and money transporting racket before he came here. The Feds paid for the charter boat and he got a reward for busting the skimming racket. He got himself a little place in the Virgin Islands but he's gonna' lose that I'll bet," Larry said.

"So you're the only one left standing. Still white on white and still stuck in Boston Mills?"

"A short life and a merry one," Larry quipped.

"What do you think of this diving outfit?"

"What are they after? Joe says they believe that the money wasn't in the SUV. That it is still lying on the bottom of the river, somewhere nearby."

'I assure you that the money came up with the Ford. There was a letter found in an old book, written in French. The letter enquires about a vessel that sank here shortly after the revolutionary war. The vessels cargo came from Versailles. They don't have any cheap stuff in Versailles."

"If you're talking about the Mademoiselle de Loire, there won't be much left of that Louis XIV furniture after two hundred years on the bottom," Larry remarked.

'When Lampert gets here, please don't let on that I told you this."

"We were talking about your father's duck hunting," Larry suggested.

Sure enough, a few minutes later, Sy Lampert came in.

"I'm sorry I'm late. I had to make some phone calls," Sy said as they stood up.

"I'm happy you could make it. I hope your supper isn't cold," Melissa said as they sat down again.

"It looks great. Lousy food on the boat," Sy said then he began eating.

"I wouldn't tolerate lousy food. I would let the owner have an earful," Larry said after a minute.

"Funny you should mention the owner. When I talked to him, he seemed enthusiastic about hiring you."

"Question one-What would he know about me?' Larry asked.

"He knows that you went down in antiquated gear and came up right as rain. My dive was aborted and three other guys died. He thinks you might know what you're doing."

"Question two-What makes him think I came up here to work?"

"He is offering you two thousand dollars for every day you dive and five percent of anything recovered."

"Five percent of river bottom mud. I never heard of a deal like this. Who is this Bozo?"

"He doesn't want his name known. At least not for now."

"Oh gosh, after what happened before? I'm okay with that-Not!"

"He's a Hollywood type," Melissa volunteered.

Larry saw Sy giving her a dirty look.

"Some lowlife producer who is always making people sue him for their money?"

"He has always paid in full before and he's paying all expenses now."

"I can trust the boy of Sidney Lampert, but how am I going to trust somebody who hasn't met me and I don't even know his name?" Larry asked.

"I'll get you a letter of agreement by morning if you like."

"Okay, suppose I bite on this. What makes any reasonable person believe that there is anything down there except worthless junk?" Larry asked.

"I can't answer that question.'

"In that case I'm getting squeamish here,' Larry said.

"The owner heard from a psychic. That's all he could tell me. Psychics usually don't go into much detail as it is," Sy said.

"Ha ha, that's real rich. You certainly inherited your father's sense of humor. I'll tell you what, they have a village idiot named Culley. You'll find him at the bar. If you buy him a beer, he'll draw you a treasure map."

Sy looked at Melissa and they both looked at him.

"Okay, but there's a proviso. When it comes to the gear and the diving, we do things my way. Nobody has ever died when I was diving and we'll keep it that way,' Larry stated.

"I'll have to consult the owner."

"Melissa has internet technology right here," Larry said.

"Do you mind if I use my phone?' Sy asked.

"It doesn't bother me but it's not my place."

"Go ahead," Melissa said.

Sy took out his phone and hit the speed dial. He began texting immediately.

'So, where was I...Oh yeah, Cindy was telling me and Joe about this guy her father knows on the other side who has this piper warrior II for a song. So I was telling Joe that he should get you to let him use your airfield for free and he could fly in those money begetting clients. If they pay six hundred for a boat ride then they'll pay that much for an airplane ride."

"I seldom let even my friends use the airfield and I certainly don't want it as an entry point for tourists. You know what my insurance would be if I went commercial?" Melissa asked.

"Have you ever heard from Joe?"

"Not since the night of August twentieth."

"Yeah, that turned out pretty rough for some people."

"You mean you?' she asked.

'Oh no, I just got wet. Les Barry, agents Rodriguez and Fredericks and Kurtz and Altieri.'

"Turner said that it's never good when you're around," Melissa reflected.

"That's because things were already messed up all to hell when they brought me in," Larry said, smiling.

They finished their supper and were having their dessert when Sy finished texting.

"Good deal. The owner sends his regards and says he is happy to have you aboard. He says we are to modify or utilize any gear or procedures that you indicate. Unfortunately, I forgot to tell you that the owner has a crew filming sometimes. The owner wishes for the filming to continue," Sy explained.

"There goes the nude diving," Larry quipped.

"I'm glad that isn't a problem.'

"I didn't notice them earlier. Tell them to remain unobtrusive and there won't be any problems," Larry said.

"Good, it sounds like everybody is happy."

"Save for the friends of Tony Raymer. How many will be willing to go back to work tomorrow?" Larry asked.

"I don't see any problems with that."

"Alright, I want to check things out then get some underwear and a coverall suit. With any luck I'll be on the bottom by tomorrow afternoon. Have a launch waiting at the pier by 0700 and a car here at my disposal."

"The boat will be ready for you. I'll have to rent another car."

"I'll arrange a hotel courtesy car for you as soon as we leave here," Melissa said.

"Good. Well, I hate to eat and run but I have some things to take care of," Larry said then they stood up.

"Certainly, let's get you a car," Melissa said, so they headed for the front desk.

"So we're chasing ghosts again."

"When they get tired of wasting time and money, they leave. We've been through this before," Melissa said.

"Idiots believe anything."

"A lot of people believe that you guys brought up a boatload of treasure in the Caribbean."

"I showed Jackie. Did she tell you?"

"She said you had a cigar box with silver and copper coins. It doesn't sound like much of a haul."

"I think if we put in some serious time and effort, it would pay out enough to be worthwhile," Larry speculated.

"How about getting help from this outfit?"

"There ain't that much. They would eat our lunch."

"That's certainly the way they work," she said as they got to the desk.

Melissa requested a car key and the young lady gave her a key fob.

Larry knew that it was the type of car with a push button ignition. They went to the back of the hotel where there was a commercial garage with four doors.

"It's not generally known that I keep a couple cars available for guests who flew in."

"Very thoughtful of you," Larry said.

He thought that her father probably did the same thing. Big wigs from New York expect that kind of thing.

Melissa opened the door on the right to reveal a silver-gray Nissan Sentra.

"Alright, a new one! That's what I call hospitality."

"Park it right outside your room. Use it as much as you like. The fob must be inside the car with you or it won't start," Melissa informed him.

Larry got inside and started it up.

"You want a ride around front?"

"No, I'll walk," Melissa said.

"Okay, catch you later," Larry said, then he pulled the car out of the garage and drove it toward the front of the hotel. He didn't make it to his room because he decided to check out the diving store and the Walmart for the things he needed.

When he got to the boat dealer, they told him that they close in twenty minutes. He went downstairs and met the same young woman that he dealt with before. She remembered him and she seemed well informed about what had happened because she treated him like a celebrity. They had dry suit coveralls and the underwear, she informed him because he had mentioned it the last time he was there. They were looking at Maris type valves when the manager told him that the store was closed. The young lady, Stephanie, informed him that Larry was the guy at the Cove a couple months ago. The manager gave him a strange look then he left. Larry learned that the two divers who died before had bought some things there. Larry told her that all he knew of his new employer was that he was some Hollywood type that was looking for treasure and he was determined to make a film of it. Stephanie named a producer who was famous for doing projects like that. When he was satisfied with the things he had picked out, the bill came to more than four hundred dollars. Stephanie said that she had a purchase order number for the salvage outfit, so Larry didn't have to use his bank card. She gave him another business card with her name and phone number and she wrote the date and the place she would be diving in the Keys, on the back. Larry thanked her then he left. If that woman had any doubts about him, Larry couldn't see it, he thought to himself as he drove back to the hotel.

CHAPTER SIX
-DESCENTS AND DARK WATERS

He decided to take the long way around and see who he ran into. As he walked past the bar, he saw Mike, Brad and some other guys from the boat that he didn't know.

"Hi guys. What's going on?"

"We were having a farewell drink for Tony," Brad said.

"Yeah, it gets pretty rough sometimes," Larry said.

"Manolete said it's not a tragedy if you're doing what you love," Mike said.

"I suppose policeman, bridge workers, all those guys have their own philosophy," Larry said.

"Sit down here. It's Sy's tab," Brad said.

Larry took the offered seat.

"You knew Sid senior?" Brad asked.

"Yes, I did."

"I heard a story about a six man Seal team that were unsuccessful at taking out these terrorists, so you went in and blew up the whole damn place," Brad said.

"President Reagan decorated me for that," Larry said.

"You killed two men here a couple months ago. None of us has ever killed a man," Mike said.

"The bitch was having to explain why I did it. I never had to do that in the navy."

"Did you run into your lady friend?"

"No, I ran into a Norwegian named Gunnar Vissten. He claims that he's a tender for someone."

"I never heard of him. What did you think of him?"

"He's Norwegian, he must suck," Larry replied.

For the next half hour they talked about diving then the other guys left, so Larry and Mike took a table. They weren't there long when he saw two women come in the door. Even from that far away he could tell it was Cindy and Sylvia. He didn't say anything until they were nearly next to him.

"These two ladies look like fun dates," Larry remarked as they stood up.

"Excuse me. Do I know you?" Cindy asked.

"You will, Baby," Larry said before embracing her and locking his lips onto hers for a few moments.

"I heard you were holding out on me."

"Holding out on you!" Perish the thought!" Cindy exclaimed as she pushed away from him.

"Oh, Cindy and Sylvia, this is Mike Schaeffer. He's a diver and he's Canadian and he's not married."

"Hi Mike. Nice to meet you," Cindy said as they shook hands.

"Hi Mike," Sylvia said as they shook hands.

"Sit down, please. I know you're here to keep two lonely old guys company."

"Actually I heard you were in town. Surprise, surprise."

"At the request of Misses M. She even sent Jackie in her plane to fetch me."

"First time I ever saw you get free airfare. What's this about holding out on you?"

"Everybody I talked to said that you had a chest of gold and jewels."

"When I came back, I took your advice and showed the box to nobody but Sylvia. When I bought a safe, the rumors became absolutely ridiculous. You were absolutely right about the beggars. You can't believe how many people have asked me for one little dubloon for a keepsake. Everything would have been gone in the first day," Cindy related.

"Tell them you don't give away treasure, you sell treasure. Then ask some outrageous price," Mike suggested.

"God, I love this man," Larry quipped.

"Confused as usual. Brown, at the jewelry store, offered to evaluate the stuff and give me a hundred and ten percent of the listed price."

"There you go, Sylvia. The four of us can plunder the Caribbean. Never have to work an honest day in our lives. What do you think of that?'

"I'm not sure how that fits into the schedule and curriculum of our college?'

"Holy cow, Mike, talk about focus. Where could we ever find two such women again?' Larry asked.

"I heard that a diver died of an embolism. Manny heard it on the police radio. What's the deal?"

"His name was Tony Raymer. His exhaust valve froze on him at two hundred feet. He was on Heliox but he came up too fast. There is always that danger."

Sylvia and Cindy just looked at him for a moment.

"I had worked with him before. In fact, he got me and Brad this job," Mike said.

"Just a bad break perhaps," Larry suggested.

"That makes three dead while trying to do the same thing you did. Who is the next nickel wit?" she asked while looking right at Larry.

He raised his hand and waved his fingers.

"Why did you do such a crazy thing?"

"I get paid to dive, I dive. I considered all the risks, of course."

'When are you going down?'

"Tomorrow afternoon, I hope. I have to check everything first. Don't worry, Mike will be there to help me."

"We have to be going here. You better stay out of trouble. What room are you in?"

"Sixty three," Larry replied.

"Okay, call me before you go down."

"Will do," Larry said as they stood up.

Larry embraced and kissed Cindy. Mike shook Sylvia's hand and they said good-bye.

After the gals left, they sat down again.

"She's your squeeze?" Mike asked.

"A diving buddy and a good girl friend."

"Real good by the looks of it."

"There's the age thing and the four hundred miles apart thing."

"Are you calling her before you go down?"

"When I come up. That way she won't worry because she'll think I haven't gone down yet and I won't worry," Larry replied, adding-"They live with their parents. I'll give you the phone number."

"Thanks, I appreciate that," Mike said, adding-"Where did you go treasure hunting?"

"The Florida Keys. I've known about the place for years. We did some advanced scouting of the area. A four man team could recover enough stuff to make it worthwhile."

"Florida has some pretty restrictive laws. They get half the take. How did you get by that?"

"It was small stuff. Just some silver and copper coins. We split it evenly. I got enough to nearly fill a cigar box. Because of the BP spill, there were state guys and Feds all over the place, but they didn't bother us too much."

"That deal sounds like it's got some possibilities. What are they giving you here?"

"I get paid for every day I dive. I have a proviso that when it comes to diving, things are done my way. I don't want any more guys dying here," Larry explained.

"That works for me."

"I haven't seen much of the bottom here, but what I've seen hasn't had too much mud. Hopefully we can find the wreck without too much trouble."

"The owner doesn't understand the problems. He doesn't know anything about cold water diving."

"He doesn't know what, if anything, is down there. That's what we'll have to determine first," Larry said.

"I don't envy you guys. I just go in when I have to," Mike said.

"Well, somebody has to get the gravy job," Larry said, smiling.

"Pike and Trelleborg should be here tomorrow. They are both Harbor divers. They have done nothing but cold water work."

"They must be young. I never heard of them."

"They're both about thirty. As far as I know, they have only worked in Canada and Iceland," Mike said.

"Good. We're gonna' need some experienced cold water divers. I have a feeling there will be a lotta' hours on the bottom."

"About what you were saying before, you would be willing to cut me in on a treasure hunting deal in Florida?"

"Some planning would have to be done, of course, but I think two couple teams could make out well."

"Definitely something I could consider down the road. I'd better be shoving off here. See you in the morning," Mike said as they stood up.

"Well rested and clear headed," Larry said.

"Roger that."

When Larry got back to his hotel room, he called his oldest daughter and told her that he would be in Alexander Bay at least another two days. His daughter was fully aware of what happened last time and she didn't like it one bit. His grandson had been hit by a car while riding his motorcycle. Thank goodness it was in a parking lot and he wasn't going that fast. The old woman driving the car didn't have a driver's license or proof of insurance. Larry had bought the motorcycle for his grandson, so that was another problem that he had to deal with when he got home. After calling his daughter, he laid down and began reading a diving magazine that Stephanie had given him. He read until he fell asleep.

Larry woke up at 0600. He took a shower and got dressed. He put his underwear and his coveralls in the diving bag. He went to the dining room and had a quick breakfast. He was surprised that he didn't see anybody there at that hour. Not an early rising crew, he thought. He returned to his room and brushed his teeth, then he grabbed his bag and left by the front door.

As he drove through town, he saw that the diving vessel was still at the municipal dock, so he parked in the parking lot and grabbed his bag and walked to the boat. Not many lights were on, but he had no trouble getting up the gangway. He walked around the stern and headed for the control room he had seen yesterday. From the passageway, he could see that there was a light on in there. When he went through the open hatchway, he saw a young man with his feet on the desk, intently studying a crossword puzzle.

"Hi, Sy and the others haven't shown up yet?" Larry said as he set his bag on the only empty space on the table.

"They were having an impromptu wake for Raymer last night. I'm Sparky Sager."

"Sparky is getting some bad connotations these days," Larry said while fully aware that it was an older term for radioman.

"Everybody likes it better than Lexius," he replied.

"I'm Larry Mayer."

"I heard Sy talk about you. We were expecting Sammy Pike and Jans Trelleborg."

"They should be along sometime today, I hear."

"Sy says you're the Chief of the divers."

"That's what we agreed to."

"Commercial divers have egos," Sparky said.

"Tony Raymer didn't have any as far as I could see. Not that it made a lot of difference."

"Sy said that you don't ride anybody too hard anyway."

"I try not to."

"I never did dive. How do you learn all those things you gotta' know?"

"Like what?" Larry asked.

"How do you know if you're too deep?"

"If you start seeing naked women swimming around you, you're too deep."

"Really?" he asked.

Larry nodded his head.

"What would you have done if you were Raymer?"

"Every time I had that problem, I cut a hole in my suit to release the pressure."

"That really works?!" he asked incredulously.

"It always did," Larry replied.

"You have to repair your suit then."

"Or your body. It's a real easy choice when you have to make it."

"You look old enough to know just about everything," he ventured.

"The first thing they taught us is that the price of carelessness is death. A diver thinks about that all the time if he expects to live long."

"That certainly sums it up…"

Sager picked up the phone.

"Venturer Two, Sager….Larry Mayer is here now…No, he's the only one so far…I recorded all the calls…Yes, very good…I'll let him know…Roger/out."

Sparky hung up the phone.

"Sy is coming. He will introduce you to the whole crew. Speech! Speech!" he quipped.

"I'll give them the old General Patton. What will they think of that?"

"You ain't nothing but a god damn coward. I'm gonna' slap your silly damn head off," Sparky said in his best Patton impression.

"That will get their attention."

Larry knew that the important thing was to get their confidence. He must act confident and friendly towards everybody and the apprehension would fade as safe and successful dives were completed. Sy came in a few minutes later.

Sy took him to the suit room and Larry looked at the dry suits that were his size. He picked out a Viking Pro 1000D in red and examined it carefully for nearly a half hour. Every seam and every opening had to be in perfect condition and this one seemed to be. Larry took the Desco lightweight helmet and fastened it to the suit with the neck clamp. Next he fastened the gloves to the tapered cuffs then filled up the suit with air to check for leaks. Everything checked out okay, so he hung up the suit in the locker provided for him and placed the helmet and gloves there as well. He checked the Heliox hose system and the hose connections at the diver's end.

"Everything looks good so far. Is everybody here?"

"Let's go check," Sy replied.

When they came out on deck, most of the crew were there to meet them. Sy began the introductions.

"You have already met Ed, the dive operator and Sparky, our Commo man. This is Ricky Fitz, tender."

"Hi Ricky." Larry said as he shook hands.

"Mark Ayers, tender."

"Hello again," Larry said as they shook hands.

"Honore' St.Martin, Tender."

"You're from Quebec?" Larry asked as they shook hands.

"Certainly," he replied.

"Freddy Fowler, our gas specialist."

"Great, I'm glad you're here," Larry said as they shook hands.

"You have met Brad and Mike of course."

"Hi guys."

"Jean Broughe, motor machinist."

"Hello there," Larry said.

"Paul Bonne, deckhand."

"Hello again," Larry said as he recognized him from the launch.

"Larnce LaBatt."

"The ones that make beer?" Larry quipped as they shook hands.

"Unfortunately, no," he said, also in a French accent.

"Hal, the other deckhand quit last night."

"It shouldn't be too hard to find another one. Everything looks good so far I'm happy to say. I want to have a meeting with the divers, tenders, Eddy and Freddy here then we'll have to discuss where we'll drop anchor," Larry said.

"Very good, we can use the mess if you like," Sy suggested.

"Great, let's move that way," Larry said.

The nine men went down a stairway, or ladder in naval terminology, through a narrow passageway that went past the galley and into the mess, where they met Rook the cook. A short little bald headed guy.

"Wake up and make the coffee," Mark quipped.

"I thought everything was better ashore," Rook said as he wiped off the table.

"We don't happen to be ashore."

"As long as this boat is docked, you're ashore." Rook remarked.

"How can we work with such a non-team player aboard?" Mark said as he poured his coffee.

"Non-team, is that a word?" Rook asked.

"Sure, I just invented it."

"Okay Larry," Sy said.

"The gear that I've seen looks to be suitable for this job. I had some questions about the gas mixtures and the treatment procedures. I see that you have cylinders of helium and oxygen. How long do you think those will last if we have divers making at least four dives of one hour duration per day?"

"The oxygen will definitely be gone in three days at that rate. The helium is lost much more slowly so that won't be any real problem," Freddy replied.

"Can you make any suggestions?" Larry asked.

"I think that trimix would be better suited to this kind of diving."

Larry knew that trimix was becoming a universally accepted gas for deeper diving.

"I concur. When I go down, I would like to try it. Can you modify your equipment to mix it 20/35?"

"I'll have to get a few things ashore, but it shouldn't take more than an hour. I'll use the air compressors and add the helium and oxygen directly from the cylinders."

"Can you dehumidify the air before mixing?"

"Yes, I can dehumidify the air to less than one tenth of one percent. We also have a water heater to heat the gas before sending it down."

"Great, that should help out a lot," Larry said.

"Will the scuba divers be using trimix?" Ricky asked.

"That's a possibility. Let's see how it works out on the bottom," Larry said.

"If there are no more questions, then Freddy, take anybody you need and get the things you need," Sy said.

Everybody got up and left. Eddy, Sy and Larry went to the control room. While Sy and Larry watched, Eddy brought up the computer generated contour map of the bottom.

"Here's the last section Tony searched, B2. He was looking at this section to the west, here, before that," Sy indicated on the map.

"Where is anchor buoy number two?"

"I'll get it," Eddy said as he tapped on computer keys.

He came up with a latitude and longitude to one one hundredth of a second and displayed it as a tiny red triangle on the map. Larry could see that they were still searching close to the place where the Expedition had been sitting on the bottom.

"How fast is the current here," Larry asked.

"Less than half a knot at the surface," Sy replied.

"Hmm, there have been no other wrecks reported here?"

"None known, but sport divers don't go that deep, so who knows."

'Move upstream about half a mile," Larry requested.

Eddy paged eastward frame by frame for nearly a half mile.

"Stop there. What's this? Some kind of an anomaly on the bottom."

"Hard to say. That water is just as deep. It could be a pile of mud. Get us a size on that, Eddy," Sy requested.

Eddy used graphics manipulation to magnify the image, then he stretched a rectangle around it.

"One hundred and two feet by twenty five or twenty six feet."

"That's about what we could expect from a two masted brig of that period."

"It could still be a rock," Sy said.

"So far, all the natural features have run parallel with the channel direction. This is about thirty degrees off of parallel. There are no other features around it. I think this bears investigation," Larry stated.

"What's the depth?"

Eddy placed the little cross right on the feature.

"Two hundred and one, point 2 feet."

"Note the position."

"Got it," Eddy said as it came up on the screen.

Larry knew that it would be automatically sent to the computer on the bridge.

"Okay, as soon as Freddy and the others get back, we'll shove off."

Eddy began whistling the old Hawaiian departure song.

"Let's go see how the others are doing."

"Sure thing," Larry agreed.

They found the divers, tenders and deckhands lounging around on deck.

"It looks like a bunch of scurvy knaves, Chief," Sy quipped.

"You can't be too quick to judge a crew. Usually the hurriers and worriers crap out and the plodders bring home the boat," Larry said.

"My father would say things like that."

"Sid was a hoot and a half. He never lost his cool. Everybody he ever knew, believed in him. That means a lot," Larry said.

"Excuse me, chief," Mark said.

"Yes."

"Everybody is saying that you killed two guys right over there. Is that right?" Mark asked.

"Yes it is."

"There were two of them and they were in scuba gear and they leaped at you from above and knocked you into the water and you still killed them in the dark?"

"Well, in truth the first one hit me unawares and knocked me into the water. The second one came in about ten seconds later, with a spear gun and I had to deal with him too," Larry explained.

"Holy cow, that's an incredible feat," he remarked.

"I have done much better than that, I assure you," Larry said plainly.

"Dad always said you were one crazy son of a sea cook," Sy said.

"He should talk. Who's tending for me?" Larry asked.

"I am," Mark said.

"I chose a Viking Pro 1000D. It's a red one. A Desco lightweight helmet and Havre gloves. I placed the gear in the first locker on the left," Larry explained.

"We have all the adaptors, so the Viking suit is no problem. We are still using the return airline?" Mark asked.

"Yes, that hasn't changed. Freddy will get things rigged up so the Trimix will handle the same as the Heliox."

"Do we have lifelines for Pike and Trelleborg?" Sy asked.

"Yes, we have two more of three hundred and twenty feet and plenty of hose if we need to make up another one. I have no idea what, if any, gear these guys are bringing with them," Ricky replied.

"Good, It sounds like we're as ready as we can be," Sy said.

It took another hour for Freddy to return with the equipment he purchased. While he was rigging it up, Sy piloted the ship to the position that Eddy had logged in earlier. They anchored at the western end of the sonar anomaly that Larry believed to be a wreck. They had dinner as they waited for the gas handling equipment to be assembled. They checked the high velocity water hose since Larry had decided to take it down with him. A new recoilless nozzle was installed. This would make it much easier for the diver to hold it underwater. After an hour of testing, the trimix system appeared to be ready for service. When Larry was satisfied he went into the diver's ready room and put on his thermal underwear and the coveralls. When he came out on deck, Mark had all his gear laid out on the facing bench. Light weight gear is faster and easier to put on, so in ten minutes he was suited up and on the breathing gas. After he stepped onto the stage, the water hose was tied to the stage and his knife was screwed into its sheath. The stage was powered, so it raised him over the bulwark and lowered him into the water with no problem. Since the helmet was equipped with a regulator, constant air adjustment wasn't necessary. Larry kept an eye on the pressure in his drysuit so he didn't get the 'squeeze'. It was a cloudy day so the sunlight didn't penetrate very far. The light green water darkened quickly to black as he descended. He checked his instruments right before he touched the bottom.

"On the bottom," he said.

"Roger that. Equipment check," Eddy said.

"Five by five. I'm moving away from the stage now."

"The ELD is not working."

"I'll release gas if necessary," Larry replied.

"Roger that."

Larry stepped away from the stage and swung the light slowly to the left and right as he slowly advanced. He hadn't gone more than thirty feet when he saw something off to his left. He went that way to investigate. He found a pile of rounded stones and heavy timbers.

"It is definitely a ship. I'm going back to get the hose."

"Release some gas, Chief," Sy requested.

"Roger that," Larry said as he turned the valve to release the breathing gas into the water."

"Okay, we see you," Sy said.

"Stand by for water pressure."

"Roger that," Sy replied.

Larry went to the stage and removed the coil of hose. He uncoiled the hose as he dragged it toward the wreck. He had decided to start clearing the mud at the nearest end, which he believed was the after end.

"Okay, let's have some pressure," he requested.

"Roger that, Chief," Sy replied.

After a few moments, a high velocity stream of water came from the nozzle. Larry directed the jet toward the timbers at the end of the stones. The mud was soft and not more than two inches thick, so it came away fairly easy. He had been at it for nearly twenty minutes when he saw something black in the mud. Figuring that it was a bottle, he backed off somewhat so as not to knock it around with the force of the water. After five minutes, he had two dozen of the bottles exposed.

"I have some bottles here," Larry informed them.

"What do they look like?" Sy asked.

"Black, like a wine bottle but the bottom is rounded."

"We'll send down a basket."

"Put a light on it," Larry requested.

"Roger that."

It took a minute or two before Larry saw a light about twenty feet away. He went to the light and grabbed the basket.

"I got it. Give it some slack."

"Roger that."

Larry took the basket to the wreck and began carefully placing the bottles in the basket. He was able to only get six in.

"Okay, take care up there," Larry said. He steadied the basket so it wouldn't drag on the bottom before lifting up. After it was on its way up, he continued hosing the mud away from the remaining bottles.

"We're sending down a larger basket," Sy informed him after five minutes.

"Knock yourself out," Larry replied.

Sure enough, a few minutes later, he saw a light in the same place. This time they had sent down a much larger basket with dividers. Larry placed the twenty remaining bottles in the basket.

"Take 'er up."

"Roger that."

"I'm returning to the stage."

"Affirmative," Sy replied.

Larry brought the hose with him and returned to the stage. When he got there, he had them pull the hose up first then they brought him up. He could come up much faster than before because the Trimix had a much shorter decompression time. When the stage was on deck, he stepped off and Mark removed his gloves then began to loosen his neck clamp. His face piece was fogging up now but it looked like everybody was there to greet him. They must be happy to see a guy come up alive, he thought. In another minute, Mark removed his helmet.

"How are you feeling, Chief?"

"I gotta' pee," Larry said.

"We'll have you outta' this in a minute," Mark assured him.

"Where's Sy?"

"He went to call the owner."

"He can tell him that he got a diver up and alive," Larry quipped.

"I think it's about the champagne bottles," Mark said as he pulled his suit down off his neck. Larry had to squirm around as he pulled the suit down by both arms.

"Those jokers can buy champagne anywhere," Larry remarked.

"This is some kind that was lost during the French revolution, they think."

Mark pulled the suit below his waist.

"We should drink it and fill the bottles with river water," Larry suggested.

"Perishable goods can fetch a high price. More than a thousand dollars a bottle."

"Who knows if they're not full of river water already?" Larry said as he sat down on the bench.

"I don't know. I'm no expert about that," Mark said as he undid his weighted boots. He pulled on the feet of the diving suit and pulled it off of his legs.

"It's just like a tuxedo. It's always great to get it off," Larry remarked as he stood up.

"I'll secure this gear in the tank room."

"Great, I'll go change in the ready room," Larry said.

Larry went to the diver's ready room and stripped off his coveralls and underwear. He took a shower and dried himself quickly with a towel. He put on his work clothes and jacket then went back out on deck.

"Sy is in the control room," Brad informed him.

"I hope he's checking on supper."

"Probably drinking all that champagne," Brad said as he hosed down his wet suit.

Larry didn't meet anybody else on his way to the control room. When he got there, Sy was looking at the diving log.

"I need to use the phone."

"Use the one next to Eddy if you like," Sy said.

"Thank you," Larry said.

He picked up the phone and dialed Cindy's number.

"Hello Cindy.....I'm just checking in, Honey bear.....No, I've been down already....Sorry, it slipped my mind....I may not be ashore tonight....I'll let you know if the plans change....Sure, everything is going great....No, we won't dive at night....I'll keep you posted......Okay, kissy bye-bye."

"I got a call informing us that Pike and Trelleborg are on the way," Sy informed him as he hung up the phone.

"Good, I've never heard of them. I want to find out what depths they have worked at."

For several minutes, Sy looked at a document consisting of about ten pages stapled together.

"What ship do you think this is?" Sy asked.

"The brig Madamoiselle de Loire," Larry answered.

"Not according to the owner."

"Screw him! I never saw him on the bottom," Larry stated.

"If those bottles contain the champagne that we think, then this is already quite a find."

"Until one is opened, how do we know it's not river water?" Larry asked.

"The hydrostatic pressure would hold the corks in tightly."

"You hope. Let's open one and see," Larry suggested.

"Those bottles could be worth thousands of dollars. The cold water should have preserved the champagne just as it was."

"Does the owner have any idea what else the brig was carrying?"

"All he was told is that there is a wreck which has some sort of treasure," Sy replied.

"That's pretty sketchy information for an outfit of this size," Larry remarked.

In fact it was no information at all. He had acted on a hunch he had from the information that Misses Kellogg had helped him obtain. Otherwise they would be nearly a half mile away and without a clue.

They heard a boat's horn.

"That's probably them," Sy said.

Sy went to greet them while Larry stayed in the control room.

Are you going ashore?" Eddy asked.

"I may sleep aboard tonight."

"It sounds like you have a woman waiting for you ashore."

"She is busy tonight," Larry said.

"There's more comfortable places to sleep."

"I was in the Navy for twenty two years, so I wholeheartedly agree."

"If the new divers sleep aboard, it could start getting crowded. At least six could go ashore in the Bayliner."

"Save Rook some trouble anyway," Larry quipped.

"He gets it right half the time. He is Sy's buddy."

"I hope he got it right tonight. I'm getting hungry."

They heard talking outside, and looked toward the hatchway. Sy came in, followed by two other guys.

"This is our control room. I don't think you have met Larry Mayer and Eddy Murphy, our diving operator."

"I have heard of you. Nice to meet you. I am Sammy Pike," one of the men said in a Yorkshire accent as they shook hands.

"Nice to meet you, Sammy," Larry said.

Sammy couldn't be more than thirty and only about five feet, eight inches tall with black hair in a crew cut.

"This is Jans Trelleborg," Sy said.

"It is a pleasure to meet you, Herr Mayer," he said as they shook hands. Jans was in his mid-thirties, blonde haired and almost the exact height and weight as himself, Larry thought.

"Are you from Iceland?"

"I spent a great deal of time in Iceland. I am from Denmark," Jans answered.

"They brought their own gear. I told them that we changed our gas to Trimix. Here is our control and communication center. You can see the topographic plot of the bottom. This anomaly is the wreck," Sy pointed out.

"The depth is two hundred feet," Jans observed.

"Have you done much work at that depth?" Larry asked.

"Yes, I have worked at that depth. Most of the work was at much shallower depth of course," Trelleborg replied.

"How long have you known each other?" Larry asked.

"Six years. We first worked together on a wreck in the Faeroes," Sammy replied.

"Good, we need experienced cold water guys. With this Trimix gas and proper suiting, I was on the bottom for an hour," Larry explained.

"We both brought a light weight suit," Pike informed him.

"Good, I believe that the ship spikes can be a problem. A lot of the wood is still in good shape so we'll have to be careful," Larry said.

"The tenders have brought all your gear aboard. Let's go see what Rook has cooked up," Sy said.

"I hope your galley can accommodate us," Jans said.

"That will be no problem. Some of the guys have gone ashore."

When they got to the galley, half the crew was there. Rook had pizza on the counter and he was dishing up stew.

"It looks good, Rook. This is Jans and Sammy," Sy said by way of an introduction.

"Hello guys. There's plenty here for you. The loudmouths went ashore," Rook said.

"Misses Macklin, at Schooner Bay hotel, has set aside some rooms to accommodate the crewmen when they are ashore," Sy explained.

"I see. I was told that you have a room ashore, Herr Mayer," Jans said.

"Yes, I do. Melissa arranged it before I arrived. I was planning on sleeping aboard tonight," Larry said as he took a bowl of stew.

"Yes, if we wish to sleep ashore, this can be arranged?" Jans asked.

"Certainly," Sy replied.

They sat down at the big table, which was the only table in the galley/mess room.

"So, where were you guys before you came here," Larry asked after a minute.

"I was raising a barge in Quebec," Sammy replied.

"How was the water?" Larry asked.

"Murky and cold. A lot of mud on the bottom."

"I had a job in Montreal. We were rebuilding a pier. There was much work with concrete on the bottom. Assembling forms and handling the hose."

"I suppose that the water was also cloudy while working on the bottom," Larry said.

"Sometimes and sometimes not," Jans replied.

"The mud isn't too thick or too persistent here. As you saw, there is a relatively large area to cover. I started at what I believe to be the stern," Larry explained.

"I understand that Tony Raymer died while diving here yesterday," Jans said.

"He had a serious gas embolism when his exhaust valve froze on him," Sy explained.

Jans looked at Larry.

"Since yesterday evening, I have been given the last word on divers and diving. No one has ever died while diving with me," Larry said.

"That is good to know, Herr Mayer."

They discussed bunking arrangements and assigned tenders for the new divers. Larry informed them that they would be diving in the morning if there were no problems. After all the details had been worked out, everyone left the mess room. Larry had been given the captain's 'action quarters' just aft of the bridge. Since the vessel was at anchor, it would be quiet enough at night. After taking his things to his quarters, Larry ran into a man with a camera on the bridge.

"Hi, you're one of the cameramen?" Larry asked.

"I'm the only one now," he replied.

"I'm Larry Mayer."

"I'm Paul Tyler," he said as they shook hands.

"I didn't notice you earlier when I was diving."

"I got some footage of you going down and coming up."

"I hope you got my good side," Larry quipped.

"For five years I was a cameraman for a sports magazine. You couldn't believe how many times I heard that," Paul said.

"Have you done any underwater work?"

"No, I never worked underwater. I guess they'll get one of you guys to do that," he replied.

"That sounds like fun. Where do you bunk?"

"I go ashore every night so I can process and edit the film."

"Good deal. We'll be seeing you tomorrow?"

"What time?"

"One of the new guys will start suiting up around 8:00," Larry said.

"Alright, I'll be here by then," Paul said.

"Okay, see you in the morning," Larry said then he returned to his quarters.

Sy came to see him before he turned in for the night. He requested that he say nothing to anyone ashore about their operation. Larry mentioned some minor problems that he thought they might encounter then Sy left. Larry slept well enough and his quarters weren't cold.

Larry woke up at 6:30 and got dressed. He went to the crew's mess and found Rook making pancakes. In a few minutes Rook put three on a plate and brought them to the table for Larry.

"They look great," Larry said as he put syrup on the pancakes.

"Enjoy the peace and quiet before the whiners get here," Rook said.

"When our children were little, Darla and I would get up early to enjoy the quiet."

"How long were you in the navy?"

"Twenty two years."

"No quiet on those ships either?" Rook asked.

"Submarines are okay. There is always something happening on ships."

"How many kids did you have?"

"Four," Larry replied.

"My marriage didn't last long enough to have kids."

"I thought Sammy and Jans would be up by now."

"I guess they're not very excited about the dive," Rook quipped.

"Cold, dark water will do that," Larry countered.

"In a couple months it will be frozen."

"That will be the end of diving until next year."

"I hear that they do a lot of fishing here."

"The charters can get five or six months a year. Everybody else fishes all year round," Larry replied.

"Finish this statement-'Give a man a fish and he eats for a day'."

"Teach a man to vote for Democrats and he eats everyday on the public dime and forgets about fishing," Larry said.

"That's better than mine. 'Teach a man to fish then the government tells him that he can't fish and puts him on welfare'."

"There isn't much difference. The end result is the same."

When Larry finished his breakfast, he went to the diving control room. Eddy and Sparky were both there.

"You guys staying out of trouble?" Larry asked as he entered.

"We decided to follow your example," Eddy quipped.

"Good, we need people who know what they're doing," Larry countered.

"Sy should be coming in with Pike and Trelleborg in another half hour. He wanted you to check these gas tables and the reserves available," Eddy said as he handed him the binder.

"That sounds like a job for him and Freddy," Larry said as he took the binder from him.

He had nearly finished when Sy, Jans and Sammy came in.

"Good morning. What do you think, Chief," Sy said.

"Freddy has been getting it right the first time. That is good to know when you're on the bottom."

"Sammy is going down first. What do you have for them?"

"I made a drawing from what I remember of this end of the wreck. I can't emphasize enough that the wood is still preserved pretty well so there is a danger from spikes. Now, the ballast stones are covered by mud so there's no telling what's there without moving them. So far, everything I have found is in this area, which I am certain is the stern. We might as well continue searching here today. Try to remember the location of everything you find. Any questions?"

"There is probably a lot of glass objects. Let's try to recover them intact. Okay Sammy, Ricky has you ready to go," Sy said then they turned to leave.

Fowler squeezed through the hatchway before them.

"Sleep, sleep," Eddy joked.

"Whine, whine," Freddy replied.

"Your end is looking good," Larry said as he passed him.

"Finally some appreciation," Freddy said.

When they got to the diving platform, all three tenders were there. Honore and Mark were tending for Mike and Brad. Sammy was using his own light weight suit and helmet. In less than ten minutes, Ricky and Sammy indicated that they were ready to go. Larry picked up the phone and talked to Freddy for a minute then replaced the phone in its box.

"Looking good. Proceed," Larry said.

Ricky secured the face plate and Sammy stepped onto the stage. Sammy gave the final Okay and Ricky signaled Paul Bonne to raise the stage. Everything went smoothly and Sammy was on the bottom in five minutes. He had difficulty locating the wreck at first because the stage had turned somewhat while being lowered. After ten minutes he requested water pressure. After forty minutes on the bottom, he requested a basket. He put two bottles and a ship's chronometer in the basket then he returned to the stage. When he was on the stage, it was raised to the surface in ten minutes. The unsuiting went well and Sammy was feeling good after the dive.

Since everything was going well and Jans was ready, Larry sent him down next with instructions to work in the same area that Sammy had been working in. This time a basket was sent down with the stage.

Jans uncovered some brass objects and some porcelain cups. He had a minor leak in his suit so he came up after twenty minutes. Sy came to the diving platform as Jans was being lowered to the deck.

"This could be very interesting," Sy said.

"Just some cups," Larry countered.

"The makers marks could give us a clue to the identity of the ship."

"I doubt if the ship's manifests documented the tea cups," Larry said.

He wondered why Sy was worried about such a thing now.

"I'll take those to my quarters and examine them then I'll call the owner. I don't want anybody diving until I get the go ahead," Sy said.

"Okay," Larry said.

"Larnce, bring the basket to my quarters immediately," Sy ordered.

"Yes, certainly," Larnce said as he picked up the basket.

"Careful with that. It might be worth a million dollars," Brad wisecracked.

Larry saw Sy give him a dirty look before he turned and walked away.

"Okay, we'll be dry for a while, so unsuit and secure here," Larry said.

"Oui, mon kapiten. Does this mean shore leave?" Mike asked as Honore began helping him remove his tanks.

"Hard telling. We may not be diving again until after lunch."

"What are we gonna' do for two hours?"

"What do you usually do?" Larry asked.

"Talk about women."

"You could do that, I suppose."

"I heard that you have sampled some of the local lovelies," Brad said as Ricky helped peel his exposure suit.

"We're not gonna' let you out of that suit if you keep talking about that," Paul quipped.

"You hear all kinds of fish stories here," Larry said.

"We saw you come in the boat with her and leave with her."

"Where did you go?" Mike asked.

"Her house," Larry replied as innocently as he could.

"Where were you before that?"

"Her yacht," Larry said.

"Uh huh, and you're not jumping that?"

"Old Talmudic law-you can't ask and I can't tell," Larry said.

"You're jewish?" Brad asked.

"I don't think so. Not anymore."

"Why?"

"I stopped getting invited to the synagogue," Larry said.

"Why?"

"I wasn't paying synagogue fees."

"They had the temerity to ask for money?" Mike quipped.

"That happens."

"I'll bet Melissa doesn't ask for money," Brad said.

"To my knowledge, she never has," Larry said.

"You think everybody stays at Schooner Bay for free?" Mark asked as he picked up Mike's tanks.

"Have you ever paid?" Mike asked.

"For what?" Larry asked.

"The room for starters."

"No, back in August I came to do a salvage job for her, so the room was free."

"I was in Reno, Nevada last year. When I asked about a room, they asked-'with or without the girl?'" Paul said.

"They're not that sophisticated here. They have the Midwest sensibilities," Larry said.

"Hey Paul, they'll let you choose between the tall skinny dweeb and the gay guy," Mark wisecracked.

"You guys talk here, but don't blow it ashore. They have cops here too," Honore said.

"What's the deal here?" Brad asked.

"Everybody knows everybody and/or are related. There's no free market, I'm afraid," Larry informed them as they headed to the diver's ready room.

"It sounds like we're S-O-L."

"Not necessarily. It's just a different game."

"Are you playing tonight?" Brad asked.

"Let's see how things go this afternoon," Larry said as they entered the Ready Room.

"I'll bet your friend Melissa can hook us up," Paul said.

Larry didn't know if he would even presume to ask Melissa something like that.

"It's not like that. I know that Sy wants nothing that will draw attention to us," Larry said.

Alexander Bay was just not a shore leave town and nobody would appreciate them trying to change things, Larry thought as they secured the gear.

"Alright Skinny, what's the good word here. Hook us up."

"Niagara Falls or Montreal," Jean replied.

"Holy cow, this is the armpit of the planet," Brad remarked.

"It's a little better in the summer time," Larry said.

"We should go ashore for lunch," Mike suggested.

"Let's go ask Sy," Brad said then the five of them left.

"It seems that your friends have left you," Jean said as he turned his attention back to the electric panel.

"I don't want to go ashore. I'll probably be diving next."

"I thought about diving all the time. My brother dived with Cousteau. An embolism left him crippled. My oldest son died in the navy. I left the navy after that. The Canadian Navy that is."

"That is too bad," Larry said.

"I have always liked ships. It was good most of the time."

"I was washed out of diving after a gall stone operation that went bad."

"I hung with Sid after I got out. I was there when Sid died. He grabbed his chest and said that he hurt then he fell down. That was it, nothing more."

"I met Tony for the first time, that morning, at the pier. The next time I saw him, he was dead," Larry said.

"This is a good outfit now that you are here. Nobody will die again."

Larry and Jean turned when they heard the other guys coming.

"We have to be back by 13:00. That gives us nearly three hours," Paul announced since he was first through the door.

"That gives you barely two hours ashore and none of you come back sloshed in the gills since we're diving this afternoon," Larry said.

"You wanna' come with us?" Brad asked.

"No, I'll have lunch here."

"Farewell Mon Kapiten," Paul said then they left.

Jean showed Larry the engineering spaces then they went to lunch. Even though the tenders and deckhands had slipped away, there were plenty of people at lunch. Jean and Larry sat across from Sammy and Jans.

"Another unavoidable delay, Herr Mayer?" Jans asked.

"Sy has to check with the owners about something. We should be diving again by 13:00."

"Sammy and I had good dives, don't you think?"

"Yes, I'm very happy with what you found. I want to go down next and then we'll see about who goes down after me."

"The tenders went ashore. Was it their turn?" Jans asked.

"No turns. Sy let them go. They have to be back before 13:00 and I told them to limit their drinking. Everybody has to be ready for the next dive."

"We were thinking about spending tonight ashore," Sammy said.

"Sure, check with Sy. It's certainly no problem for me."

"There was some trouble here in August, Herr Mayer?" Jans asked.

"Yes there was. It has nothing to do with this operation."

"The tenders say that you killed two men here. Is this so?" Jans asked.

"Yes, but it wasn't while I was diving," Larry answered.

"I hope there's none of that rot. I didn't sign on for that," Sammy stated.

"I'm sure everything is above the board here," Larry said.

After lunch, Larry returned to the control room and checked on things.

"They get you out of bed, Sparky?" Larry joked.

"You know how it is. You gotta' be a team player while somebody else kisses ass."

"Okay, you can dive for me this afternoon while I play the back nine," Larry quipped as he looked at the computer.

"Sy plays the back nine all the time. Just FYI, don't count on him."

Larry knew that Sparky would only say that because nobody else was there to hear it.

"He should be back soon and we can get started," Larry said after a minute.

"I take it that you know about sharks?"

"Enough to come out the winner so far," Larry stated.

"Your gang were discussing which shark is the worst. I figured that you had your own opinion about that."

"The Bull shark."

"Nobody mentioned that one," Sparky said.

"Its temperament is totally bad. Most sharks will hesitate to attack if you look like you can take care of yourself. I've never seen one break off an attack unless it was severely injured. You've seen film of people swimming with sharks and touching them? That will instantly set off an attack with a Bull shark. They will come into freshwater rivers to hunt. They're not intimidated by people at all. The Hammerhead gets second place in my book."

"So the Bull shark is the bad ass of the sea?"

"No, the Killer Whale is the King Shit of the sea. He'll rip up any shark out there. Don't let that Sea World Shamu horse crap fool you."

"Have you ever killed one?" Sparky asked.

"I have shot them from the deck. They left in a hurry so I don't know if they died," Larry explained.

He set the computer to the bottom topographic program then he picked up the phone and tried to call Cynthia. He heard a message about the voice mailbox being full, so he hung up. He went to the Diver's Ready Room and checked his suit and helmet and weighted boots. Everything looked good so he went aft. When he got there, he saw Sy, Paul Tyler and Eddy coming in another boat. A modern fiberglass boat fishing boat called a Boston Whaler. The boat came alongside and they boarded by the ladder. They immediately headed up the steps to the upper deck. Larry figured that they were going to Sy's quarters. He couldn't dive until the other guys got back anyway. In a couple minutes he saw the Bayliner come into view. They tied up at the stern as usual and the six guys came aboard.

"How are things on the outside?" Larry quipped.

"Great! If we had another hour, we'd have all got laid," Paul, the deckhand, said.

"Sy said to get you ready to dive," Mark said.

"Let's do it," Larry said.

He wondered why Sy hadn't said anything to him. Since the air lines were already at the diving platform, Mark, Honore, Ricky, Mike and Brad went to the Ready Room with him. Larry put on his long underwear and the diving coveralls then the tenders helped carry his gear to the diving platform.

As they were suiting up, Larry watched the others. Everybody seemed on the ball and ship-shape. Before he put his helmet on, he picked up the telephone and talked to Freddy for a minute.

"Everything is good," Larry said as he hung up the phone.

"Here ya' go," Mark said as he handed him the helmet.

Larry checked the gas flow and checked the regulator again.

"Okay, check it all the way around," Larry said as he set the helmet on the neck gasket of his suit. By the feel of it, the helmet was seated properly all the way around.

"It's a go. Clamp on?"

"Clamp on," Larry responded.

Mark slid the clamp on and tightened it up. He attached the diver's knife and tool bag to his belt then helped him put on his gloves. Paul swung the stage over and Larry stepped onto the stage. Larry saw Sy and Eddy come out on deck so he gave them the high sign. Paul raised the stage and swung it overboard.

When Larry got to the bottom, he took the hose and went to the wreck.

"I'm at point A3. Give me some water pressure," Larry requested.

"Water pump on," Eddy relayed to him as the water started coming from the nozzle. He turned the water jet on a peculiar looking hump just to his left. After a few minutes, Larry could see that is was a timber, approximately a 4X4, with the thin bulkhead sheeting attached to it. The timber was well preserved so he had the hose shut off while he moved the wreckage. The timber was completely saturated so it showed no tendency to float but it moved easily. Larry had the hose turned on and he began to hose away the mud he had exposed. He soon uncovered two large locks which further cleaning showed were attached to an iron box. He managed to remove part of the lid which was badly rusted. His light revealed that the box contained silver coins. He informed them of his find and requested a large basket be sent down. While he waited for the basket, he slipped two of the coins into the cuff guard of his left glove. When the basket arrived, he moved the strong box by easy stages until he had it in the basket.

"It's heavy so take it easy. Haul away," Larry said.

The basket was raised slowly and Larry watched it in his light until it was out of sight. When they told him that the basket was on deck, he returned to the stage and requested to be brought up.

In ten minutes he was on deck. Everybody else was there too. Mark removed his helmet.

"This looks like a good find," Sy said as he turned toward him.

"Gold would be better," Larry said.

Mark unhooked him then pulled the suit down below his pelvis. He sat down and Mark removed his boots and pulled his suit off the rest of the way. Larry and Mark carried his gear to the tank room by themselves because Sy had detailed Ricky, Honore, Paul and Larnce to carry the strongbox to the safe in his quarters.

"Sy is sure getting anal," Larry said when they entered the tank room.

"I guess gold and silver will do that to people," Mark said.

They hung up his suit and his boots to dry.

Larry took his gloves and rolled out the cuffs.

"This is what is in there," Larry said as he pulled out the coins and handed one to Mark.

"Sy will have a shit fit," he said as he took the coin.

"I'm supposed to get five percent but don't show that to anybody just yet."

"That box must contain thousands," Mark said.

"No telling now but it's pretty heavy."

Larry saw someone in his peripheral vision so he turned that way.

"Sy would like to see you in his quarters immediately," Sparky said.

"Immediately? Does he think this river is gonna' dry up in the next five minutes?" Larry quipped.

"See you out on deck later," Mark said as they left.

Sparky went back to the control room and Larry took the steps topside to Sy's quarters. When he got there the door was open and Sy was talking on the phone. He knocked and Sy turned and gave him the 'one minute' sign. Sy talked for another fifteen minutes before hanging up.

"Come in, Larry. Sorry to keep you waiting," Sy said as he stood up and held out his hand.

"Haven't we met before," Larry quipped as they shook hands.

"Congratulations on your find. The owner is convinced now that we have the right ship," Sy informed him.

"So what's the Grand Poobah's instructions?"

"Keep you out of trouble."

"Our million man Navy couldn't do that," Larry joked.

"There's some new suits in the Ready Room. You might like one of them better than what you have now. You can change and clean up while you're in there. We'll see you when you come out," Sy said.

"If you insist," Larry said then he left.

When he got to the Ready room, he removed his diving coveralls and his long underwear. He put on deodorant and washed his face and put on his work clothes and his heavy jacket. There were so many diving suits hanging in there now that he couldn't tell which was which.

When Larry came out of the diver's ready room, he wasn't greeted by Sy or his tender as usual. They must be drooling over the box of silver francs, Larry thought, so he headed aft to the staging area. When he got there, he saw the Ricky and Mark talking to Gunnar Vissten, the man he had met a couple days ago. Sitting on the bench in a Viking dry suit was a young woman about twenty two years old.

"What's going on guys?" Larry asked.

"Herr Mayer, It is good to see you again," Gunnar said, extending his hand.

"Gunnar, what is going on here?" Larry asked as he shook his hand.

"Allow me to introduce Brigitte Svenson. I am tending for her." Gunnar said as they shook hands.

The young woman said something in Norwegian.

"I am in charge of the divers. I didn't hear anything about this," Larry stated.

"Her father is the diver, Cleng Svenson."

"I never heard of him. Is he aboard too?"

"No, of course not," Gunnar answered.

"Then let's talk about her. Who brought her aboard?"

"Herr Lampert."

"Where is Sy?"

"He is making a call ashore," Ricky said.

"He could be doing that all day. Is she ready to go?" Larry asked.

Gunnar said something in Norwegian and she said something to him.

"She is ready," Gunnar answered.

"Okay, get the rest of the gear on and check the breathing gas in her helmet. Don't let her go down until I come back," Larry ordered.

"Yes sir," Gunnar replied.

"Jerk!" Brigitte said.

"Save it for your husband. Proceed," Larry ordered, then he headed for the diving control room. He was wondering if he was sounding snappish when he got there. Freddy was watching the gas analytical instruments while Eddy was making notes in his logbook.

"Sy get lost again?"

"You gave him more work to do," Eddy said.

"Counting his money," Larry quipped.

"The adjusted mixture is right on the money," Freddy informed him.

"Good. Did either of you know that a woman diver was going down?"

"Sy mentioned that a Brigitte Svenson had come aboard. I asked him about checking with you. He said that he would take the responsibility of informing you," Eddy said.

"The responsibility of not informing me. Anybody could have informed me," Larry said.

"I'm sure Sy will hear you out," Eddy said.

Larry didn't feel like yelling at anybody.

"Good job, guys. I'll be out on deck," Larry said then he left the control room.

When he got back to the staging area, Brigitte was still sitting on the bench. Gunnar looked at him.

"Everything is good with the Trimix. Any problems?"

"We are waiting for your approval," Gunnar said.

"Are you ready, guys?" Larry asked.

"We are?" Mike replied for the both of them.

"Okay Gunnar," Larry said.

He wanted to check out her gear himself but he hadn't done that with Pike or Trelleborg.

Gunnar put the helmet on her and slipped the clamp on and tightened it. He used snoop to check for leaks. When he was satisfied, he pulled the gloves onto her hands. He helped her onto the stage then fastened her knife and tool bag onto her suit. The water hose was already tied to the stage. When Gunnar looked at him, Larry gave the go ahead sign. Ricky raised the stage while Gunnar watched his diver. She got into the water and to the bottom with no trouble. Larry let Gunnar listen with the spare headset since he didn't know Norwegian. Brigitte found the wreck and was using the hose to clear away the mud. In a half hour she found two more of the black brandy bottles and a large gold pocket watch.

"Tell her to beware of ship's spikes," Larry warned.

Gunnar said something to her in Norwegian. Larry heard the phone ring and he instantly grabbed it.

"Mayer....Roger that. Any other problems?....Alright, we're bringing her up."

Larry put the phone on the hook.

"Tell Brigitte to secure there and return to the stage. We're bringing her up."

Gunnar said something in Norwegian.

"She is returning to the stage, Herr Mayer."

"She is cold. When she gets up here, get her under the electric blanket immediately."

"Very good, Chief," Gunnar replied.

Mike and Brad waited by the railing in their scuba gear.

"Stand by until we get her up."

"Right Oh, Chief," Brad said.

In fifteen minutes the diving stage was being swung onboard. Ricky and Gunnar helped get her out of her suit and put the heated blanket around her. Gunnar took her to the ready room while Ricky secured her gear.

"You guys will have to wait a few minutes."

"Alright Larry, way to go the extra mile for us!" Mike quipped.

"She looks a lot better than anything I've bunked with so far," Brad added.

"Bunking is up to Sy. I wouldn't be surprised if he has her sleeping ashore."

"That's okay, we're going ashore tonight," Brad informed him.

They heard the Bosun's whistle and turned to see Sy approaching.

"How is Brigitte?" he asked.

"She got cold, so I had her brought up. There's the stuff she brought up," Larry said, pointing to the basket.

Sy looked in the basket.

"It is probably brandy. That watch looks interesting."

"It would be interesting to see if the springs and gears have survived," Larry said.

"I am glad that there wasn't any problem about her diving."

"There will usually be no problems if I am informed first."

"I would have told you myself, but I had an important teleconference with the owner. Her father, Cleng Svenson, is an old friend of the owner. For the sake of the film, he wanted a woman diver."

"I don't care who her father is. Things have gone real well and we don't want any mistakes now. I'll talk to her at mess," Larry said.

"Yes, of course," Sy agreed.

They went to the control room while the tenders secured the gear.

"Brigitte and Gunnar are bunking ashore?" Larry asked as Freddy handed him the clipboard.

"At least for tonight," Sy replied.

Larry looked at the gas consumption figures and the gas available.

"We'll have to count on at least a third more consumption," Larry said.

"With all you dainty breathers, it shouldn't be a problem," Freddy quipped.

"You sampled the unused tanks, good," Larry said after a couple minutes, adding-"Yeah, three more days, I concur," then he signed the bottom of the page.

"You brought up quite a payday for us," Freddy said as he took the clipboard from Larry.

"That much silver would only pay for a day of operating this outfit."

"I'll bet there's a lot more stuff down there," Freddy speculated.

"Let's stow all the talk about what came up. Especially now, we don't want hundreds of boats out here. It will be much more difficult if that happens," Sy snapped.

When Sy was done making log entries, he went with Larry to the Diver's Ready Room.

"I think we have one or two that will fit you," Sy said as he looked at the suits.

"Jans said that he brought his suits and he wears the same size as me."

"Yeah, this is a heavy suit. It must be Jans. How is your suit holding up?"Sy asked.

"So far it is doing fine and the fit is good."

"I guess we won't have time for another dive."

"No, it's too close to dark now," Larry agreed.

"Diving after dark is more risks. I just don't want to take any more risks," Sy said.

"All of us divers wholeheartedly agree," Larry said.

After looking at the diving suits, they went to the mess room. Sammy and Jans and the six guys who went earlier, had went ashore. Larry and Sy sat across from Gunnar and Brigitte.

"The others went ashore. We wanted to sample the cooking here," Gunnar said.

"I hope you find it satisfactory," Sy replied.

Gunnar translated for Brigitte.

She looked at Larry and said something.

"She wants to know why you do not like Norwegians, Herr Mayer."

"I don't dislike Norwegians. I don't understand why two economically stable countries like Japan and Norway feel that they must hunt whales," Larry replied.

Jans translated for her.

"Apparently whale hunting is an old tradition that some wish to preserve," Jans translated.

"It is slaughter. The bogus fucking U.N. allows it to be called research and it's horse shit," Larry stated.

Brigitte said something to him.

"In fact, Brigitte agrees with your point of view, Herr Mayer."

"Where is she from?"

"Trondheim."

"How many jobs like this has she worked on?" Larry asked.

"This is only her second job. Her first job was a fjord pipeline. A much shallower depth but the mud and the current were worse."

"It's just as well that she's a rookie in this outfit. I never lost a diver when I was the Chief," Larry said.

Jans translated for him and Brigitte said something.

"Uh, how many years were you diving in your navy?" Jans translated.

"Twenty two. I retired in '96 because I was washed out of diving," Larry explained.

Jans translated for both of them again.

"Brigitte was born in '91. She is impressed with your experience and your ability, Herr Mayer."

"That's very kind of her. When I went to Torpedo School in '74 there was a sign above the door that said-'The price of carelessness is death.' It's not very romantic, but it's the best way of saying it that I have ever heard," Larry explained.

"Her father drilled a similar maxim into her when she was learning to dive," Gunnar said.

For the rest of the time they talked about her father's diving and things that Larry did in Norway. When they left the mess, everybody seemed to understand each other much better. Sy and Larry had agreed to Brigitte and Gunnar going ashore for the night so they can get the clothes that she will need for diving. Larry stays onboard and talks to Sy and some of the other guys about the diving he did in the navy. When he slept he was plagued by odd dreams about being in strange places and dealing with people he didn't know.

Larry got up at seven and went to the Control room to get himself a cup of coffee. Sparky was the only guy there.

The phone rings and Sparky picks it up.

"Venturer Two…No, Larry is here now…alright, I'll tell him…just two other calls from the boss…See ya' when you get here."

Sparky hung up the phone.

"You're getting to be a popular man. Sy wants you to go down first this morning."

"Following our normal rotation, Pike and Trelleborg should go down."

"You know how it is, some of these people can't get outta' bed in the morning. Gunnar and Brigitte will be coming later also. Sy and the others are coming now."

"As long as everybody is happy. No calls for me, I suppose?"

"An ugly old dude like you? You gotta' be kidding," Sparky joked.

"It's getting hard to be loved."

"Ya' gotta' stop killing people, especially when you're on vacation."

"You ever kill anybody?"

"No, I hit a kid on a bicycle but he lived," Sparky replied.

"You get sued?"

"No, they took what my insurance gave them. He came into the street from between two parked cars. Thank goodness I was going slow. I was delivering pizzas."

"That doesn't sound like much pay," Larry said.

"About what the pay is here. I get fifteen hundred and month and Brad and Mike get a thousand a month."

"Underpaid salvage divers, simply deplorable," Larry remarked.

"Especially when they're drinking it up. Sy doesn't always pick up the tab for them."

"Now that the owner is convinced that we have the right ship, maybe he'll be more generous."

"I heard that you get paid by the day."

"Where did you hear that? Larry asked.

"Actually I overheard it."

"In fact I do get paid for every day I dive, but I had to take on the responsibility of looking out for the other divers and I had to find the Brig for them."

"How did you find the wreck?" Sparky asked.

"I was checking out the gossip in old newspaper articles."

"Sy will grab all the credit he can. If I was getting paid by the day, we'd still be upriver."

"I'm a results oriented kinda' guy," Larry quipped.

"On this boat it's no money and no fucking thanks."

"It's the golden rule. Those with the gold think they make the rules. Don't deal from a position of weakness."

"Melissa Macklin is the strong suit here?" he asked.

"She sent Jackie Dunlap in her plane to pick me up. Melissa isn't particularly generous with her time and money either," Larry said while intentionally omitting any involvement with federal agencies.

They both turned to look when they heard someone approach.

"Good morning, gentlemen," Jean said as he came in.

"The rats are coming out of the hold. This boat must be sinking," Sparky joked.

"I brought some paperwork that Sy requested," Jean said as he set a folder on the desk.

"It's too late to run, Sy will be here in a couple minutes," Sparky said.

"You're looking well. Are you diving today?"

"Yes, it looks like Sy wants me on the bottom this morning," Larry replied.

"Let's have more of those money begetting dives."

"What did you dive for in your navy?" Jean asked.

"Usually to spread death and destruction," Larry replied.

"None of that King and country crap here. This is a money deal," Sparky said.

They heard the horn of a boat.

"Sy and his band of rough necks. I'll bet they're hung-over," Sparky remarked.

A few minutes later, Sy and Eddy came in.

"How is everybody doing this morning?"

"Ship shape," Larry replied.

"Good, Sparky gave you the message?"

"Yes he did."

"As soon as you and Mark are ready, we'll get started."

"Did Freddy come with you?"

Sy looked annoyed at the question.

"Eddy, see if you can find him."

"I'm on it," Eddy said as he went to the computer desk. Sparky stood up and moved aside.

"Get some sleep, Spark. You're looking a little punchy," Eddy said as he sat in the chair.

"Sleep, what's that," Sparky said then he left with Jean.

"Pike and Trelleborg take a vacation?" Larry asked.

"They'll be along."

"Did Svenson get everything she needed?"

"According to Gunnar, she did."

"Okay," Larry said then he erased their names in the AM slot and wrote his name.

"So much for that."

Mark came into the control room.

"We're waiting for Freddy," Larry informed him.

"He should be here pretty quick. Everything looks good in the Ready room."

"Great, as soon as Freddy gets here and we check the gas, we'll be ready to go," Larry said.

"Roger that," Mark said then he left.

Sy was looking at the computer and not looking happy.

"I've texted him but he hasn't replied yet," Eddy said.

"I'll be in my quarters. Let me know when he gets here," Sy ordered.

"Will do," Eddy replied.

After Sy left, Larry went aft. The divers and tenders were waiting at the diving platform.

"I brought your gear out since you're the first one going down," Mark said.

"Very good," Larry replied, adding-"How were things ashore?"

"This place really sucks for shore leave," Paul declared.

"It's too small for that. You have to have three grandparents in the cemetery or nobody is talking to you," Larry said.

"We didn't run into Brigitte at all," Brad said.

"She and Gunnar were supposed to go shopping for some warmer underclothes."

"Sy didn't pick up the tab either," Mike said.

"Good, that kept drinking to a minimum," Larry quipped.

"I was talking to Gloria, the girl at the desk," Brad said.

"He struck out with her too," Mike chided.

"She said that you got around quite a bit in the five days that you were here last time?"

"Alas, what a difference a couple months makes," Larry sighed.

"Everybody is expecting trouble when they see you now, she says."

"What a terrible thing to say. I'll have to spank her for that."

"Have you heard from Cynthia or Sylvia?" Mike asked.

"No, in fact I haven't. Have you?"

"No, it's probably a busy time in school for them."

"Yeah, that's what I figured," Larry said.

In truth, he didn't know what to think. He had expected to hear from Cindy much sooner, even if it was to get the brush off.

"I hope we get some time off soon. There's gotta' be a place where the girls are friendlier," Paul said.

They saw the Boston Whaler approaching. They could see Freddy and Paul the photographer on board.

"That's okay. Take all morning," Ricky harassed them.

"First time I ever saw you in a hurry," Freddy said as the boat came alongside.

Paul set some equipment on deck then came up the ladder. He was followed by Freddy.

"Hi guy. Sy wants me to go down first so we have to check the gas mixtures."

"Yeah, Eddy texted me. I don't know what their damn hurry is now."

"No telling. Take all the time that you need. I want to be sure that everything is good before I go down."

"Alright, let's go to the control room," Freddy said.

When they got to the control room, Freddy ran the GC on the gas samples while Larry got into his diving clothes. Everything was looking good for the dive. Sy came in when they were about to leave.

"Everything is looking good with the gas mixture," Larry informed him.

"As I expected. Everything was good yesterday."

"After what happened to Tony, we will take no chances," Larry said.

"Of course, you're absolutely right," Sy said quickly.

The three of them headed out to the diving platform.

"Alright, let's suit up here, guys."

Mark helped Larry while Ricky and Honore helped Brad and Mike. Larry waited until they were fully dressed before he had Mark put his helmet on. After the function tests he stepped onto the stage. Mark affixed the tool bag, light and knife to his belt. Mark asked him for a final check then he fastened his face plate. The stage was lifted and Larry was lowered into the water. He checked his light then turned it off and returned it to his belt. In five minutes he was on the bottom.

"On the bottom," he said as he tried to turn on his flashlight.

"Blasted! My light isn't working," Larry said as he tried the switch several times.

"Would you like to come up," Eddy asked.

"Negative. Send Brad or Mike down with another one, if you would."

"Stand-by…Roger that, Mike is coming down with another light," Eddy said after a minute.

"Acknowledged," Larry replied.

He waited in the total darkness for nearly two minutes then he saw a light right above him. Mike came right down to the bottom and Larry handed him the broken light. Mike handed him another light from his belt. Larry turned it on and gave the okay sign. Mike had written-'Are you OK' on the board. Larry wrote-'Fine, thank you'. Mike indicated that he was returning to the surface and Larry gave him the 'Okay' and patted him on the shoulder. He watched briefly while Mike ascended.

"Mike is coming up," he informed them.

"Roger that," Eddy replied.

Since he had descended in the dark, he didn't know that he was facing in the wrong direction until he shined the light right in front of him and there was nothing there. He swung the light to the left and moved it around. He was surprised to see a white face about ten feet from him. He studied it for a moment then grabbed the hose and moved toward it.

"Moving away from the stage."

"Roger that."

"Stand-by for water pressure."

"Standing by."

Larry studied the face for a moment. It looked like neo-classic period and white marble.

"Interesting. Let's have some water," Larry requested.

"What is interesting?" Sy asked as the water started.

"I got a Babe down here," Larry replied.

"Would you like to come up?"

"Not without her. I'll need the hook, three slings and a coil of rope. I'll let you know when I'm ready."

"Roger that," Sy said.

They must think I'm crazy, Larry thought as he continued to hose away the mud. At the base of the statue he saw the initials A. Cambi and the year 1730 had been chiseled into the stone.

"Hmm, she looks pretty youthful for 1730," Larry remarked.

"Where do you see that?" Sy asked.

"On the base naturally," Larry replied, adding-"Another couple minutes."

When he had hosed away enough mud, he requested that the water be stopped. Topside, they lowered the hook with a light attached to it. Larry retrieved the hook and the slings. He carefully slid the slings under the statue and hooked them. He requested the slack be taken up. When the slings started lifting the statue, he told them to stop then he tied the slings together and tied the statue to the slings.

"Steady as she goes. Haul away,"

"Steady as she goes, Roger," Sy replied.

The statue tried to drag, but Larry held it until it was off the bottom. He held the light on it as it was raised. Sy called out the depth as it was raised.

"On the surface. Bring it alongside and raise it to the platform," Sy ordered.

Larry could imagine the excitement onboard. He grabbed the hose and returned to the stage. He waited a few minutes for someone to call down.

"Are you there, Larry?" Eddy asked.

"Where else would I be? I'm ready to come up."

"Stand by."

"Sy requests that you return to the stage."

"I'm already on the stage and ready to come up."

There was another pause.

"Roger that. We're bringing you up."

"Good idea!" Larry snapped.

There was another half minute delay then the stage began ascending. In ten minutes, he was being swung over the side. Everybody seemed to be on deck now. The stage was lowered and Mark opened his face plate.

"You hit another home run, Chief," Mark said as he loosened the neck clamp.

"It must have put everybody to sleep," Larry said.

"Everybody was so excited that they forgot about you. Everybody except me, of course," Mark explained as he started pulling his suit down. Sy didn't send anyone to help him.

"That could be a big mistake on their part," Larry said.

Eddy came out and said something to Sy then he came over.

"You got everybody pissing their pants."

"That's why I'm the Chief. I get results," Larry said.

"I can't argue with that. Sy wants you to go ashore with him later," Eddy said as Larry sat down and Mark pulled the suit off of his legs.

"Sure."

"I'll let him know," Eddy said then he slapped him on the shoulder as he left.

When he was down to his coveralls and booties, he helped Mark carry his gear into the tank room and secure it for drying. He had seen that Sy had the statue laying on the foam rubber mats and he appeared to have every available man trying to do something.

"What are they doing?" Larry asked Mark as they came out on deck and headed that way.

"Sy wants it crated up so it isn't damaged," Mark explained.

"Fortunately this is fresh water and cold, so there wasn't any solution damage that I could see."

"They still want it crated and shipped ashore for preservation," Mark said.

They watched as Sy directed the crew to raise the statue a couple feet then they removed the rubber mats and slid a heavy wooden base under it. They had four inch timbers, cut to the approximate contour of the statue and padded, placed on the base and the statue lowered. Once Sy was convinced that the statue was laying properly on its improvised cradle, the crew began nailing a frame work together and nailing the boards to the framework. They were nearly done before Sy turned and looked at Larry.

"Six hundred pounds or a little more," Larry said.

"It has to be taken ashore for preservation."

"Being it's freshwater, It doesn't look like it will require much work," Larry said.

"It has to be examined by the experts to decide that," Sy said.

"Of course," Larry said.

Sy seemed a little too preoccupied and in too much of a hurry. Not the way he usually is, Larry thought. When they had nailed on the last boards, Sy sent most of the crew below for lunch. Larry sat across from Brigitte and Gunnar. Pike, Trelleborg and four of the tenders had gone ashore already.

"Well Chief, you certainly found deh big one," Gunnar remarked.

"God only knows how much more is down there," Larry replied.

Brigitte said something in Norwegian.

"Herr Lampert looks excited."

"Excited isn't the word. He looks unsure of himself," Larry said.

He was wondering why Sy was running to his quarters after every dive instead of tending to diving operations like he should have been. After lunch, he went topside and knocked on the door of Sy's quarters. Sy opened the door and looked at him.

"We need to discuss diving operations for the rest of the day."

"I'll have to talk to the owner again before we plan anything," Sy replied.

"I can't see why the owner would give a damn about who's diving next."

Sy looked at him incredulously.

"I'll need you to come ashore with me in an hour. We'll discuss it then," Sy said.

"Very well," Larry said then he turned and left.

This seemed to be very unusual behavior. If the divers were bringing up real treasure then why would the owner delay the divers. He remembered what Sparky had said about not trusting Sy. As he descended the steps he saw that the sky was cloudy and it was getting cooler. It's upper New York in November, he thought. When he got to the Control room, Eddy and Freddy were still there.

"Diving is stopped for now. I'm going ashore with Sy in an hour."

"Sy already told us," Freddy said.

It's strange that he didn't tell me, Larry thought. He went aft to the diving platform. Mike, Brad and the tenders were there.

"When we asked you to find us some women, this is not quite what we had in mind," Brad quipped.

"He likes those women that you can sharpen your pocket knife on," Ricky said.

"She's a little stoned but her virtue is rock solid," Mike added.

Larry didn't mind the guys ragging on him like that.

"It looks like Sy is stopping the diving for today so I won't be able to do any better than that I'm afraid."

"We can go ashore early then," Paul said.

"Me and Sy are going ashore. He didn't say anything else," Larry said.

"Honore was saying that you don't like Norwegians because they hunt whales?"

"That's right," Larry replied.

"Nantucket is famous for whale hunting. That's being hypocritical don't you think?"

"American whaling ports got over it. They moved on a long time ago."

"You saw whaling ships when you were in the navy?"

"Yes, I did."

"You saw the Green Peace guys trying to fight them?" Paul asked.

"Yes."

"Green peace is a bunch of liberals."

If they are not against us then they are for us, Larry thought.

"Animals like Whales need to be protected from men. If it was up to me, I would have sent the whalers to the bottom."

"You'll never get a Norwegian girl like that," Brad quipped.

"I was married too long to worry about that now," Larry said.

"Misses Macklin was married four times. Did she tell you that?" Paul asked.

"No, I heard it from the townies last time I was here."

"How much did it cost you to get married?" Mike asked.

"Twelve hundred dollars."

"It lasted thirty three years, you said. That's pretty good."

"Unlike these Hollywood types, I was trying to get my money's worth."

"Have you heard of a guy named Joe Cole?" Ricky asked.

"Of course, he brought me here in August. We enlisted together in '74."

"Where is he now?"

"The Virgin Islands."

"I heard he is CIA."

"No, he was never a spook," Larry lied to not complicate things.

"A lot of people say he is," Paul insisted.

"They say all kinds of things about me. The only federal job I ever had was as a diver in the navy. That ended in '96 and I have never worked for any federal agency since then," Larry stated.

"They don't pay worth a fuck here. What was the pay in the navy like?" Brad asked.

"Enough to get by. I never bought a house then because we lived all over the place."

"I was convinced that this was a glamour job. See places that most people only dream about. Write your own ticket. Take care of your family. I never knew a diver who wasn't divorced. Nobody could stay married on this pay," Brad said.

"All those sunny tropical places we were promised. Where the hell are they now?" Mike asked rhetorically.

"We got us a mutiny started," Mark joked.

"I dived with some guys who went on to do deep saturation diving for Oil companies. They seemed to make out pretty good. Darla just didn't want me to be a professional diver, so it was the pilot plant for me," Larry explained.

They heard a horn and saw the fishing boat coming. It was Pike, Trelleborg, Svenson and Gunnar. The boat came alongside and they came up the ladder.

"The work is already done. You slackers might as well have stayed ashore," Paul said.

"Herr Mayer, we have heard great things about you," Trelleborg said.

"Just a garden statue. It's all crated up now," Larry said as he pointed out the crate.

"That is very encouraging, Herr Mayer," he said then the four of them headed forward.

"If you and Sy go ashore, we won't have nothin' to do but watch TV," Mike said.

"The only movie they have is the one where New York get flooded then it goes down to minus a hundred degrees," Brad said.

"All those Obama loving bastards all die. Good, I like a happy ending," Larry said.

"It's one of those feel good movies," Mike said.

"How about the 'Three hundred'? Spartans, prepare for glory!" Ricky said.

"Let's not and just say we did."

"You can ogle Brigitte," Paul suggested.

"Your time is up. Sy is coming," Ricky said.

They saw Sy coming down the steps.

"Somebody has to drive the boat," Larnce said.

"Sy will drive it," Brad said.

"Okay, Larry. We will probably be docking later to unload this stuff, guys," Sy said then he followed Larry down the ladder.

Chapter Seven
–You'll Never Work In this Town Again

Sy piloted the boat ashore. Larry waited for Sy to talk but he didn't say anything until they tied up at the municipal pier.

"We have a teleconference hook-up in one of the private dining rooms," Sy said as they stepped onto the pier.

"We should be salvage diving and not chatting," Larry suggested.

They went to Sy's rental car and drove to Schooner Bay.

"Have you seen Melissa?" Larry asked as they got out of the car.

"No, I haven't."

Larry was getting even more suspicious. He knew that she was never around when there was trouble. When they walked by the front desk, Larry smiled and said hello to Gloria. Sy said nothing. When they got to the dining room, Sy told Sharon that they were going to the reserved private dining room. She nodded but didn't say anything to them either.

"Is anybody else coming?" Larry asked.

"No, just us," Sy replied.

When they entered the dining room, Sy closed the door. On the table, there was only a laptop computer.

"Let's sit down at the computer," Sy said.

Sy sat down to the right of Larry and grabbed the mouse. After a couple clicks on the mouse, an image from an office appeared. Sy typed something on the keyboard then a man in a suit sat down in the chair.

"Good morning, gentlemen," he said in a German accent.

"Good morning, Herr Straussel. This is Larry Mayer," Sy said.

"Good morning, Herr Mayer. Unfortunately I must tell you that your services are no longer required in this salvage operation."

"There is a little manner of money," Larry snapped.

"When the operation is concluded, our accountants will determine what is owed to you," Straussel said.

"Three days diving at two thousand a day. You don't need an accountant to figure that out!"

"I think I made myself clear on how this will be done," the German said.

"Listen you Kraut son of a bitch, I have contacts in three federal agencies that can shut down this outfit in an hour. I'm not dealing from a position of weakness here. I'll have people put in jail!" Larry exclaimed.

"Your threats do not impress me, Herr Mayer."

Sy waved his hand at him.

"Johan, I gave my word to Herr Mayer. I'll take the money from the operating fund."

"This is not the way I was instructed to handle this matter, Herr Lampert."

"I can avoid a lot of trouble this way, so I'm handling it this way," Sy snapped.

"Perhaps I can meet you one day, Herr Mayer," Straussel said.

"God have mercy on your Nazi fucking soul if that day ever comes, asshole," Larry shouted at him.

The German got up from the chair and left.

"I'll write you a check on the credit line," Sy said, taking out his debit card.

"You better make it a cashier's check," Larry snapped.

"I'll have to go to a bank for that."

"There's one on the way," Larry said.

"Alright, I'll call Mark and have him get your clothes," Sy said as they left the room.

On the way to the bank, Sy called the ship and arranged for Larry's clothes to be brought ashore. By the time they got back to the municipal pier, the Bayliner was also there. Paul handed him his diving bags with his clothes.

"You ask for too much," Sy said.

"Exactly what you welching cocksuckers offererd three days ago. Don't spin horse shit to me! Fucking presidents didn't get away with that!" Larry snapped.

Sy looked at him and said nothing.

Larry looked at Paul.

"Maybe I'll see you guys again before I leave," Larry said before he turned and walked away.

The nerve of these fuckers to make an agreement then go back on it so quickly, he thought. By the time he got to the courtesy car, he thought he would go see the sheriff and report that there was something questionable about the salvage operation.

That afternoon he drove to the sheriff's office in Watertown and made out a complaint. While Larry was doing this, Trelleborg was making a dive. When he got to the bottom, his air hose separated and he barely managed to save himself by shutting off his air and breathing the air in his suit as he came up. When he was back up on deck, it was apparent that the hose had slipped off of the barb and the clamp was missing. Ricky insisted that he had checked the clamps when he brought the hoses out. Pike and Svenson refused to dive.

That evening the Venturer was brought in and docked at the municipal pier. An hour after it docked, the Sheriff brought a court order to cease the salvage operation and confine the ship to the dock. Sy was furious. He called the Sheriff's office in Watertown and he was told that the Venturer had to remain docked and he must remain onboard or in town.

The next morning when the Sheriff arrived to determine who and what was on board, he found out that Sy had left before first light on another boat. Larnce told the Sheriff that Sy had taken a heavy box with him. Since he was seen headed for the Canadian side, the FBI had been called in.

Early that afternoon, Larry was summoned to Watertown. He was interviewed and asked to detail everything he did, saw and heard on the salvage operation. After the questioning about that, he was asked numerous questions about his relationship with Cynthia, Jackie and Melissa. He managed to de-emphasize the fact that they had been looking for treasure in Florida. He mentioned visiting Joe and seeing Luis in the Virgin Islands. While the FBI detained him in Watertown, he heard that Sy was picked up by the O.P.P. after attempting to flee by car. Nothing was said about him having any treasure in his possession. Larry was given take-out pizza for supper because he needed to remain in the building. A couple hours later, he was taken into a room and a video tape was played for him. A man who was apparently French addressed him:

"Hello Mister Mayer. According to the treaties of 1763 and 1783, any French vessel in the St. Lawrence, whether afloat or on the bottom, remains the property of France forever. It has been a pleasure working with you. In case you are wondering, we have recovered the items in question. The marble statue will be returned to us as well. We have convinced your government to allow you to keep the money given to you. As in your Navy, you are not at liberty to divulge the existence of this operation or to discuss any part of it with anyone. We know that you will cooperate fully in this. 1097366, out."

Great, It sucks enough to deal with agents of his own government, and now he has to deal with the Special Branch of the Surete invoking Nauticus Obscura. As usual, he takes the risks and does ninety five percent of the job and a government will reap the benefits now that the treasure has been found, he thought. When he got back to Schooner Bay it was very late so he decided to wait until morning to make some phone calls.

The next morning, Larry dialed the number for Cindy's house. A man answered.

"Hello."

"Hello, I am Larry Mayer. Is Cindy there, please?"

"No, I'm afraid not. You should talk to her mother."

Larry noticed a change in the tone of his voice.

"Okay, sure," Larry said.

"Mister Mayer, I'm Josie, Cindy's mother."

"Hello, call me Larry if you like."

"I'm afraid that Cindy has received some news. She has an opportunity to go to school out of state. I'm afraid that this is an awkward situation for the both of you."

"Oh no, I would never want to put Cindy in an awkward position. If she is there, I would like to tell her so myself."

"I'm afraid that she is unavailable at the moment, Larry."

"Well, tell her I said good-bye and good luck in everything."

"I will. I certainly will."

"If she ever needs anything, a recommendation or reference, anything, then let me know. She knows my phone number, address and email," Larry said.

"I'll tell her. I know she will appreciate that."

"Okay, good-bye," Larry said then he hung up.

He called his daughter's house and left a message then he went to the dining room and got some breakfast. In spite of the fact that the Venturer was docked, he saw none of the crew there. After breakfast he walked to the municipal pier. He walked up to the policeman that was guarding the gangway.

"Good morning, I'm Larry Mayer. Is anyone onboard?"

"No, they all left."

"Thank you," Larry said.

He decided to return to Schooner Bay. Larry came in by the front entrance and waved at Gloria as he walked by the desk.

"Excuse me, Mister Mayer. You have a message from Misses Macklin," she said as she held up a folded piece of paper.

"Thank you. Do you know where the rest of the crew went?" Larry asked as he took it from her.

"All I was told is that they were all checking out last night. I haven't seen any of them this morning."

"Thank you," Larry said.

He unfolded the message and read it-'Larry, I had to leave town on business. Please let Gloria know when you plan to check out. Melissa.'

"Today," Larry said.

"Check-out time is 12:00," Gloria informed him.

"Okay," Larry said then he put the message in his pocket and went to his room.

After he had finished packing, there was a knocking on the door.

"Enter," Larry called out.

There was no response.

"Come in," Larry said.

The door opened slowly and a young man, about nineteen or twenty years old stuck his head in.

"Excuse me, Mister Mayer. I'm Frank Blair.... I'm here to pick up the car.....I do Tim Lesher's job," he said haltingly.

"Okay, I suppose I can take a cab to Watertown," Larry said then he tossed him the fob.

"Oh no, I'll be glad to take you. No problem at all. Let me take your bags," he offered.

"Okay, if you want."

Frank came in and picked up his bags.

"You can leave the card key in the box outside," he said.

"Okay, good," Larry said.

He shut off the light, closed the door and put the cardkey in the box. Frank put his bags in the trunk then they got in the car.

"To the bus station, Frank, and don't spare the horses," Larry quipped.

Frank chuckled at that remark as he started the car.

"The wind has shifted around. The temperature will drop and we'll get snow or sleet by tonight," he said as he pulled out onto the road.

"Duck hunters, moose hunters, bear hunters, it won't bother them," Larry said.

"You knew Tim?" Frank asked.

"For only a couple of days. He helped Joe Cole tend for me when I dived back in August," Larry replied.

"They say he was drowned by one of the guys you killed."

"The story was that he cut a hole in the ice and pushed the SUV into it. He was involved in a plan to steal the money while the SUV was on the bottom," Larry explained.

"Holy cow! He should have known better than that."

"Yeah, it cost him."

"Do you mind me asking about it?" Frank asked.

"No, ask anything you want. I like expressing my opinion," Larry quipped.

"I heard that the sheriff shut down the salvage diving you were on."

"They had already fired me. It turns out that that particular wreck still belongs to France. I just had to find it for them."

"Ouch!" Frank remarked.

"I didn't run into Eric Edwards or Charlie Clapton. What happened to them?"

"Clapton got a free year at SUNY Buffalo. Edwards joined the Navy."

"It sounds like they made out Okay." Larry said.

"Everyone says that you and Cindy Morrow were an item," Frank ventured.

"Were is the operative word here. I only saw her once, for only a minute."

"All the guys say she is a hot babe."

"Well, it's free market now. In fact, I never got in anybody's pants that the whole time I was here. I guess I should have tried harder," Larry quipped.

"Everybody says that she came back from Caribbean with all kinds of treasure."

"Not that much in fact. We didn't have the time to do a good job," Larry replied.

"Whatever the details, her stock has gone up tremendously."

"She's fun to dive with."

"You heard that Misses M left town?"

"On business, no doubt," Larry said.

"Everybody says that you and her will pair up."

"Me and her are the only two that apparently don't think so," Larry quipped.

Frank was silent.

"There's an old saying that says Thousand Island girls marry Thousand Island guys."

"What happened to your wife?"

"She died from a heart condition a couple years ago."

"Wow, there aren't too many men who would turn down a chance to snuggle with Misses M," Frank said after a minute.

"Four guys weren't too successful at it. I never asked her if she has done any diving."

"I never heard anybody say anything about that."

Larry thought again. Were the people just leery of him because of the things that happened or did his age make him unworthy of having enjoyable experiences with other people.

The Next day

He called his daughter when he got to the bus station in Brecksville. It was six o'clock in the morning, windy and a freezing rain falling as they walked out to his car.

"I spent the night at your place. I checked your mail," she said.

"Nothing, I'm sure."

"A Shirley Douglas sent you an email."

"I wonder how she knew my address."

"An old friend of yours," she asked.

"An old acquaintance who wants to meet me again, apparently."

"She invited you to visit her on Nantucket Island for Thanksgiving."

"Great, I'll leave one cold, wet, windy place for another. Why don't I have friends on Aruba?" Larry asked rhetorically.

"She says that if you can get to Boston or Hyannis, she'll do the rest. Why don't you go and check it out for me. I always wanted to go there. I'll drive," Meghan said as she reached for the handle of the driver's door.

Larry opened the back door and put his bag on the seat then he got in the passenger's side. You gotta' be made of money to live on Nantucket. This Shirley must be single, at least thirty seven and have an airplane. Normally this would seem ideal for him, he thought.

"How did Mister Slick make out with the bike?" Larry asked.

"The dumbass woman didn't have any license or proof of insurance. Bob Jr. wants to take them to the cleaners."

"His mother must be so proud," Larry quipped.

"They only offered him eight hundred to settle."

"Let's gouge the shit outta' them just for insulting us like that."

"I know you'll get it outta' them," Meghan said.

"We'll buy a place on Nantucket," Larry joked.

"Spending next summer on Nantucket! I could definitely handle that."

"Aah ye whalin' folk?" Larry quipped.

"Eh-yuh, eh-yuh." she replied.

Haul away to Nantucket

Meghan backed the Nissan out of the parking space and headed out of the bus station driveway. The sleet was getting worse but there weren't many cars on the road since it was early Saturday morning.

"I answered Shirley's email for you. She's not on Facebook."

"Good, I don't want the whole damn world to see it."

"You sound tired. It was a rough trip?" Meg asked.

"Yeah, it turned out that way."

"Did you see your friends, female and otherwise?"

"It turns out that I don't have any friends there."

"Ouch!" Meghan exclaimed.

"Yeah, that's one way of putting it," Larry said as he closed his eyes.

"Everybody is getting sick with this lousy weather."

"Nantucket is the same damn thing. Why don't I have friends on Aruba?"

"She said that she can pick you up from Boston or Hyannis. You gotta' go and check it out," Meg insisted.

When they got home, Meghan set his gear bags on his bed. Larry took off his clothes and laid down next to them. He heard his daughter turn on the computer in the next room.

"I'm gonna' put on a pot of coffee."

"Hmm," Larry said as he faded off to sleep.

When he woke up, he rolled over and looked at the clock. It said 1:06. Lousy Saturday afternoon, he thought as he rolled over and closed his eyes again. When he woke up again it was 2:00.

I feel like crap. I must be getting sick, Larry thought as he stretched out.

'And so the great warrior was laid low. Not by the arms of the world but by a little urchin with the sniffles,' Larry thought to himself as he sat up in bed.

He decided to check his email then check his cupboards. He should have plenty of food but sometimes his daughters or grandchildren would come over and remove everything edible. Since it was too late to take a shower, he got dressed and turned on his computer. Checking his email, he found two from FlyGirl, AKA Shirley Douglas, and one from his younger daughter, Beth.

He moved those to the top. The other nine were for male enhancement and borrowing money. It's much too late for that he thought as he deleted them. His younger daughter had heard about him making apple pies, so she requested some.

The first email by Shirley had been answered by Meghan. She informed Shirley that her father was indeed the former Master Chief and diver. She had given her his address and telephone number and told her that he was doing a salvage job in the Thousand Islands and expected to be home by the weekend. The second email had been sent last night. Shirley had heard that there was some trouble with a salvage operation in the Thousand Islands because the wreck in question was in fact in federal waters. Larry wondered if she had heard from Jackie or did she have some connections in the federal law enforcement business. She also sent photos of herself in front of a 'cottage' and one of her standing on the wing of a Beechcraft G58 Baron. He pulled a couple pictures out of his photo bucket and sent her a short Bio with as detailed an explanation of the salvage operation as he could write. After sending the email, he turned off the computer and checked his cupboards and made a list of things he wanted to get then he left.

When he returned home, the miserable sleet had started again. He took the bushel basket and the bag from his car and headed up the steps. Meghan was there to hold the door for him.

"What have you been up to?" she asked.

"Sinfully wasting money."

"Please tell me it was an airline ticket to Mass."

"Frozen pie crust and apples," Larry replied as he handed the bag to her as he walked through the doorway.

"Agh, you're killing me here," Meghan said.

"I'll make you an apple pie, that'll revive you."

"Make that Shirley an apple pie. She'll be eating out of your hand. I made some Sailor's stew."

"Bless your heart. I got some Italian bread."

"Excellent, I hope you're ready to eat."

"It's after four. We might as well." Larry said as he set the basket of apples in the kitchen.

"I have some clothes in the washer. Could you get them for me?" Meghan asked.

"Sure," Larry replied.

While he was in the basement he policed the area. When he came up, she was dishing up the stew.

"I'll get the Italian bread," she said as she went back into the kitchen.

Larry remembered overhearing several women pilots on the LDH-4 joking about being 'Italian Bred' or 'French Bred'.

Shirley must have been the one with long brown hair, he thought. If she remembered him and Joe flying out to CVN-68 in an NE-1 then she must have been there too. How could he have missed her among four thousand men, he thought.

"How's the stew?"

"Great," Larry replied.

"I didn't get to those bed clothes yet."

"That's okay. It's nothing pressing."

"There was a woman in your bed?" she asked after a minute.

Larry nodded.

"Young Cindy?"

"No, Jackie Dunlap, Melissa's pilot."

"They must have had you suckered from the get-go," Meghan suggested.

"I got the money, so I ain't complaining."

"How did that work out?"

"Federal waters. If you bring up anything from a wreck in federal waters it belongs to the government and they don't have to give you crap.

This one still belonged to France because of a treaty. Nice guys those French," Larry explained.

"So, it was three thousand last time and six thousand this time. That sounds like a decent take."

"Three men dead this time and five dead the last time. I guess there was a price to pay."

"You gotta' stay away from that place. I'm talking sense here," she stated.

"I couldn't agree more," Larry agreed.

"Nobody gets killed on Nantucket."

"I wouldn't be too sure about that. All those liberals running around over there, God knows what goes on."

"Anyway, you gotta' go and check it out. This Shirley has got to be loaded," Meghan said.

"Her father left her the house. He was a big wheel at Sikorsky. Wife number two wanted Long Island so Shirley got her inheritance early. Her husband died in an airline accident and she got another pile of money."

"She was born with a silver Joy stick in her hand," Meg quipped, adding-"I like that airplane."

"Yes, it's half again the plane that Melissa's Seminole is. Half again as fast, half again the range and twice the price."

"Couldn't she just fly out here and get you?"

"She could if she wanted to," Larry replied.

"Let's see, you said fuel is six bucks a gallon and that would take about a hundred gallons of fuel one way."

Larry figured that she used the fuel consumption of the Seminole as the basis for that calculation.

"It's a little more than that if you figure 6.1 miles per gallon at a cruise speed of 180 knots and seven hundred and fifty miles."

"How long would that take?"

"Three and a half or four hours depending on the wind," Larry said.

"Boston would be nothing. Fly straight across Cape Cod. It's probably not a hundred miles."

Meghan thought for a minute.

"You took us to Cape Cod when I was twelve. Why didn't you take us to Nantucket then?"

"Round trip was a hundred dollars for an adult and eighty dollars for a child."

"Pheew! Five hundred and twenty bucks. That's a lot of clam chowder in Chatham."

"It turned out that it was," Larry agreed.

"I met my first boyfriend there."

"It was only four weeks. Kinda' dumb to get that started."

"I was just learning about those things. Give me a break here."

"Sure, no problem," Larry said.

He thought about her drug addict husband who ruined her financially then hanged himself rather than face the responsibility for what he did.

"Are they on Eastern Standard Time over there?"

"Yes they are," he replied.

"I'll check your email later."

"She probably ran for the hills. I sent her some pictures and told her about Alexander Bay."

"Oh, don't do that. Let me send your replies from now on," she suggested.

"Sure, the weather is here, I wish you were beautiful."

"You gotta' turn on the charm here. You gotta' sell yourself," Meg insisted.

"Grandma and Grandpa Davis said that I couldn't sell ice water in hell. That's the only thing they ever said that was true."

"I never put much stock in them anyway."

Larry thought about when Meg needed help five years ago. Darla's parents were worse than useless so Larry had to help her, and Meghan was still paying him back.

"Charm her like that cashier at the dollar store."

"I just told her that she was a very pretty young lady and she didn't need those piercings."

"Yeah, use the psychological approach. They don't see you as a potential mate but more like a friendly uncle so they're not afraid to open up to you then you move in for the score."

"Meghan's Love Line. Let's take the next caller," Larry quipped.

The fact that Shirley had communicated through Jackie and got his email address seemed to indicate that she was interested in more than just a 'hook-up', Larry thought.

After supper, Larry put some of Meg's clothes in the washer while she did the dishes. Afterward, Meghan got on the computer.

"We're going hot over here," Meghan said as she started typing away.

"What's on the tube?" Larry asked as he looked at a magazine.

"Shirley answered and now she's live. She only has a couple minutes. Hop to it, Romeo," Meg urged.

"Oh bother," Larry said as he walked into the computer room.

"She is impressed with your last email. Read her reply so you can go live!" she exclaimed.

Larry read her email at the top of the screen while Meghan continued to stall for time. Shirley was still single and uncommitted as far as men were concerned. She was enthusiastic about having him as a dinner guest for Thanksgiving. She wasn't put off by the death and destruction that seemed to follow him around. She had talked to Jackie again while she was flying back from Montreal. Larry had Meghan type while he dictated.

"Hi, I didn't expect to hear from you so soon. What did Jackie have to say?"

"She was leaving Montreal with another diver. She said that you were the Chief in that outfit."

"Chief in name only. They shoved me out the backdoor right before the feds came through the front door."

"Good lord! Can't you stay out of trouble?" (Smiley face)

"Who ever got anything done in this world by staying out of trouble?"

"Too true, too true."

"How's the weather over there?"

"Same damn thing as Ohio. Come and see."

"I understand that there's always a gale blowing around Thanksgiving time."

"Sometimes. This G58 will fly through anything. I'll get you here."

"What's my window here?"

"Logan Airport, any time Tuesday."

"Sounds good. I'll have to get a ticket."

"What airport?"

"Probably Akron/Canton."

"I'll get you one at the regular price with FlyRite. They rip-off people around the holidays."

"That would be great. Let's pray for good weather."

"Absolutely. Your daughter said your wife died. How long ago?"

"Yes, going on three years now."

"When Adam died, I moved here permanently."

"Inheriting a house on Nantucket. You can't beat that."

"Taxes and utilities suck like anywhere else. Jackie says you handle twin engines pretty good. Do you want to fly out of Logan?"

"A big airport like that! I would probably pee my pants!"

"It's just like an aircraft carrier. You gotta' fly between the big guys."

"That time on the Nimitz in '95 was my only carrier landing. I thought I did pretty good."

"The Skipper was pissed. The CAG didn't care if you went into the ocean."

"That's why they didn't get a pizza."

"You and Cole didn't get on anybody's Christmas list. Where were you headed?"

"Newport on that occasion. We returned the NE-1 unscathed. We were at mess with the pilots but I don't remember you being there, I'm afraid."

"I had just landed an H-3 before you landed. I was still in the cockpit when you got out with the pizza."

"I remember you on the LDH-4. You were talking to the two other women Helos."

"You looked dashing in your uniform. Real old school navy."

"As well-heeled in the aviation business as you were, what were you doing in the Navy?"

"That was for appearances. Like Prince William and Prince Harry have to be in the Army."

"That bites!"

"Not really, I met a lot of great people."

"Like your husband?"

"No, he was never in the military. I met him on a business trip with my father."

"I was always happy with Darla. I seems like we didn't want for anything. I hope it was like that for you."

"He was away a lot. Of course, since he was at Bell, I had to move to Fort Worth when we married. It never felt right being that far inland."

"I missed being at sea when my fitness for diving was taken away. I couldn't do anything else but retire."

"That must have been very difficult for you. I have to attend a dinner party for a neighbor who's retiring."

"Certainly, don't let me hold you up."

"I'll have the airline contact you about your ticket."

"Great, I'm really looking forward to it."

"Good-bye for now."

"Good-bye Shirley," Meghan typed then she logged off.

"That almost didn't suck. You gotta' leave out the weepy, creepy stuff and concentrate on how much you love Nantucket," Meghan stated.

"I love Nantucket?"

"Sure, the windmill, the sleigh rides, the reds, the Lightship baskets, you love it!" Meghan exclaimed.

"Maybe you should go."

"I can't get away until next summer. Like John the Baptist, you gotta' preparest the way. Make straight the path for the one who follows, which is me."

"I've never seen you so full of the holy spirit," Larry quipped.

"Yeah, that's another thing, don't try to be funny. You come off as offensive or cornball. Remember that you're a mid-western conservative and that's not an animal they like up there."

"You're your mother's daughter."

"When are those pies gonna' be ready?" she asked as she put on her coat.

"With all this jerking around on the tube it'll be tomorrow evening."

"Okay, good. Can you bake some more before you leave?"

"That shouldn't be a problem."

"Okay, I gotta' get this stew home. See you later," Meghan said as she hugged him.

"See you tomorrow and tell your sister that I'll stop by in the morning."

"Okay Daddy," she said as she went out the door.

Since the computer was on, Larry decided to check out the diving conditions around Nantucket. The island is roughly a bent half-moon in shape with the rounded side to the south. A barrier island on the northeast end cuts off the sea and forms Harbor Bay and the only decent sheltered anchorage for sailing vessels in previous centuries. The fact that the island is composed mostly of sand meant that the bottom was sand. Water conditions could range from clear to silty and visibility from four feet to more than a hundred. Currents were variable depending on the location and the tides. A wreck could be covered with twenty feet of sand in a year. There were almost six hundred wrecks around the island.

The most desirable one and the only one mentioned in any detail was a British vessel that ran aground on Horseshoe Shoals in the winter of 1780. The vessel carried gold, silver and Rum for the redcoats who were laying waste to the shore on the mainland. The locals came out and 'captured' the British and as much rum as they could. Overnight the ship capsized and broke-up. Doubtless the records archived on the island would be the best source of information on the wrecks, Larry thought.

He thought about going to Nantucket to visit Shirley. He had made trips in the past to visit old navy buddies. Sometimes they came to visit him, but not so much anymore, except for Joe. He wouldn't tell Joe about this. Not yet anyway. Even after finding out that Joe had not been up front with him about the things he had been involved in, Larry would never place him on the same 'shit list' as the other folks in Alexander Bay. He thought about a time when Bush Senior was president. A time before anybody had heard of Somali pirates. He carried out a demolition operation on a pier. When he got there, he was low on air and there were people all over the pier and they were armed. He jettisoned the TXP package under the pier and armed it. When he returned to the pick-up point the raft wasn't there. Using his radio locator, he managed to get a fix on the raft. When he found it, he quietly took one of the paddles and tapped Joe on the back.

"You're a half mile from the pick-up point"

"You're an hour late," Joe countered as he helped him into the raft.

"I got invited to a wedding. It was a blast."

"So I saw. Where's my piece of the cake?" Joe asked as he took off Larry's tanks.

"Sorry, the caterer allowed no doggie bags."

"Remember the caterer at Flynt's wedding?" Joe asked.

"Yeah, you screwed her in the coatroom," Larry said as he dropped his BCD.

"Let's do it again. Okay you jokers, the Chief's here so put your backs into it," Joe ordered. They got back to the submarine before daybreak.

He made a mental note to tell his daughters to not say anything about this trip to anyone except immediate family since Larry wouldn't be able to make it to his mother's for thanksgiving.

The next week, nineteen people were terminated where he worked. Larry was one of them. He got a severance package that would be good for a year. The day after he lost his job, airline tickets came in the mail. This is such a sucky way to go into the holidays and end the year, he thought. He didn't know if he should tell Shirley. He hesitated to tell his own mother. He tried to call Joe, but the phone message said the number was no longer in service.

Things just weren't going well. He spent the next week taking care of business then Meghan drove him to the airport and he got on the plane to Boston.

When they reached their cruising altitude, Larry tried to put his head back on the headrest and he closed his eyes. He thought of people he knew in the service. It was always the same thing in those days-'Old Charley' didn't re-enlist, 'Old Charley' retired, 'Old Charley' died. It wasn't much of a problem until he was 'Old Charley' forced to retire. His life, the people he knew and the things he did could be symbolized as a jigsaw puzzle. A piece gets taken out and another piece gets put in. A kind of homeostasis as it were then the puzzle got turned over and all the pieces fell out onto the floor. He wasn't the Chief anymore. He wasn't a brick in a wall, he was a brick trying to fit into a complex mosaic.

The fellow in the window seat, tapping on his arm, woke him from his trance. He wanted to go up to first class and get himself a drink, so Larry let him out. Larry looked at his hat to make sure he hadn't gotten any dust on it. He saw that the Flight Attendant, with the drink cart, had stopped and looked at him.

"That looks important," she said.

"This is the only way my friend will recognize me, I'm afraid."

"What does that badge mean?"

"Those are my Dolphins. I was a diver for twenty two years."

"You have been a lot of places, I'll bet," she said.

"Just about every place that you can dive."

"I did some Scuba diving in Hawaii. How deep have you been?"

"Two thousand feet. That was in Hawaii, in fact," Larry replied.

"Wow, that's amazing!"

"There wasn't anything down there worth seeing. The Caribbean is my Favorite place to dive."

"I'll have to check it out," she said then she pushed the cart ahead.

Larry thought about Nantucket again. The last and only time he was actually there was in '95 when he and Joe flew an NE-1 into there, from Newport. He had been careful to not deceive Shirley about who he was and how he looked. Nothing in her emails showed that she had the slightest doubt about anything he said or a loss in her enthusiasm. From the Seaman recruits to the Admirals, he always had a reputation as a straight shooter and a plain talker. He always believed that anybody who was worth a shit never had any problems with him. For all that, Shirley could take a look at him and walk the other way. 'Oh well, I have faced the largest predators on the planet, so how tough can this be, he told himself.' He read a magazine until they landed.

As usual, the Flight Attendant walked backward down the aisle, allowing people to get their overhead bags and get in line. When she moved past him, Larry got up from his seat, put on his Master Chief's hat and took his carry-on bag out of the overhead compartment.

"Take care," he said.

"You too and have a nice holiday," she said.

"You too," Larry said then he joined the line in the aisle.

When he got to the front, the pilot shook his hand.

"You take it easy, Chief," the pilot said.

"What a wonderful world that would be," Larry said, smiling then he turned left and stepped onto the passenger bridge. As he walked into the concourse, he saw a woman with a long leather coat and a summertime squadron's hat. Suddenly all his apprehension was gone.

"Shirley, you're looking great!" he blurted out.

"Larry, you old son of a Sea Cook, how the hell are ya'," she said before throwing her arms around him.

"Still above ground," he said as he dropped his bag so he could embrace her.

"It's been such a long time."

"It doesn't seem like it now," Larry said as they both released their embrace.

"So, how are you doing?"

"Ninety nine percent good," Larry said as he looked at her.

"What's wrong?"

"A week ago they eliminated nineteen jobs. One of them was mine."

"Oh my goodness, was there a severance package?"

"One year's salary and one year's medical benefits," Larry replied, adding-"I didn't know how to tell you."

"Well now you don't have to be in any hurry to get back to Ohio," she said.

"No, I suppose not."

"Luggage is downstairs," she said, indicating to go right.

"Great, where's your plane?"

"You can see it on the other side," she said, looking toward the windows.

"Oh yeah, the red and white one."

"Have you had any time in Glass cockpits?"

"Zero, I'm afraid."

"It's no different than conventional instruments and you got a lot more runway to play with."

And a lot more people to see me fuck up, Larry thought as they stepped onto the conveyor.

"You can handle it easily. I never saw anybody land an NE-1 on an aircraft carrier."

"It was the siren call of that giant flight deck," Larry quipped, adding- "And it was good weather for landing."

"There is no fog on the island and the wind is manageable so that won't be a problem."

"I don't know the procedures for dealing with the ATC at a large airport like this."

"I'll have my headset on so I'll handle that for you," Shirley said.

"You have plenty of gas?"

"Eighty seven percent. I'll go over the checklist with you. I'll be there if you hit the chicken switch."

"It looks like I'm volunteered," Larry said as they started down the escalator.

"I told my father and Joan about you."

"Good, spare them the shock and awe," Larry quipped.

"Dad is a lot like you. Not a lot of BS."

"He sounds like my kinda' guy."

"Like your Mr. Cole?"

"Joe was a mole for the Treasury. He said nothing about that when he asked me to come to Alexander Bay in August. Divers don't withhold information like that, ever," Larry said as they stopped at the belt.

They heard the horn but the belt didn't start moving.

"How long have you known Jackie?" she asked.

"Only since I went up there in the middle of August."

"I've known her for about two years. I met Melissa last month in Puerto Rico."

"On the seventh, at 1:30 in the afternoon," Larry stated rather than asked.

Shirley looked at him quizzically.

"I happened to be there with Joe Cole and another woman. I saw a Seminole pass nearly overhead and watched it land. I swore it was Jackie, and when she came to Ohio, she told me that it was indeed her," Larry explained.

"Melissa flew up from Costa Rica with a guy named Allen Weaver. Jackie introduced us. I already knew Allen."

"Can you imagine that! What a blow-out that would have been if we had all met in San Juan."

"Like two ships passing in the night."

"That's just too much. I can't believe all the times I've run into people at airports," Larry said as the belt began moving.

"It happens a lot when I leave the island," Shirley said.

Larry saw his big suitcase come through the portal.

"There it is. Excuse me just a second," he said as he reached between a man and woman to grab it.

"I only brought one suit," he said as he turned back to Shirley.

"That should be enough. You can buy clothes on the island."

"Super," he said.

They stopped at a computer station and Shirley used her Phone to send her Flight plan. They exited by a ground level door normally used only by ground crews and flight crews. Larry hoped that their hats and his Burlington Pea coat looked convincing as they passed people along the flight line. He said 'Hi' to people that looked at them. When they got to the airplane, Larry opened the 'cargo doors' on the starboard side.

"Oh, that's a big one," he said before he put his suitcase and gear bag in the passenger compartment and closed the doors again. Unlike the Seminole, normally luggage is carried in a compartment in the nose

"The cockpit is no bigger than the Seminole. Very cozy. The heating is great for a twin. Go ahead," she said.

Larry stepped up onto the peg and then onto the flap. It had a flush door handle which was smaller than he was accustomed to. He opened the door and ducked down to look in before entering. Sometimes pilots put the restraining belt through the control wheel when the aircraft was parked. The cockpit looked small but the seats looked big enough for him.

He crouched down even more as he entered. Being careful where he placed his feet and knees, he moved over to the pilot's seat.

"That's the spare headset. The checklist is in the pouch," Shirley said.

Larry took out the Checklist and went over everything in the cockpit then they got out and did the preflight check. It was cold and there was a little wind, but no precipitation. When they got back inside, Larry plugged in the headset and put it on. He turned on the Master Switch and checked the instruments. Shirley called Ground Control and requested clearance for Baron 338 Lima to start engines. It took a minute before the tower gave them clearance to start engines. The procedure was nearly the same as Melissa's Seminole. Larry made sure the parking brake was set then he started the left engine and a few minutes later, the right engine. He ran up one engine at a time and checked the rudder, flaps and ailerons. Shirley had him call the tower this time.

"Baron 338 Lima requests runway 1-5."

The ATC told him to hold for November (something), and Larry acknowledged.

"Do you know who that is?" Shirley asked.

Larry shook his head.

"That's Caroline Kennedy."

"You would think she has had enough of flying."

"She's a real advocate of general aviation," Shirley said as they watched the large twin come from their left and make a left turn in front of them.

"She has the money, I suppose," Larry said as the other plane taxied away from them. They waited until the other plane got to the end of the runway.

"Baron 338 Lima, taxi into position and hold," the ATC said.

"Roger that, Tower. Baron 338 Lima, out," Larry replied.

He released the parking brake and advanced the throttle slowly. The Baron moved ahead easily and readily. He kept the speed down to the max taxiing speed for the NE-1. It didn't require much of a turn to the right to get lined up with the runway. When they got to the yellow line, the other twin was starting their takeoff run. Larry backed off the throttle even more and let the plane coast to the white line. He brought it to a stop and set the parking brake.

"Okay, check your wind direction."

Larry looked at the indicator.

"About ten degrees to port," Larry said.

"That's good. The props turn clockwise so it may save you some right rudder."

"Great, just like the NE-1."

"Check your trim."

The trim was right on the control wheel. They saw the other aircraft climbing into the air.

"Baron 338 Lima, you are cleared to takeoff on 1-5," the ATC said.

"Roger that, Tower, Baron 338 Lima, out," Larry said.

He ran up the engines to 2200 rpm and checked the controls again. He released the parking brake and the plane surged ahead. A little heavy handed, but this is the time to pour on the coal, Larry thought as he advanced the throttle even more. He was keeping it right on the centerline and watching for any tendency to pull to the left.

"You're doing great," Shirley said.

A few moments later they felt the Baron lift off the runway. It just seemed to have a natural urge to fly, Larry thought. He glanced down at the Garmin and saw that the airspeed was already eighty five knots. He gave it an ever so slight back pressure on the wheel and the nose started coming up. They were gaining altitude even more rapidly than the Seminole. When he glanced down again, they were doing ninety five knots. He raised the switch for the landing gear.

"What did you think of that?" Shirley asked.

"God, she grabs for air like a jet!" Larry exclaimed.

"You can set up for cruise climb."

Larry slowly pulled back the throttles until both engines were 2400 rpm then he set the props manually and turned on the autosynchronization and the yaw dampener. He made a climbing turn to the right and set their course for 170. At five thousand feet, he set the mixture for that altitude.

"You must have flown one of these before," Shirley said.

"No, just two hours in Melissa's plane with Jackie. That's it."

"I'm sure you know that the airport is on the south side. Barring any traffic, we'll come in from the west and turn to port and glide in from the sea."

"That sounds like a plan," Larry said.

"You can handle it. Wake me when we land," she quipped.

"Don't bail out on me now, Baby."

"Is that what you told Jackie?"

"She didn't say much either. Pretty laid back like you."

"Is that the way you like it?" she asked.

"I don't like the control freaks. You can say something encouraging. I don't like to look away to see if you're frozen in fear."

"You don't mind me talking while you're flying?"

"No problem at all," Larry replied.

"Do you mind talking about Alexander Bay?"

"Ask anything you want or about anybody you want."

"You were a guest of Melissa Macklin?"

"I was, on both occasions."

"Do you know that she was married four times?"

"I was told that the morning after I arrived."

"Did that put you off?"

"It didn't because we didn't do anything, ever," Larry said.

"How about Jackie?"

"The fifth night I was in Alexander Bay and the night she spent at my house last month."

"You don't have to say anything that you don't want to say."

"She wasn't married or 'committed' to anybody else and neither was I. As far as I'm concerned, that's Free Market. In fact, she came to me on both occasions," Larry explained.

"There was never any talk about love or commitment?"

"None whatsoever."

"The way Jackie talked about you, it seemed like something had happened between you two."

"I now have grave doubts about the sincerity of her and Melissa. A diver doesn't like to associate with people that they feel that way about."

"No more 'Hello Sailor?'"

"Not from any woman in Alexander Bay, I'm afraid."

"When Adam died it seemed like there were all sorts of men, but as you say, I had doubts about their sincerity. A couple days before Jackie texted me, I visited the dying mother of my stepmother. She told me that my next man would be revealed to me during a flight that week. I didn't see any credibility in that, of course."

"Maybe you heard about more than one man in that week."

"No, in fact that was the only day I left the island and that was a fluke."

"It was only a few hours before I took off with Jackie that I even knew I was going to Alexander Bay. How strange is that?" Larry asked rhetorically.

"Some people say that God works in mysterious ways."

"I know a catholic who says that, but he's CIA so how can you trust him."

"Everything is black or white with you. You don't have a different color umbrella, do you?"

"No, I don't pretend to believe anything or to be anybody. It's too hard to remember what the pretense is. I learned that in elementary school," Larry said.

"What do women think of that?"

"That's why I stuck with Darla all those years. I can't change and I don't expect anybody else to change to suit me. If anybody doesn't like it, they will walk," Larry said, adding-"They have this down to a science in Alexander Bay."

"I understand that there were other women."

"Little Karen and Cindy Morrow. Both were diving buddies and rather short affairs."

"What was the problem?"

"As Joe said, one day they're gonna' wake up and realize that they're in bed with some fucking old man."

As they approached the Lower Cape, the clouds made a ceiling of three thousand feet. Shirley told him to fly under it. After they passed the Cape, Martha's Vineyard was off to the right.

"It's a good view from up here. I hope we don't run into any Kennedys tooling about," Larry said.

"Let's keep a lookout," Shirley said as she looked at the navigation screen.

The only aircraft he had seen was an airliner, far off to their right and climbing rapidly. Larry saw her change the 'page' on the NAVCOM screen.

"The wind is from the southwest, five knots, occasional gusts. After we turn, we'll start descending," Shirley said.

"What if we miss your tiny little island in all these clouds," Larry quipped.

"We shall discuss an appropriate punishment," Shirley said in a man's voice.

"Oh no, that guy was a bastard," Larry said, smiling at the joke.

Actually, they could see the island now, off to their left. A few minutes later, Larry turned left and began descending. He called Memorial tower for Approach Confirmation. Flight control was obviously taken aback that they weren't hearing Shirley, but they acknowledged the intended runway and confirmed that there were no other aircraft in the vicinity.

"They obviously expected to hear you. There will be guns drawn when we land," Larry quipped.

Larry knew that the ATC's have absolutely no sense of humor.

"You're ornery"

"You must have me confused with that other guy, Chief Lanamai," he quipped.

"I remember that. I forget what it means."

"It is 'I am anal' spelled backwards."

They heard the Flight controller talking to another aircraft also requesting approach confirmation.

"They're behind us," Shirley said, adding-"Go ahead for final."

"Baron 338 Lima to Memorial Tower, requesting clearance to land."

"Memorial Tower to 38 Lima, you are cleared for landing on runway two-four, out."

"Roger that, Memorial Tower, Baron 338 Lima, out," Larry said then he took his finger off the button on the left side of the control wheel. He looked out the window to get a visual on the airport. It was looking murky down there, but he saw the yellow lights of the Meatball, so he turned left about thirty degrees and lined up on them on a heading of 061. He held their altitude as they crossed the coast heading north east.

"There's no obstacles in the glide path," Shirley said.

"I didn't want to lose altitude too quickly."

"It's not that far, continue as you were," Shirley instructed.

Larry put the Beechcraft in the nose down glide that they were in before and turned off the yaw dampener. The wind was coming from nearly behind them, which was better than a crosswind. He lowered the flaps ten degrees then lowered the wheels and checked his airspeed again.

"The wind is pushing us a little bit. Don't let that worry you," Shirley said.

When it looked like there was nothing but the end of the runway ahead of them, he crammed on full flaps and they began to lose altitude faster.

Larry saw the runway numbers pass just beneath them and he pulled back on the control wheel slowly.

"Gently now, it's getting the idea," Shirley said right before the main gear touched down. Larry held it for a couple seconds then pushed the control wheel forward to bring the forward wheel down. The plane continued to slow. Shirley told him that they would turn off toward the hangars ahead on the right. Larry raised the flaps and adjusted the props before making the turn. He turned right again then turned left to park it on the apron in front of the hangar that Shirley had pointed out. He set the Mixture to idle cutoff and shut down the magnetos for both engines.

"That was good. A simple approach, but that tailwind didn't help any," Shirley said.

Larry was reminded of those 'Twelve o'clock High' episodes where the 'flak happy' pilots can't let go of the control wheel. He knew how they felt as he reached for the checklist in the door pouch. They turned off the landing and taxiing lights and checked the flaps before turning off the Master Switch. When they got out, Shirley handed him the cover for the Pitot tube and he put it on. Larry opened the 'cargo doors' and removed his luggage. Shirley closed the doors for him.

"My car is over there. The black SUV."

"Oh, a Mercedes," Larry said as they started walking that direction.

"Adam bought it. I drove it up here. It doesn't have much mileage on it."

"I had a 240D. I got rid of it. It wasn't a driver friendly car. It wasn't an anything friendly car. I was really disappointed in it."

"Adam developed this 'only the best and most expensive' kick," Shirley said.

"Trying to impress his coworkers, that sort of thing?"

"He was trying to keep ahead of me, I'm afraid."

"Oh, the petty, jealous, ego thing. I had to slap the crap outta' a couple son in laws for that. Be assured that whatever our relationship, your financial situation doesn't bother me in the least. I don't even think about it," Larry assured her as they got to her vehicle.

Shirley took out her remote and opened the doors. Larry went around back and opened the hatch and put his bags in there then closed it.

Shirley waited for him to come around to the passenger side and they both got in. Normally, if he was driving, he would have got the door for her. As she started the engine, he noticed that the SUV had every option he could think of and looked new inside and out.

"Adam really pimped out this baby," Larry quipped.

"Yes, he took care of it," she said, looking distracted and not moving the car.

"You're the one looking worried now."

"It's that 'whatever our relationship' part ..."she hesitated.

"Well, I was talking about money and I didn't want to sound presumptive. What have you told friends and family? Am I an old friend, an old Navy buddy stopping by for a few laughs?"

"I just told them that I was having a guest for a couple days."

"Well, it's your house and your rules, that's no problem for me," Larry said.

"You're more laid back than I thought. Adam was such a control freak about relationships and I'm afraid that he made me one as well."

"I don't want you to feel uncomfortable about anything. If there is any issue that comes up, sing out and we'll resolve it pronto."

"It's a deal," she said as she shifted it into reverse.

"Great...Hey, they're towing your plane into the hangar," Larry observed as she backed out of the parking space.

"Yes, I have them get it in as soon as possible in this weather."

"Good idea. It's a great plane. I'm sure you know that Melissa has her own airfield and hangar. My sister and her husband have their own airfield. It's only twenty two hundred feet but he flies small aircraft anyway," Larry said.

"All empty land is usually set aside as a wildlife preserve. I would play hell getting the county council to let me build my own airfield. My father got my hangar space 'grandfathered' in so it doesn't cost that much. I just pay a monthly service fee."

"Good deal. Fuel and everything else for aircraft is so expensive," Larry said.

"You will probably think a lot of things are costly here."

"I'm feeling it already," he quipped.

"There are a lot less tourists here now so the Islanders relax things a little bit."

"I'm really looking forward to seeing this place. I haven't been to the Cape in years and I've never been up here at this time of year."

"My cottage is on the north shore. Some of my neighbors are coming over this evening. Casual clothes will be fine."

Invasive Species Part Two

"That's good, I never like to wear a suit at home."

When they got home, Shirley showed him the house and gave him the back bedroom to stay in. Larry changed his clothes and got ready for supper. An hour later her other guests arrived. A young man and woman.

"Larry, this Brian Berg and Kristen Kauffmann. This is Larry Mayer, a friend from way back in my Navy days," Shirley said as Larry stood up.

"Hello, it's nice meeting you," Larry said as he shook hands with Brian and then Kristen.

"Sit anywhere at the table," Shirley said and they sat down.

The wine and the appetizers were already on the table, so they began to dish up themselves. It took a few minutes before everyone was finished.

"I hope the weather gets better," Kristen said.

"It won't," Brian said.

"Did you see the rainbow earlier?" Kristen asked.

"Yes, it was very pretty," Shirley said.

"That one must have reached the ground," Larry said.

"Rainbows don't reach the ground," Brian said.

"Yes, they do sometimes," Larry said, wondering why Brian thought he was lying about that.

"Prove it," Brian demanded.

"They have been photographed many times. I'm sure you could find it on the internet. I have been in the end of a rainbow. Well, the yellow and the red were there for sure," Larry stated.

"Did you find a pot of gold?" Kristen asked.

"No, you get a wish."

"You didn't wish for gold?"

"No, I was twenty years old. Stupid me wished for a wife," Larry said.

"Did you get her?" Kristen asked.

"For thirty three years."

"Where are you from, Mister Mayer?"

"Larry please. Boston Mills, Ohio."

"I can tell you are not from here. How is the weather there?" she asked.

"About the same as here."

"Larry had some rather interesting experiences in the Navy. Earlier this year, he had some rather interesting experiences while salvage diving in Alexander Bay, New York," Shirley said.

"What does 'Interesting experiences' mean?" Brian asked, looking at him.

"People died," Larry replied.

"Does that happen a lot?" Brian asked

"Sometimes."

"I never did any scuba diving," Brian said.

"Larry can walk around on the bottom like we walk around on the beach," Shirley said.

"Is that right?"

"Sometimes it's a little more complicated than that."

"At Cambridge I was an activist in environmental issues, including the effects of man-made global warming on the oceans."

"Oh, it's man-made this time?" Larry asked rhetorically.

"You deny that it is due to pollution by man when there is absolute proof that it is."

"There is no proof whatsoever. Historically climatic fluctuations have always occurred and this warming cycle is occurring in the expected time frame."

"Climatologist all over the world agree that pollutants like carbon dioxide are driving this warming trend," Brian insisted.

"Because Climatologist are given money by governments to say that carbon dioxide is the culprit. CO2 is less than two tenths of one percent of the atmosphere and samples of trapped air from past centuries have a similar CO2 composition. The NOAA did experiments which showed that water vapor is the only 'greenhouse gas'. This has always been accepted until the liberal fools in governments decided to make global warming another issue. Apparently gun control and illegal immigrants wasn't enough for them," Larry concluded.

"You are saying that all these people are lying!" Brian exclaimed

"Exactly, politicians lie all the time to make a political issue out of something that is an issue for scientists. Has been politicians like Al Gore are always finding some issue to keep themselves in the money. It is truly disgusting," Larry stated.

"I can't believe you can say that!"

"In '77, 78 and '79 we had three very cold and snowy winters. The Climatologist were saying that another Ice Age was coming because of that. Now if we have a bad winter, climatologists will say it's due to Global warming. A hurricane is blamed on global warming. People have to face facts, in spite of what Al Gore says, the polar icecaps are still there," Larry stated.

Rosa and Olga brought in the main course which was Beef Wellington and the side dishes. It took a few minutes for everybody to get dished up then the servants left.

"At home we never knew what we were having on thanksgiving," Kristen said.

Since nobody else commented, Larry jumped in.

"My family always insisted on turkey."

"Larry has nine brothers and sisters," Shirley informed them.

"You have children, Larry?" she asked.

"I have four children and seven grandchildren," Larry replied.

"I don't want children. I don't think I want to bring children into a messed up world like this," Kristen said.

"What do you think of that, Larry," Brian asked smugly.

"Oh gosh, I'm sorry this isn't a perfect fucking world for you. Do you think it was a beautiful world when your mother had you? If you don't want children, that's your right. Don't be hypocritical about it by blaming the rest of the world," Larry said.

"I'm not sure that I understand what you are saying," she said.

"I have been all over the world and I have seen people who had nowhere to live and not much to eat. Now you look like someone who has never wanted for anything in your life and I am certainly no socialist so you don't have to apologize for that at all. If you feel that it will mess up your body or take up time that you need for other things then look in the mirror and admit it to yourself," Larry explained.

"Wow, and you were married for thirty three years! What do you think of that, Kristen?" Brian asked sneeringly.

Kristen looked at him then looked at Larry.

"Well Larry, I can't tell you if I agree with you, but you're more of a man than I've seen in a while," Kristen said.

"You're too kind," Larry said.

"I'm getting a stomach ache. If you'll excuse me," Brian said, standing up.

"Certainly," Larry said as he stood up also. "I have good luck with Rolaids," he added.

Brian just looked at him then walked away.

"Larry, you can still clean out a house," Shirley remarked after a minute.

"He talked about the 'spirited debates' they had at their supper table," Kristen said. "How could they have any meaningful dialogue if they all had the exact same opinion?" Larry opined.

"What do you think of that, Kristen?" Shirley asked.

"You certainly don't hold back your opinion, Larry."

"If it's understood that religion or politics is not discussed at the table then I won't."

"My father always talks about socialism," Kristen said.

"The most wrong-headed concept ever."

"He always said that this country is moving toward socialism."

"Exactly what is wrong with this country," Larry said.

"Karl Marx said-'From each according to his abilities. To each according to his needs'."

"Doubtless Marx never had to wait in line for two hours for bread, three hours for milk and four hours for meat. People used to do that in Moscow, before they got rid of that stupid socialism."

"Socialist seem to ignore the fact that the Soviet system was politically oppressive," Kristen observed.

"They have their head very far up their ass. That's why they're socialists in the first place."

"So political oppression is the only way to enforce socialism?" she asked.

"Whenever you have one portion of the population trying to oppress a larger portion of the population, the oppressors are a bunch of uptight fuckers. You could see this Sparta and in some southern states before the Civil War," Larry explained.

"We have to write a paper about the Vietnam War. The question is, was it a Civil War or a Revolutionary War? What do you think, Larry?"

"It was neither a Civil War or a Revolutionary War, it was a Thirty Years War in the Jungle. I have met very few Americans who know anything at all about the Thirty Years War, but we should. That war covers just about every possible question and consequence that can arise in a war. Three biggies are, why are we getting into this war, how are going to prosecute this war and how are we gonna' get outta' this war when we no longer want to be in it. Presidents Kennedy, Johnson and Nixon were Second World War veterans and had absolutely no knowledge of what happened in the Thirty Years War."

"What happened ultimately?" Kristen asked.

"At the end, all the major powers pulled out and left areas of Germany, Poland and the Czech Republic devastated and depopulated."

"I see the similarity there."

"My old history Prof said that all you really need to know is the French Revolution, and the Thirty Years War, but you have to know them well."

"Rosa, bring the pie," Shirley requested.

"Certainly Mam," Rosa said.

"It's been an hour and a half. It should be just warm enough," Larry said.

"Larry made the pies," Shirley said.

"Is that right? You are a man of many talents, Larry," Kristen said.

"My daughters say that pies are my specialty, which is to say, that is the only thing I know how to bake. What do you like to cook?" Larry asked.

"Oh, I don't cook," she replied.

Larry looked at her for a moment.

"Why don't you cook?"

"I just never got into it."

"My father would have had a field day with you. Before me and Darla were engaged, I took her home to meet my family. I had already told them that she was a great cook. The first thing my father says to her-'Can you make gravy'?" Larry said.

"Larry grew up on a farm," Shirley said.

"And my mother cooked!" Larry added, "and took care of us and worked on the farm."

"That sounds like a lot of work," Kristen said.

"What, if anything, have we learned here, boys and girls?" Larry asked rhetorically.

"Be prepared to do anything," Shirley said.

"Yes, but it was a rhetorical question," Larry replied, smiling.

"I'm starting to miss the Navy. Bless your heart."

Rosa came in with the pies already dished up and set the plates in front of them.

"Is Mister Brian coming?" she asked.

"Perhaps, set one for him," Shirley replied.

"Yes Mam."

After Rosa left, Kristen pushed the whipped cream off of her pie with her spoon.

"When I went to school, we had to stand up when asking or answering a question and we had to address the teacher as Mam. I never let anybody call me 'Mam'.

"What do you think of that, Larry?"

"Well, I went to public school, but I suppose it makes you sound like some fricking old lady," Larry replied.

Shirley laughed at that. Kristen didn't see the humor.

"Larry, you haven't changed one bit. You have the answer for everything."

"My grandchildren say that I'm a big, ugly Yoda."

"I always found the speeches of President Kennedy to be very inspirational,"

Kristen said after a minute.

"That's all speech writers stuff. He said-'There's always a son of a bitch." Now that's some wisdom you can hang on to. Ronald Reagan's '64 Republican convention speech is what you wanna' read and remember. 'One day you will tell your grandchildren that you remember when America was free.' That still scares me," Larry said.

"What do you think of this 'Arab Spring'?" Kristen asked.

"Remember the French revolution? These political coups almost never go off as the revolutionaries think then they go through chaotic stages then a military strongman takes over."

"Interesting, I'll have to bring up that idea in our next class discussion," Kristen said.

CHAPTER TWO

The cold air blew on their faces as they walked along the beach in the dark.

"What do you think of young Kristen?" Shirley asked.

"Well, she won't have children, she won't cook and she won't be called 'Mam'. I can only remember three things, so she will have to start compiling a list here pretty soon."

"She can hand out a sheet of paper when she meets people," Shirley joked.

"She might need a book."

"Some women can't man up. She needs some time away from mommy and daddy." she suggested.

"She hasn't felt the hard edge of life. I envy her."

"You seem to get it enough. So, what's your thoughts on life?" she asked as she took his hand in hers.

She hasn't heard enough already! Larry thought.

"When I lost my rating, it was like the ground opening beneath my feet. When I lost Darla, it was the same thing. Now it's happened again. A short life and a merry one and another fucking train wreck."

Larry looked straight ahead rather than look at her.

"The Japanese are liberals," Shirley said.

"Yes, I believe most of them are."

"What's your definition of a liberal?"

"Well it's not my definition, but I found it amusing to hear a liberal defined as somebody who knows nothing about history, nothing about math and nothing about pulling their head out of their ass," Larry said.

"That may be the best description I ever heard. Their philosophy seems disjointed and their ideas unworkable."

"That's the 'head up their ass' part. Jesus said that there will always be wars, poverty and injustice in the world. The only thing you can hang on to is the truth and the truth is the last thing a liberal wants to hear. You see it all the time. Black people objecting to any mention in history books that they were slaves at one time and people having hissy fits because the Declaration of Independence says 'All men are created equal.' That's the truth, that's the way it is, deal with it and get over it," Larry stated.

"Those are some very strong words," Shirley opined.

"An old admiral said-'Larry, if deeds spoke louder than words you would be king of this country.' Now Franklin, he was a man of words. I always wished for his eloquence."

"My stepmother has some unusual philosophy. Her name is Joan."

"Nietzsche said that it is normal and usual to protect the status quo, therefore progress can only be made through the abnormal and the unusual," Larry said.

"I don't know about Nietzsche, but my step mother is Apostolic Pentecostal. They believe that you can't question the Bible and you can never start questioning God's will. To her, my mother died because it was time for her to be my father's wife. Adam died because it was time for me to have another husband."

"I don't know how much comfort that is to you and your father, but it worked out for Joan," Larry quipped.

"Her aunt was crushed by a semi-truck, but they didn't sue because their church doesn't allow that."

"I wonder how they feel about taking a man's head off with a Smatchet? They sound like a bunch of church nuts. Another Westboro Baptist church."

"Something like that. I just wanted you to be forewarned."

"Where did he find her? Mismatch.com," Larry quipped as they started up the steps.

"She really isn't a bad person, I suppose. Dad is happy with her."

"She didn't force daddy to embrace the faith?" Larry asked.

"He is Catholic, of course."

Larry figured that you don't stop being Catholic unless you're excommunicated. He wondered how her stepmother felt about her having a male house guest as they went in and took off their coats.

"As far as me being here, is there any adjustment necessary?"

"They know I'm not some teenager. They have always let me live my own life."

"Good, that saves the awkward part," Larry said as they went into the living room.

Larry watched television while Shirley chatted with the servants then made some phone calls. Later she sat next to him on the couch.

"You must be tired."

"Getting there," Larry said.

"You can use the big bathroom if you want a bath."

"A shower will be fine for tonight."

"Were the accomodations satisfactory at Schooner Bay?" she asked.

"Yes, they were."

"Melissa had two husbands that killed themselves according to Jackie."

"The first and only time she really talked to me, I told her about my family. She was an only child and wealthy, so her family life had been very different. I had already been told by the townies that she was married four times. She seemed unhappy about not having a good life in that respect."

"My early life wasn't quite that bad. We traveled a lot. I missed not having brothers and sisters. Adam was adamant about not having children," Shirley explained.

"That's too bad. You could have some very pretty children," Larry opined.

"How about Jackie and those other women?"

"Same as Darla, it was up to them if they wanted children."

"How is Melissa gonna' handle it without heirs?" Shirley asked.

"I never thought of that. That shows you how much I didn't concern myself with her affairs."

"In the morning I need to get some things in town."

"Great, Meghan wanted me to get her some Nantucket Reds," he said.

"Do you know her sizes?"

"I always buy them one size bigger because she lies about that. Intentional underestimation as Joan Rivers says."

"My mother would do that then she would secretly exchange the clothes for the proper size."

"I wonder if people who do that know how much they're driving up the price of everything?" Larry asked rhetorically.

They talked for twenty minutes then Larry went upstairs and took a shower and went to bed. About half an hour after he was in bed, he saw the door open part way.

"Who comes?"

Shirley came in and closed the door. She got into bed with him without saying a word.

"Are we alone?" he asked.

"Rosa and Olga went home"

Larry embraced her under the blanket.

"Jackie didn't say anything about you disappointing her," she whispered.

"I have a baby making shawl at home. Guaranteed to work every time. I wouldn't let Jackie touch it," Larry said.

"That's so silly," she said as she slid over and sat on top of him.

She pulled off her night gown over her head and laid on him.

"I've been feeling undersexed for quite a while."

"Deplorable, simply deplorable," Larry said softly then there wasn't much meaningful conversation after that.

CHAPTER THREE

As they came out of the Toggery, they ran into two women.

"Hi. Larry these are my friends Heather and Shelley."

They were both about five feet, nine inches tall in their boots. Heather had red hair and Shelley had blonde hair.

"Nice to meet you, Larry. Where have you been hiding him, Shirl?" Heather said.

"Larry is from Ohio."

"Is that right! I've never been there. What brings you here, Larry?"

"Oh, I'm just a holiday guest of Shirley's."

"Oh no, we must see more of you here," Heather insisted.

"He'll be here for a couple days," Shirley said.

"We'll be off-island for a couple days. Will you be here after Thanksgiving?"

"If I haven't worn out my welcome by then," Larry said, smiling.

"Wonderful, see you in church. Must dash," Heather said.

"Nice meeting you two," Larry said.

They both waved then hurried off.

"Such friendly people. I haven't heard 'see you in church' in years."

They had lunch at a seafood diner. The waitress brought them large bowls of clam chowder and buttered bread.

"The Clam Chowder has always been good here," Shirley said.

"Good, I can't find decent Chowder in Ohio."

"This is one of the few real old-time places left. I thought you would like it," Shirley said

Larry saw a man in a suit come through the door and start walking past the counter like he was going to the tables in back. He stopped and looked at them.

"Shirley, fancy meeting you here," he said.

"Oh, hello Bruce. This is my old friend, Larry Mayer."

Bruce just nodded at him. Larry saw that he was an inch or two taller than him and he could smell his cologne.

"Why don't you join me at my table."

Larry thought he was only talking to Shirley since he didn't look at him.

"I'm afraid we have already ordered," Shirley said

"I could have it brought to my table," he suggested.

"Maybe some other time," Shirley said.

"Yes, we should have dinner soon. We have a lot of things to catch up on. I am director of my department now."

"That's good. Maybe I'll run into you sometime," Shirley said.

Bruce hesitated. He didn't look happy and he wasn't hiding it.

"Sure, I'll give you a call," he said then he went back the way he came.

"I guess he changed his mind about lunch," Larry quipped after he left.

"One of those guys that started hanging around after Adam died."

"Yeah, he looks like the type that lets that suit go right through him," Larry said.

"God help him if a hair gets out of place."

"He's wearing make-up too. I would have liked to have him in my outfit."

"What he lacks in guts he makes up for with arrogance and churlishness," Shirley joked.

"We'll see," Larry said.

After they finished their lunch, they went to Ollie's second hand store. Another gray shingled place.

"This is one of those old fashioned places with that bucolic charm that you were talking about," Shirley said as they entered.

Shirley began talking to the woman at the glass case. Shirley introduced her to Larry. An older man was putting things on an old wooden shelf behind her. The old guy turned toward them after a minute.

"You say you were a Master Chief?" he asked.

"Yes I was," Larry replied.

"I got something here that you might like," he said as he looked around on a lower shelf. He picked up an old knife in a sheath and handed it to Larry.

Larry pulled it out of the sheath and looked at it. He saw a price sticker that said $45.

"Yes, it's an old USN mark 1 utility knife," Larry said.

The sheath said 'Made in Germany' and was darkened by age. It wasn't original at any rate, he thought as he sheathed it and handed it back to the man.

"I haven't seen one with a wooden pommel like that," the old guy remarked.

"Some of them had wood. There were so many made and so many different designs and manufacturers that collectors won't even look at them."

Larry would expect to see one at a garage sale for $8-$10 in Ohio. The old guy showed him a Burnside Fifth Model. The bore was in bad shape but the action was workable. The owner came up with an old cartridge box that had two Burnside cartridges. Larry showed him how the cartridge fit into the breech block instead of the barrel. In spite of its rather unconventional action and cartridge, it proved to be sturdy and reliable. Even with its bad bore, that one could still be loaded and shot, Larry explained. Shirley bought two whale oil lamps and she bought him a replica of an old pocket watch plated in gold.

After they returned home, they visited a man named Frank Folger. Folger was supposed to know more about the diving around the island than anybody else. He had heard of Larry through an old article in a diving magazine. He explained that the Guinness Book had recorded the deepest dive being 554 feet by a British diver. The article stated that Master Chiefs Larry Mayer and Chris Hartmann had used various experimental mixtures of gases to make dives down to two thousand feet. Larry confirmed that in fact they exceeded the depth in Guinness on every dive. Unlike a lot of deep divers, Frank showed no competitiveness or secretiveness and Larry liked him right off. Strangely, Larry had little diving time in the area, while most of Frank's diving was in the northeast. Frank had dived on the U-boat which was too deep for sport diving. The conning tower had been blown off, leaving a large hole in the pressure hull so divers were able to enter the engineering spaces and photograph the diesel engines. Larry told him about diving on the Madamoiselle de Loire.

"Damn, it's too bad the Froggies found out about that. I'll bet there was some serious gold down there and you were that close to finding it," Hank speculated.

Frank's wife insisted that they stay for dinner. They discussed how severe the winter would be and if the seals and sharks would leave soon. How much snow and cold a Monkey Puzzle tree could take and how many people would come for the Christmas Stroll. After supper, Frank had to help a clam fisherman with his boat. He told him that they could meet at the Red Gull after seven o'clock if he finished in time. Since there was a good chance that he could run into other guys who knew the bottom around the island, he decided to check it out. Shirley had other things to do so Frank dropped him off in front of the bar and went on his way.

Larry went in and introduced himself to the owner, whose name was Ed. Most of the people in there seemed too young to be divers or have any knowledge of the bottom. He talked to a few people about being in the Navy and about flying. At seven o'clock, Ed told him that Frank regretted that he couldn't make it. He decided to sit at a table and finish his Modena Chianti. The 'old sea dog' ambience was really lacking here, he thought as he checked out the décor in the rest of the room. He caught a movement in his peripheral vision. 'Spruce Bruce' had come in and was getting himself a drink. 'What a putz. The man wears make-up and gets his nails done by a manicurist. I'd have loved to have him in my outfit. He'll never sit with me, too beneath him,' Larry thought as he headed his way.

Bruce surprised him by sitting down at his table without even asking.

"I wasn't expecting you here."

"I can say the same thing," Larry said.

"Are you enjoying our weather?"

Not enjoying the company, Larry thought

"If it would get better."

"I'm surprised you are friends with Shirley," Bruce said.

"I've known her for a long time," Larry said.

"Old acquaintances don't carry any weight here."

"And your point is?" Larry snapped.

"You're way outta' your league here."

"I've been told that I'm outta' my league, outta' my class and outta' my mind, all my life." Larry replied.

This is a one-sided conversation. This jerk isn't even listening to what I'm saying. A habit honed by many years of being a prick asshole at work, Larry thought as he went into a slow burn.

"You're just a little fish from a little pond. An insignificant…"

Larry threw his wine into his face then backhanded him across his mouth. He slammed his face down on the table.

"Now that you're listening. I've been all over this world and I've always had arrogant pricks like you trying to get over on me. Now you stay right there until I leave."

Larry got his coat and walked out of the bar. It was more than a quarter mile walk. Although it was after dark, Shirley was sitting on the porch when he came 'home'.

"A little chilly for the porch. Folger didn't make it to the Red Gull so I left," Larry said as he came up the steps.

"I heard there was some trouble there."

"Oh, not really. Old Spruce Bruce had too much to drink. He hit his face on the back of my hand then fell and hit his face on the table. I'm sure he'll be feeling better in the morning."

"The sheriff told me that nobody got a clear enough view of it to make out a report. He hopes there isn't any more trouble like this," Shirley informed him as she opened the door

"Certainly, I abhor violence," Larry agreed as they went into the cottage.

"So it was that 'two males wanting the same female' thing?"

"For him it was. The prick bastard told me that I was some kinda' inferior human being that didn't belong here. He has obviously been doing that with coworkers for a long time. It didn't work." he said as he took off his coat.

"So you were getting one back for what happened to you at work?" she asked as they went into the kitchen

Larry hesitated, "Perhaps."

"You could start a dating service, 'It's just punch'," she said as she turned around right in front of him. He gently put his arms around her waist.

"That's very funny. That's the first time I've seen you make a joke."

"The Sheriff knows about the fiascos in Alexander Bay and that you killed a seventeen year old kid in 2007 and severely wounded two men in 2009."

"They were criminals trying to rob me. Did he tell you that I didn't get no loving the whole time I was there last month?"

"What about Cindy 'Whatsherface'?"

"She only talked to me for a minute in the hotel. I got the brush-off via her mother."

"Ooh, she got the treasure then she dumped you."

"You could say that."

"Did it occur to you that she knows where the wreck is now?" Shirley asked.

"She may have looked at the GPS, but she doesn't have the know-how to carry off an operation like that," Larry replied.

"How about your buddy Joe?"

"Don't worry about Joe, I trust him fifty percent," Larry quipped.

"So he knows about the wreck in Florida?"

"He saw us diving there and he knows about another prospect in St. Lucia," Larry replied

"Jackie doesn't trust him either."

"What does Jackie say about me?" Larry asked.

"She says that you're white on white and you wouldn't touch any money that doesn't belong to you."

"I have heard that before."

Larry wondered how much she knew about salvage laws.

"Do you have any interest in salvage diving?"

"Not really," she replied as they sat on the couch.

"I have heard about a couple more interesting wrecks around the island."

"Everybody wants to dive that U-boat," Shirley said.

"What good is a fricking U-boat?"

Shirley blew into his ear.

"Maybe there's Nazi gold is in there. Maybe the Amber room from the Winter Palace is in there," she whispered.

"Maybe the rotten bones of some stinking Nazis are in there. If I found anything of value, under the Four Powers Treaty, they decide who it belongs to and I don't get shit."

"I'll always make sure you get all you want," she said before she latched onto his neck.

"Oww! If you're that hungry let's go to the kitchen," Larry said as she shifted around for another bite.

"You sleep with me tonight," she said when she let go.

"I'll have to tie you up so I can get some sleep."

"Remember, it's my house and my rules."

"All those years and I never remember making any rules about that," he said.

"How about 'forsaking all others until death do you part'?"

"Me and Misses Mayer had an agreement-I stay faithful and she let me live," Larry said.

"Oh yeah, I like that one. I never touched another man until Adam died. I don't know about him, though."

"Joe Cole was faithful to his wives. As soon as they thought they found a better proposition, they ran off. It didn't take them long."

"And what, if anything, have we learned here, boys and girls?" Shirley asked.

"Knock her up before you marry her."

"What if you get me, you rascal?"

Larry wondered if she meant 'if' or 'when'.

"I want red and white carnations," Larry said.

"Do you know how hard it is to get those here?" she said as she goosed him in the ribs.

"Just for that, I'm gonna' bite you as hard as you bit me," Larry said as he pushed her down on the couch.

"Oh no, I'm not ready!" she exclaimed.

"Save it for the Obstetrician," he said as he held her down.

The next day was Thanksgiving and they got up late. Since dinner was at two o'clock, they showered and got dressed. Larry began making the pies while Shirley left to get more things and pick up her father and stepmother at the airport. They arrived right at dinner time. Shirley introduced him to her father and stepmother then they went into the Dining Room and sat down to wine and rolls.

"How are you keeping, Mister Mayer?" she asked.

"Not bad and call me Larry."

"What do you do, Larry?"

"Right now, nothing."

"What did you do before nothing?"

"I made polymers for computer chips for fifteen years."

"He was in the navy before that," Shirley said.

"What did you do in the Navy?" Joan asked.

"I killed people." Larry replied.

"Why did you do that?"

"They looked like they needed killing, I suppose."

"How could you tell?"

"When I was a kid I saw a dog killed. Everybody said it was a mad dog and it would try to kill people so it had to be killed. That criterion seemed to fit."

"Did you have permission to kill these people?"

"No, that horseshit was back in the Clinton days. They wanted us to call the White House and ask if we could kill somebody. Naturally a lawyer will always tell you that you can't kill them, so I ignored that procedure," Larry explained.

"What did President Clinton think of that?" she asked.

"I never got to ask him. We were standing formation and Clinton says something to my buddy, Joe Cole, so Joe calls him a lying, cheating, doping, whoring, punk hillbilly. Him and Clinton got into it right there. That really blew me away, I'll tell ya'," Larry explained.

"You haven't accepted Christ as your savior?"

"No, I was jewish."

"You were jewish?"

"I guess, I stopped getting invited to the synagogue."

"You must accept Christ as your savior."

"Or Mohammed, or Buddha? I killed religious nuts. Happy is in and holy is out in my world. We used to say-separation of church and state. That means everybody has their own ideas on religion and politics and keep them to yourself."

"Don't get the wrong idea. Larry is a Midwest conservative. He made Ronald Reagan blush," Shirley said.

"Larry, Shirley told me that you flew her Beechcraft here from Logan," Albert said.

"You let him fly an airplane!" Joan asked, incredulously.

"Yes, I must admit that I was a little nervous."

"Larry is the only guy I ever saw, land a Piper Cub on an Aircraft Carrier. He just brought it in like nothing to it and took off a couple hours later the same way."

"That is rather unusual these days," Albert said.

"It was fun," Larry said.

"It was never a quiet ship with Larry there," Shirley assured them.

"We stopped here and got a pizza. We had to buy our own pizza and pay for the gasoline ourselves. The ATC told us to gas up and get," Larry said.

Rosa and Olga started bringing in the turkey and the other entrees. They had to wait for the servants to dish them up rather than the 'help yourself 'style he was accustomed to. Larry had them hold the sweet potatoes. The conversation was stopped until the servants were finished.

"It looks like the looneys in the state house are considering gay marriage again," her father said.

Joan looked at Shirley. Shirley smiled at her.

"What do you think of gay marriage, Chief?" Albert asked.

"Marriage is between a man and woman who are in love and who are one hundred percent committed to each other."

"None of this 'same sex' stuff?" Joan asked.

"I already stated the conditions and that ain't one of them."

"These people think they can change marriage," Joan said.

"Marriage has been affirmed by six thousand years of human nature. Gay marriage, open marriage, it's all horseshit. None of it is any good. None of it can work," Larry stated.

"I wholeheartedly agree with you. What do you think, Shirley?" Joan said.

"The Chief has the correct answer as always," Shirley agreed.

"So many young people are living together without being married," Joan said.

"Fornication has always been popular," Larry quipped.

Joan turned red at that remark. Shirley had to bite her tongue to keep from laughing.

"How about you two?"

"Really, I just arrived two days ago! I hardly think that we have discussed cohabitation!" Larry exclaimed.

Shirley couldn't hold back laughing at that.

"Of course, I wasn't suggesting any such thing," Joan said, adding- "There are numerous other sins."

"I'm sure if the subject ever comes up, God will find fornication well down on the list," Larry asserted.

They ate in silence for a few minutes.

"Thou shalt not kill' is another commandment," Joan said.

"I like 'smite the Amalykite. Spare not even the women and children.' Such a charming little passage," Larry stated.

"Do those you killed haunt you?"

"No, those who died on September eleventh, ten years ago, haunt me," Larry said.

"Yes, well, enough said. Your flowers are lovely, Shirley. It must be hard to get good flowers this time of year."

"Yes, the greenhouse has less of the good ones every day," Shirley replied.

"Thank goodness we always have flowers available on Long Island."

"Chief, what sort of flowers do you have on your place?" Albert asked.

"Roses, Darla was crazy about roses. Since she died I'm afraid that they have become rather scraggly. She was the only one who knew how to take care of them properly."

"In the picture of your daughters on the porch, your roses look so lovely," Shirley said.

"That's very kind," Larry said.

"Shirley told me that you made the apple pie, Larry," Joan said.

"Yes, I did."

"Some men find it embarrassing to admit that they cook," Joan said.

"They should find it embarrassing that their wife or girlfriend doesn't cook."

Daddy was telling me that you had a rather embarrassing moment at the Women's Supper Club," Shirley said after a moment.

"I was in the ladies' room and I had a zipper failure on my Armani dress. I couldn't get the zipper up so I had to wait for another woman to come in and help me and she couldn't do much with it either. I was supposed to be out there making a presentation. It was quite embarrassing, I assure you," Joan explained.

"Well that certainly sounds embarrassing," Shirley agreed, adding- "Can you top that, Larry?"

He decided to leave out the gross stuff.

"I gave my daughter a couple grand so she could give it to her friend as a wedding gift. It was for a security deposit on an apartment. Well I got invited to the wedding and at the reception I was introduced to this young woman who was a nurse in Maternity. So I said, 'Well you must like a lot of babies.' I meant to say, 'You must like babies a lot.' It wouldn't have been so bad except a hundred people started laughing. I felt so stupid."

"Events like that are always remembered for the things people say," Albert said, adding-"Chief, I understand that you have quite a gathering for the holidays."

"My mother has ten children, thirteen grandchildren and eight great grandchildren. Eighty percent of us are likely to show up on any holiday," he replied.

"I suppose you know that Shirley was an only child?"

"Yes, she mentioned that."

"Since we were talking about embarrassment, would you like to say something, Father?" Shirley asked.

"We're old guys. Don't rush us," Larry quipped.

"Your mother wanted Grandchildren. You promised her that."

"Oh, so we're getting down to brass tacks now. Okay Larry, are you still fertile?" Shirley snapped.

"Check," he replied in Navy fashion.

"If I tell you I'm pregnant, is that going to be a problem, Chief?" Shirley asked like an officer asking a CPO.

"No...er, I mean it never has been so I don't see why it should be," Larry replied.

"Alright, the question has been resolved," Shirley declared.

Her father and Joan looked at her, incredulous.

"Too bad you can't make it to the farm for Christmas. It's always a riot," Larry said as casually as he could.

All three of them looked at him now.

"I'm sure they would love you folks. I mean people pronounce 'R's over there. You would probably think it's funny," Larry quipped.

"I have been to Nautheast Ohio," Albert said.

"Everybody has guns in Ohio. How many guns did you say you have?" Shirley asked Larry.

"Only nine now," he replied.

"We were at Ollie's and old Glen showed him this rifle. What kind of rifle was it Chief?" Shirley asked.

"A Fifth Model Burnside."

"Right, a Burnside. Larry showed him how to load it and shoot it."

"I've heard of the Burnside," Albert said.

"It was an unusual design. The cartridge has an obturating ring at the bullet and tapers to almost half that size at the rear. It is loaded into the breechblock rather than the barrel. The design is so rugged that in spite of the rough rifling in the barrel, that one could still be loaded and fired," Larry explained.

"Was this a cavalry arm?" her father asked.

"Some were, but this was an infantry rifle. Soldiers started to get leery of standing erect and shoulder to shoulder while advancing into cannons. The Burnside allowed them to kneel or lay down since it could be loaded like that," he replied.

After dinner, her father and stepmother were supposed to go shopping and visit more friends for supper. When it came to those two subjects, the women could talk all night apparently. Larry was standing by the front door and talking with Albert.

"That watch chain brings back memories. My grandfather had one," Albert said. "My mother has one that was her grandfather's. This one was given to me by a diving buddy. A young lady named Cynthia Morrow."

Larry didn't feel like giving out any more information about Cindy.

"I haven't seen one in years."

"The bridle is supposed to be gold plated. I was thinking of having it redone in fourteen carat gold."

"That would look nice," Albert agreed then he looked at his watch.

"She dawdles around so much, the store will be closed, and it's open 24 hours," he said.

Larry laughed at that.

"That's very funny. Shirley has an occasional sense of humor. She usually catches me quite by surprise as well."

"She is thirty seven. I'm afraid she might be getting too old to have children," her father said.

"My cousin had three boys and she started in her late thirties," Larry said.

"I wasn't an only child in truth. I had a younger brother and sister that died as children."

"That's rough, Al. Grandchildren don't come when you want or think and they don't always come with benefit of clergy," Larry said.

"Joan will be thrilled to hear about that," he said sarcastically.

"They're still your grandchildren and you have to love them just as much," Larry stated.

"Are you ready to go, Al?" Joan asked as they came into the room.

"Certainly," he replied.

"A lovely dinner, Shirley," her stepmother said before kissing her on the cheek.

"Thank you. I hope we can see you again before too long," Shirley said.

"It was nice meeting you, Larry," she said before kissing him on the cheek also.

"Great meeting you. Maybe we can dive sometime," Larry said.

"Yes, take care. Bye bye," she said.

"Bye," they both said as Albert and Joan went down the steps.

Shirley watched them as they got into their car then she waved again before they backed out. After they were gone, she closed the door.

"You wanna' go down to the club and play some tennis?" Larry quipped as they embraced?"

"I'm still bruised and sore from last night, you brute."

"Is it rough for girls and gentle for boys or the other way around?" he asked.

"After all those children, you need to ask me!"

"Actually your father was asking," Larry replied.

"What did you tell him?"

"I told him that grandchildren aren't that predictable."

"What were his specs?"

"Two boys then a girl," Larry replied.

"Can I do this in one shot?" she asked.

"Babies and babies and babies," Larry said, adding-"You'll have to come for Christmas and meet my mother."

"Serious drugs here."

"Drugs are bad for you," Larry said.

"And where did you get this information?"

"Brook Shields told me that."

"And she is a reliable source of medical information?" she questioned.

"Certainly, she wouldn't lie about that."

"You can't trust those Hollywood types."

"You mean I can't keep up with the Kardashians?" Larry joked.

"Her wedding cost $12 million and lasted two months. That doesn't seem cost effective," Shirley opined.

"Mine was $1200 and it lasted thirty three years. I was trying to get my money's worth."

"Maybe she would go diving with you."

"That's it, fashion scuba gear to go with fashion swim wear. We'll make a million!" Larry exclaimed jokingly.

"I thought that bunch were one of your pet peeves?" Shirley asked.

"No, Band Aid and that song by John Lennon."

"Is that just a seasonal thing?"

"Four fifths of the world aren't Christian so it's not even their holiday! Do you know how many places Christians get tortured to death in Africa? Screw them, screw the song and screw the artists who did it."

After her parents left, Larry and Shirley went to the theater to see plays put on by the elementary and high school students. The youngsters put on an adaptation of The Little Christmas Tree which lasted about half an hour. In the intermission before the high schooler's rendition of the Thanksgiving story, Shirley introduced him to several people in the lobby.

"Hello folks. Larry, this is Dorothy and Melanie Shook. They have the Knit Fits, a shop that sells real wool scarves and hats."

"Hello, nice meeting you," Larry said.

"Are you the man that leaves dead bodies lying around the countryside?" Melanie asked.

"In years past it has gotten a little sticky," Larry replied.

"Dot and Mel lived next to Beth Lochtefeld," Shirley said.

"Oh yes, I remember that she was killed by a Mr.Toolan, from New York."

"My goodness, we have had two homicides and an attempted murder. I don't know what craziness is afoot here these days," Dot stated.

Obviously they felt that Larry's presence didn't augur well for the violent crime problem. He decided that he wouldn't tell them about killing Kurtz and Altieri in the water in August.

"I'll try to restrain myself," Larry quipped.

"I heard about an incident at the Red Gull," Dot said.

"There's always the fellows who occasionally gets too full of themselves," Larry replied.

"Our father is a selectman."

"That's good. I always wanted a family member that could address such problems."

"Are you ready for the Christmas Stroll?" Shirley asked.

"You know how that is. We always think we're ready," Melanie replied.

"Larry has a crocheted shawl which he claims will bring babies to any woman who wears it. That would be a real draw for your shop."

"Such a thing would be worth a million dollars if it were only true," Dot said.

"It has worked for nine different women. I keep it locked up," Larry said.

"Are you afraid that it will get loose," Melanie joked.

"Women always want to touch it and put it on."

"It's really beautiful. It's five feet square, white and three shades of brown. All natural colors and all hand worked and hand spun yarn," Shirley explained as she took out her cellphone.

"That kind of craftsmanship is rare these days," Dot said.

"On this island it's non-existent," Melanie stated.

Shirley handed Dot her phone. Melanie took out her glasses.

"Let's see, there's the box stitch, treble shell and the pineapple stitch. It certainly looks well made. It's not for sale?"

"No, it's just for show. I never let it leave the house now."

"Where did you get it?" Dot asked.

"A woman named Mavis Matheson on the island of Jura and four of her friends, made it for me. I recovered some things for them in a diving operation."

"So they imbued it with this progeny producing power?" Melanie quipped.

"That's what they said. Women seem to be attracted to it for sure."

"We would certainly like to see it," Dot said, adding-"Here's the Commodore."

"Commodore, this is my friend Larry Mayer," Shirley said.

"Call me Larry," he said as they shook hands.

"I talked to Albert earlier. He said that you were a navy diver."

"Yes I was."

"I was an engineering officer back in the sixties."

"I was a Master Chief."

"I never could conn a big vessel. How deep have you dived?"

"Two thousand feet. That was in Hawaii."

"That's fantastic!"

"Commodore, I thought you would be in Florida by now," Shirley said.

"The boat and Diane are in the intercoastal waterway. I'll be heading there tomorrow," he replied.

"Do you still have a place in Boca Raton?"

"Yes, that's where we're heading," he said.

"Larry spent some time in Jacksonville. He was an instructor there," Shirley said.

"I have dived all over Florida," Larry added.

"If it wasn't for hurricanes, it would be the greatest place in the world," the Commodore quipped.

"There's a lot of good diving and decently priced accomadations."

"Larry is still suffering from off-island sticker shock," Shirley explained

"It takes some getting used to. I have to check in with the boss."

"Catch you later, Commodore."

"Nice meeting you," Larry said as they shook hands.

"I don't think the Commodore ever gets it out of the intercoastal."

"He looks pretty old," Larry said.

"Mid seventies…Well, here is another pair of birds who forgot to fly south," Shirley said.

"I can't flap my arms like I used to," the man said.

"Larry, this is Ike and Jessie Chambers. Jessie painted the landscape in the living room."

"I noticed it right away. I thought it was a Van Wittel," Larry said.

"I have been told that our styles are similar," Jessie said.

"Are you staying for the walk?"

"No, we're locking up the house and leaving tomorrow for St. Petersburg," Ike said.

"Are you spending the winter here, Larry?" Jessie asked.

"My house is in Ohio. I'll have to return eventually."

"My brother moved to Florida twenty years ago. He likes it there, summer and winter," Jessie said.

"I lived there for five years. I never got bored with it."

Another woman came over to them.

"Larry, this is Margaret Sullivan. Margaret, this is Lawrence Mayer," Shirley said.

"Nice to meet you Mr. Mayer. Did you enjoy the presentation by the fourth graders?"

"Yes, very entertaining," Larry said.

"Margaret has been the art director for years," Shirley said.

"Maybe you can do something about that pile of trash out front," Larry suggested.

"You mean 'Leaves of knowledge?' That was done by Felix Moore," Margaret informed him.

"He should have been whipped."

"Don't you see anything when you look at that?"

"Yes, I see a degenerate and decaying society that would allow such a piece of junk to be displayed as art," Larry said.

"I hope you enjoy the seniors," she said then she left.

"Scratch one friend," Shirley remarked.

"I can't stand somebody trying to pass off schlock as art."

"It's Miss Sullivan by the way."

"Why doesn't that surprise me?"

They heard the bell and filed back into the auditorium. They took the same chairs that they had before.

"These folding chairs are murder on our backs. I hope they make this quick," Larry said.

"That's the first time I've ever heard you complain about aches and pains," Shirley observed.

"A miserable chair is something I don't need."

The thanksgiving play was well done and the writing was at an adult level. Larry was impressed with the costuming and the acting. They stood up and applauded at the end. At the door they ran into Miss Sullivan.

"What did you think of the play Mr. Mayer?"

"It was very good. Obviously you're a master at the performing arts," Larry said.

"As opposed to visual arts?"

"You said it, I didn't."

"What do you do, Mr. Mayer?"

"Right now, absolutely nothing."

"What did you do before that?"

"I made polymer for silicon chips."

"Larry was a navy diver and a Master Chief for twenty years," Shirley added.

"I suppose you have been all over the world?"

"Yes I have."

"Did you see much art?"

"Everywhere I went. Rome, Florence, Paris, London. I have visited cathedrals all over Europe. Mosques in Istanbul, temples in China and India, museums in the former Soviet Union. I checked out the art and architecture in places that most people never heard of."

"My goodness, that certainly sounds impressive. Perhaps you could do a presentation on some of the things you've seen."

"Well, I'm returning to Ohio so it will probably have to be next summer. Keep in touch with Shirley and she'll let you know when I'm available," Larry said.

"I'll do that. Thank you and good night."

"Good night," they both said and they left.

They got in Shirley's SUV and she started the engine.

"You smoothed things over with Miss Sullivan pretty good," she remarked.

"I should have groused her off. Instead she volunteered me into doing a presentation, duh," Larry said.

"I'm looking forward to that," Shirley quipped.

"You'll help me practice. Why is she still Miss Sullivan?"

"Nobody dares ask that question."

"Does she got money?" Larry asked.

"Not that much."

"Too bad, I could get Joe Cole interested," Larry suggested.

"AC doesn't mix with DC," Shirley said as she put it into reverse and backed out of the parking space then put it into drive and headed home.

"Miss Sullivan doesn't want to live in the Virgin Islands?" Larry asked rhetorically.

"Everybody wants to live in the Virgin Islands. Joe is a two-time loser. I don't think he wants a woman like Margaret."

He wants a woman that's loaded, not a woman with a steady job, Larry thought.

"Have you heard from Joe lately?"

"No, he makes himself scarce until he wants to see me. The sun will keep him warm, so I'm just worried about me," Larry said as he gently placed his hand on her leg.

"You gonna' watch that hand, buddy," she quipped.

"No need, we can both feel it good enough."

"You bad."

"You talk. Now I gotta' bring Darla's shawl," Larry said.

Shirley flew back to Ohio with him and she spent Christmas in Ohio and New Years with Larry in Florida. At the end of January they were forced to part company. Larry took her to the airport. Shirley was still wearing her pea coat. Larry was wearing a Chief's overcoat. A woman who looked to be about fifty years old, came up to them.

"Excuse me, are you going to Boston?" she asked.

"Shirley is," Larry replied.

"You both look like you're in the navy," she remarked.

"We both were in the navy at one time," Larry informed her.

"I'm a school teacher."

"That's good," Larry said.

"My nephew was crippled in Iraq. He lost an eye and can barely walk now."

"That's rough," Larry remarked.

"I can't go to church. I can't believe in God anymore."

"Jesus said that there will always be war and poverty and injustice in the world. Do you hate him because he told you the truth?" Larry asked.

She just looked at him.

"You cast aside the only thing that can let you be happy again. Does anger taste so sweet or embitterment feel so pleasant that you would wallow in it?"

"Does God make these wars?" she asked.

"Heaven forbid! God is not a murderer. Only Muslims believe that nonsense."

"What do you pray for?" she asked.

"The grace to do all that I have to do and bear all that I have to bear," Larry replied.

Another man came up to them.

"Ethel," he said

"Grace, yes that's it. The grace that's bigger than all your troubles... Oh, I must be going. Take care," she said.

"Good-bye," they both said.

"A most extraordinary man..." the woman said as they walked away.

"I didn't know you had such a grasp on theology," Shirley said.

"It's a good philosophy. I don't always follow it, but it's good still."

Shirley looked at him.

"Is this the first time you've seen a hypocrite?" Larry quipped.

"So if it's not God's fault, it's Bush's fault?"

"Obama is the president so it must be Obama's fault," Larry said.

"People around here greeted him so enthusiastically."

"That's called the 'Old man in the cave' syndrome. It's from the Twilight zone episode where the people in this little town get tired of living how they have to live to survive in the post-nuclear war apocalypse. They listen to this stupid colonel instead of the computer that has kept them alive."

"I'll have to watch that episode," Shirley said.

They chatted contentedly while they waited for the plane.

"This sucks," Shirley said as she picked up her carry-on after the boarding call.

"It's better than the navy. We can keep in touch."

"I'll write you every day if I can."

"I'll write you too," Larry said.

"We sound like teenagers."

"Don't we?" Larry said then they kissed again.

"First class must board now," the stewardess said.

Shirley turned and hurried toward the gate. She showed the other stewardess her ticket then she went through.

"Have you known each other long?" the first stewardess asked.

"Seventeen years now."

She looked at him quizzically.

"You never got married?"

"We should, now that we have the opportunity," Larry said as he fixed his eyes on the airplane.

He waited until the airplane taxied out of sight then he left.

During the winter and the spring he lived off of his navy retirement and the severance money. At this time he sent his diving gear to Nantucket in three shipments. He arranged for his youngest daughter to live at his house over the summer.

CHAPTER FOUR NEXT SUMMER

In the beginning of June, Larry flew to Boston with Meghan. Shirley flew them to the island. Meghan was chomping at the bit, so Shirley let her use the car and Larry gave her some money to go shopping.

"Meghan should be busy for a while," Shirley said.

"She could spend six hundred dollars on supper," Larry quipped.

"She is certainly healthy and robust looking."

"Yes, having two children was no problem for her."

"Are all your children like that?" she asked.

"Yes they are."

"That's good. I left your gear in the boxes."

"Good, I'll tend to it tomorrow. When is supper?"

"Right now," Shirley said as they went up the steps.

"Great, I had a bottle of rootbeer for lunch."

It was well after dark when Meghan got back. Larry and Shirley were sitting on the porch. Shirley had the baby shawl draped over her shoulders.

"Well, the prodigal daughter has returned. You get lost?"

Meghan looked at Shirley then at him.

"You should have left that thing back in Ohio. You'll never guess who I ran into."

"The sheriff," Larry quipped.

"Bob, old Shaughnessy's son."

"You haven't seen him since eighth grade."

"I knew him as soon as I saw him and he recognized me too."

"Is he still on the Cape?" Larry asked.

"Yeah, he's just here for another day or two. He was gonna' show me the island tomorrow."

"You're a guest of Shirley, not Bob," Larry reminded her.

Meghan looked at her.

"Oh go ahead. You're here to have fun," Shirley said.

The next morning, Bob came by and picked up Meg. Later that afternoon they came by and picked up her bags. They took the ferry to the Cape.

"It looks like you lost Meghan," Shirley said at supper.

"It's hard telling with that girl. They looked like teenagers. They couldn't take their eyes off of each other."

"She has two teenagers back in Ohio."

"Reality will kick in here, sooner or later," Larry said.

"She's daddy's girl."

"Heavens no, not like me at all."

"She wouldn't touch this at all," Shirley said, indicating the shawl.

"Yeah, her and her sisters won't let their children touch it. Tell Dot and Melanie to keep it in a display case and under no circumstances allow it to leave their shop."

"Will do," Shirley acknowledged.

After supper, Larry went to see Frank Folger. Frank arranged for a short dive the next day, on an old trawler which was in sixty feet of water. Finding nothing interesting on the wreck, Larry filled his net with the starfish and brittle stars which were numerous on and around the wreck.

The next day his diving buddies began spearing fish on a nearby shoal. This activity began attracting sharks. A seventeen foot, great white shark made a real close pass and Larry impaled it behind the gills with his lily iron. Larry hung onto the line and steered the shark into shallow water. Unfortunately there were a lot of people on the beach so they had a lot of spectators as they drug it ashore and cut off its tail and skinned it. Larry refused to talk to the tourists as they worked. The proprietor of a local bait shop offered him a hundred dollars for the jaws, so he cut them out then they dragged the carcass into the sea and left it to sink to the bottom.

In spite of his refusal to talk to anyone, there were pictures and an article in the newspaper the next day. That day they dived in an area known as the 'junkyard'. Larry disposed of two ten foot gray sharks in a similar manner as before, but there was hardly anybody on the beach there to report their activities.

The next day he rescued a ten year girl that had fallen off a boat. This also earned him some more unwanted attention from the newspapers.

In the evenings he researched wrecks around the island. He found that much of the information about the nature and location of the wrecks was conflicting or ambiguous. The older fishermen told him about the Samosett wreck. The Samosett was a small coastal steamer that foundered south of Tuckernuck Island just days before the start of the Civil War. According to old newspaper articles, the captain's safe contained a large number of gold coins when it went down in two hundred feet of water. Old Misses Macy told him about her father, Joseph Sommers. He had tried to locate the wreck for years. According to her, the gold was Morgans' gold so her father had an agreement (that she showed him) to get half of any gold or silver recovered. At the start of the Second World War, her father quit looking for the wreck. All he told her was that he had searched in the area south of Tuckernuck Island. That could mean half of the Atlantic Ocean as far as Larry could figure. He found it mentioned in the sailing directions and the Life-Boat station logbook from that period. The locations where fishermen reported fouling their nets were so numerous and widespread as to be no help whatsoever. If it was constructed like other small steamers of that era, it shouldn't be any problem to reach the captain's quarters, Larry figured. When he thought he had a good idea of the location, he went looking for a boat. Since Frank had left for a couple days on some off-island business, he had to look for another boat.

For $150 an hour, Henry Gardner and his son Pete crewed their old fishing boat for diving. They piloted the boat to the location that Larry had determined. Pete was at the wheel.

"Two hundred feet seems like a lot," Pete opined.

"Carpe diem," Larry said from below.

"What does that mean?"

"Sieze the day. You could be a millionaire by the end of this one."

"That would start my life with a bang," Pete said.

"What gives my life meaning?" Larry asked rhetorically.

"Whassat?" Pete asked.

"When I was a kid I lived on a small farm with my nine brothers and sisters. We worked, ate and slept. There was no purpose to life but that little farm. When I was in tenth grade, a rather philosophical history teacher asked-'what gives my life meaning?' I don't think I could answer that even now," Larry said.

"It doesn't sound like any question to waste any time on. All that matters now is this little dive," Hank declared.

"I hope you don't have any problems below," Pete said.

"If this turns into a disaster, I was opposed to the idea," Hank said.

"Duly noted. Let's not mention anything about getting paid," Larry quipped.

"How did you determine this location?" Hank asked as Larry came from below deck wearing his drysuit now.

"I took the map from the old piloting book and used wing dividers to transfer the distances. You know, the old 'three distances from three different points will give you only one point' principle," Larry explained.

"That old map could be off by more than a mile and the slightest error in scale would increase it by that much again," Hank said.

"Let's hope they were sticklers for accuracy," Larry said as he looked around.

"It's fair weather for this."

"I was looking to see if anyone was hanging around," Larry said.

There was only a large sailing boat far off in the distance.

"Relax, you were the only one who knew the location before we left the dock."

"An old Navy trick," Larry said.

"It's less than a mile now. What's the depth?"

"Uh, 2-2-6 now," Pete called out.

"Are you sure this fifteen-fifty trimix will work?"

"It always has."

"How long will you have on the bottom?"

"Twelve minutes, I figure," Larry replied.

"That doesn't seem like much."

"I have to allow a margin for safety."

"Good idea since neither of us can go down to rescue you. Does Mrs. Douglas know about this?"

"In a general way."

"So you didn't bother telling her?"

"I'll tell her when I get back."

"She'll be waiting for you with a stick."

Pete started throttling back. Henry looked at the GPS. Larry saw Pete pick up a sheathed knife. He recognized it as the one in the junk store.

"Those are junk," Larry remarked.

"This is a genuine Navy mark one Knife."

"Yeah, it's trash."

Larry pulled out his knife.

"This is a Randall utility knife which was given to me by President Reagan. You can see that the blade, bolster, tang and pommel are one piece of steel. This knife will cut through a Plexiglas canopy and it won't break. Those knives have a tiny little tang that will break easily. I would put that thing in a drawer and leave it there," Larry suggested.

"It was nice of Reagan to give you a knife," Pete remarked.

"Yeah, he just had a Urethra catheterization, so he was really a being a great guy."

"Are you ready, hero?" Hank asked.

"Let's do it," Larry said.

Because the oxygen level was slightly low for normal breathing, he would wear an escape bottle on his right hip for the surface and above a hundred feet. Hank helped him with the gear as they had practiced. Larry checked his instruments then put on his slate, knife and light.

"Everything is good," Larry said.

"It looks good," Henry agreed after he walked around him.

"Just keep watching for my bubbles," Larry said then he brought his full face mask down and fitted it carefully to the sealing surface of his drysuit. He turned the valve on his escape bottle and inserted the regulator and turned it one quarter turn clockwise and engaged the latch. He turned and stepped through the gangway opening and took a big step into the water. The air in his BCD made him come to the surface again. He made another check of his equipment then signaled by putting his hand on his head. He saw them wave to him. He let the air out of his BCD and he began sinking. The water was fairly clear but he turned on his light anyway as he descended. When he got to a hundred feet, he put more air in his suit and turned off the escape bottle and turned on his hundred cubic feet tank with the trimix. The water was a darker green down here. He kept a lookout for sharks even though he was told that the sharks around the island had vanished. He wasn't feeling any discomfort from the water temperature when he reached the bottom. The bottom was sand and he had to watch out for rays and sea urchins that were down there as he swam a couple feet over the sand. He checked the time then began swimming in circles to cover the area. It was dark but the clarity wasn't too bad. He stopped to check his instrument console again when he saw something in his peripheral vision, off to his right. He swam about thirty feet and came to the nose of an airplane. It looked to be a Piper Arrow and it hadn't been there long, he guessed. He took out his slate and wrote down the registration number. He looped he end of the buoy line around one of the propellers and inflated his diving buoy using a sparklet bulb. He let go of the buoy and paid out the line until it went slack then he dropped the reel. He checked his console again then began to ascend slowly, letting the 'air' out so his dry suit didn't inflate. At one hundred feet he switched to the escape bottle again. When he got to the surface, he was about sixty feet from the boat. He inflated his BCD and took off his mask and regulator. Suddenly Henry and Pete saw him and began waving and shouting. He swam toward them and stopped next to the boat. They reached over and grabbed his arms and pulled him up before he could remove his fins.

"We're sure in the hell glad to see you. We lost your bubbles. We didn't know that you were on the starboard side," Henry said as they still held him.

"I'm in no distress here," Larry assured them.

"We'll help you get this stuff off," he said.

"Take it easy, guys," Larry said as they began removing gear hurriedly.

He figured that they were over excited due to inexperience. They were trying to remove his dry suit when he stopped them.

"Enough guys, you're hyperventilating," Larry declared.

They both looked at him strangely.

"What happened?" Henry asked.

"Nothing, I'm fine," Larry replied.

They both hesitated again.

"Did you find anything?" Pete asked.

"Yes, I did."

"The wreck?"

"No, an airplane."

"An airplane," they both said as they looked at each other.

Larry picked up the slate and showed them the FAA registration number.

"What does that mean?" Henry said.

"Someone lost an airplane, a Piper Arrow, here in the last few years."

"Do you remember anything about that, Dad?" Pete asked.

"Can't say that I do," he replied.

"I left a buoy and we'll get the exact fix on it and the FAA will be able to tell 'who and when' so our job is done," Larry said.

Hank wrote down the exact GPS fix then he called the Coast guard and gave the information to them. A few minutes later the Coast Guard station called them and asked them to repeat the information so Henry did. He also told them that they were on their way in. When he came in the door, Shirley looked at him.

"What have you been up to?" she asked.

"Oh, just paddling around."

"Looking at aircraft?"

"No, we weren't near the airport," Larry said.

"Not what I heard from Ellington at the FAA."

"I never heard of him. Is he a Duke?" Larry quipped.

"Reporttt!!" she bawled.

"Okay, me and Henry and Pete were out doing an exploratory dive and I found an airplane out there. We had to report it, that's all," Larry said.

"You didn't say anything to me about exploratory diving," she snapped.

"I didn't want you to worry. It was a routine dive. No problem whatsoever."

"It was more than two hundred feet of water!"

"Well, that's routine for me."

"You're supposed to tell me every time and you had two guys who couldn't dive if you had trouble. What does the sign say in Torpedo School?" Shirley demanded.

"Point well taken…"

"I can't hear you!"

"Mam, the price of carelessness is death, Mam," Larry sang out while standing at attention. Larry hoped this would placate her enough.

"Max Ellington is coming over later and you had better have some answers for him."

"I can only tell him the truth," Larry said.

"Yeah, you do that and in complete detail," she demanded.

"Certainly, no problem."

CHAPTER FIVE

A man about 6'2" tall, wearing a suit came to their door. Larry was there before he knocked.

"Hello," Larry said.

"Good afternoon, I'm Max Ellington. I'm looking for Lawrence Mayer."

"I am he."

"I need to talk to you about the aircraft that you reported on the bottom of the ocean."

"Certainly, would you like to come in?" Larry asked.

"Thank you. I know an Investigator named John Mayer."

"I know a Duke named Ellington."

Ellington just looked at him.

"Sorry, I couldn't resist that."

"Is this your house?"

"No, it belongs to my friend, Shirley Douglas," Larry replied, adding "Sit down here at the table if you like."

"Thank you," he said as they sat down.

He opened his brief case and removed a folder and a tape recorder.

"Now this is a copy of the report of the missing aircraft bearing the registration number that you reported. For security reasons the names have been deleted. Did you look into the passenger compartment?"

"No, I did not."

He made a note.

"Did you touch or remove anything from the aircraft?"

"Other than tying the buoy line to the prop, no."

He wrote something again.

"Why were you diving there?"

"I..er, we were looking for a wreck from a couple centuries back."

"This aircraft has only been there since last October."

"Obviously not what I was looking for."

"How did you come to that particular location."

"Using the old piloting book and a chart for that area, I used wing dividers to mark out distances from three points on land and came out with that point as the location of the Samosett wreck."

Larry reached over to the end table and picked up the old piloting book for the island and his chart with the markings and he showed them to Ellington.

"Can I take these for now?" he asked.

"No problem," Larry said since they weren't much use to him now.

Ellington wrote for a minute.

"The only thing we have is a flight plan that says their destination was Virginia. They were coming from Florida."

"Oops, somebody messed up. Virginny is a big target," Larry commented.

"It has happened before," Ellington said.

Larry had always figured that if an aircraft strayed out over the ocean, all the pilot had to do is turn to the west. The North American continent was pretty hard to miss. Ellington continued to write for a few minutes.

"Alright, if you will sign this affidavit that you willingly gave evidence and the evidence is true," Max said.

"I would like to see everything you wrote first," Larry said.

"Certainly," he said as he gathered up the material and handed it to Larry.

"Be it recorded that Lawrence Mayer is reviewing the material that he gave in this investigation," Ellington said so that the recorder would pick it up.

Larry read everything then signed the affidavit. Ellington got up and Larry saw him to the door. As he was going down the steps, he passed Shirley. Larry opened the door for her.

"So, now you come."

"I was here all along. I watched you from the security camera in the back room."

"What did you think of Ellington?"

"I've never heard of him. Usually Brockman comes from Hyannis," Shirley said.

"He's a barrel of laughs."

"I don't know what he is," she said.

In spite of the local rumor factories and the presence of a Navy diving ship from Newport, there was no mention in the newspaper of the airplane or how it was discovered. It took four days to recover the aircraft. It was temporarily stored in a hangar at the airport. The next day a man who identified himself as Harry Brown, called the house and said he needed to talk to Larry. When Larry got to the airport, Brown took him into a small storage room. There was nothing but a card table and folding chairs in the center and file cabinets and shelves along the walls. Harry placed a transistor radio in the little window and turned it on.

"Sit down if you will," he said, so Larry did.

"I am sure that you saw the aircraft being brought ashore."

"Yes, I did," Larry replied.

"According to the statement you gave, you did not look in the aircraft or remove anything from the aircraft."

"That is true except for the fact that I did not give a statement, I just answered questions."

"You stated that you used an old map and wing dividers to determine the location of the aircraft."

"Wrong again. I used an old map and wing dividers to try to determine the location of the Samosett wreck. I had no idea that anything else was down there," Larry stated.

"I find that highly unlikely," Harry snapped.

"I'm not surprised."

"What do you mean by that!" he exclaimed.

"You are obviously one of those lying, sneaking, manipulating suck faces and you can't imagine that anyone else isn't," Larry said plainly.

"Is that what you really think?" he said jumping up from the table.

"Bingo."

"Do you know who was in that plane?"

"Not interested," Larry stated.

"I think I'll tell you."

"Don't trouble yourself."

"Joe Cole and Luis Valero," he said.

Even Larry couldn't hide his surprise for a moment. He thought Harry was messing with his head. Another con by the CIA, he thought.

"What do you think of that, Chief?" he said with a sneer.

"Your credibility is zero."

It looked like Harry wanted to hit him. He would stomp him if he did, Larry thought.

"Does that piss you off, Shorty?" Larry snapped.

Harry turned his back to him and looked at the wall for a minute. He was still looking at the wall when he began talking.

"We're gonna' stop the crap here. Now tell me how you knew about the plane."

"I have already said that I knew nothing about the airplane and I certainly didn't know who or what was in it," Larry repeated.

"Would you take a polygraph?"

"No need to, I'm telling you the truth."

"Marita Valero said that you visited Luis last October. That was five days before he went missing."

"Yes, I ran into Joe in Panama City where I was diving with my friend, Cynthia Morrow. He took us to supper and we flew to the Virgin Islands via Puerto Rico the next day. We ran into Luis at a gas station. Luis invited us to his house that afternoon. We did some shooting in his back yard. That's about it," Larry explained.

"What do you mean by 'you ran into Joe'?"

"We had just docked and Cindy went ashore to change clothes. I was sitting in the boat, washing our regulators in a bucket of freshwater when Joe walked right up to the boat," Larry explained.

"You didn't think this was unusual?" he asked.

"Joe would do that all the time in the Navy. Since then he frequently had financial problems so it wasn't unusual for him to drop in unexpectedly," Larry explained.

"As far as you could see, what was his relationship with Luis?"

"Joe talked about him like he was a boy scout," Larry replied.

"What did you think of Luis?"

"I never much liked Spooks."

"You must be a racist."

"We both know what it means," Larry said.

"You will be on the island for a while?"

"Here or Boston Mills, Ohio. I can't afford to go anywhere else."

"One more thing, do you recognize this?"

Harry handed him a picture. It was somewhat water damaged but he recognized it as a picture of Joe, him and Cindy on Luis' Verandah.

"Yes, that is us at Luis'house," Larry said. He secretly wished he had one.

"Your girlfriend seems a little young. What happened?" he asked.

"They frequently wake up and realize that they're in bed with some fricking old man," Larry remarked.

"That's for sure. You will say nothing about what you or I said here."

"Sure, it isn't that interesting," Larry said then he left.

"What did that Harry want?" Shirley asked when he got home.

"The usual CIA shit. He's trying to find a patsy so his boss will be happy."

"That's quite a coincidence, anchoring right over a lost plane like that," Shirley said.

"You don't know the one percent of it."

Shirley looked at him strangely.

"According to Harry, Joe Cole and the spook, Luis Valero, were in that plane."

Shirley looked as shocked as he felt. She didn't talk for a minute.

"Is that the guy you talked about meeting in the Virgin Islands?"

"Yes it is."

"That's just too weird," Shirley stated.

"Yes, it would appear to be. Luis said that God works in mysterious ways."

"That takes it, even for God!" she exclaimed.

"In our operations, Joe and I always vowed to come back for each other."

"I know CIA operatives aren't that dedicated, but you would think they would try to search for wreckage."

"They were supposed to land in Virginia, so the fact that they went down three hundred miles from where they were supposed to be didn't help, I suppose."

"You look worried." she said.

"Joe is a real hero. He must be buried properly. I can't let him be thrown into some landfill."

"If you have his SSN, I'll call my friend in the Department of Justice," she suggested.

Larry gave her Joe's social security number.

CHAPTER SIX

After supper he met Frank Folger and a couple younger guys at his boat shop.

"Hey there, Roughneck, meet Billy and Howard," Frank said as Larry came in the door.

"Hi guys," Larry said as he shook hands with them.

"I saw you in church," Howard said.

"I hate that 'Stand Up For Jesus'. I have to stand up," he quipped.

"How hard is that for an old Jew like you?" Frank countered.

"I'm kinda' between synagogues at the moment."

"Upsetting the Rabbis, tisk tisk. We were just talking about your little find. We were wondering how you did it with Hank and Petey," Frank quipped.

"It could have been you. Your name would be a household word."

"Eh-yuh, everybody would be talking about me sitting in security detention. Oh joy."

"Don't answer questions that already state that you are guilty," Larry advised.

"What kind of question would that be?" Billy asked.

"Have you ever sucked a dick bigger than mine?" Larry asked.

Howard laughed at that.

"I see what you mean. That's a good example," Billy stated.

"Another thing they taught us in the navy."

"Our spies claim that you knew the two guys in the airplane." Frank stated.

"Your spies know quite a bit. They obviously didn't get that reading the newspaper."

"They don't get any Pulitzer Prize for investigative reporting. What's the poop?"

"A guy named Joe Cole and a guy named Luis Valero. Joe was in the navy with me and Luis was a CIA operative that I ran into a couple times. Nobody says that they know what they were doing in an airplane way out here, but that's the way it goes sometimes. Sometimes you never find out the answers," Larry explained.

"I saw the airplane. It must have been a pretty soft landing, everything was intact. When they got it to the airfield, they cranked the wheels down by hand," Frank informed him.

"Just another strange set of circumstances in this SNAFU."

"Did you ever work for the CIA?" Billy asked.

"Indirectly, I never worked for them up front. They're just not my kinda' people."

"I was reading about this four man Seal team that got annihilated in Afghanistan. I didn't think that ever happened," Howard said.

"Eighty percent of their operations go to shit on them," Larry said.

"I thought they were some sort of supermen who never failed."

"That's what they thought when planning the Mogadishu operation. All these wonderful helicopters and super soldiers against uneducated and untrained savages with Ak's and RPG's. How could we lose?"

"How did you do it?" Frank asked.

"I liked to work underwater. The bastards aren't sophisticated enough to work underwater."

"Yeah, nobody likes to work underwater. There's not too much underwater in Afghanistan," Frank stated.

"We gotta' stay outta' Afghanistan. It's just like Africa. It's just a bunch of stupid tribes and the only thing they do is grow Opium. It's just a bad deal from any angle," Larry said.

"The conspiracy people say that Alexander the Great wrote about a giant vein of gold in Afghanistan. All these Ivy Leaguers had to learn ancient Greek and some of them read his chronicles," Billy said.

"Old Al was quite the real estate acquirer. Ancient Greek isn't quite a secret code.

If such a thing was true, I'm sure the locals would have found it by now," Larry said.

"They're only interested in growing Hash. We should send Kerry over there to straighten them out," Frank quipped.

"He hasn't done too good of a job with the Israelis," Larry said.

"They just have to put up with him on an occasional visit. The son of a bitch lives here," Frank said.

"Are you looking in the same area south of Tuckernuck?" Howard asked.

"I don't think so. Even if I found something, salvage would be too expensive."

"Other people are talking about diving there. Some serious divers are looking at it." Howard said.

You only go round once in life, so you gotta' grab for all the gusto you can get," Larry opined.

"I was heading to the Red Gull. Are you guys coming?" Frank asked.

"Are your friends gonna' be there?" Larry asked.

"Very likely," he replied as they left the shop.

Frank had an F-150 with the crew cab. Joe had one like it in Alexander Bay. Larry wondered if it was his or government property.

"Bench seats front and back. You can't beat that," Billy said.

"I was gonna' buy one like this. A half hour before I got there with the down payment, some tourist bought it with cash," Howard said.

"Does that sound familiar, Larry?" Frank asked.

"A minute late and a dime short is the story of my life."

On the way to the bar, Frank got a call on his cellphone, so he dropped them off in front of the Red Gull and left. They took a table near the front. Larry told the barmaid to bring them a pitcher of Whale's Tail Pale Ale.

"I'm only eighteen," Billy said after she left.

"Wear your hat more to the side and down in front," Howard suggested.

"If you drink this stuff, you'll be lucky if it stays on your head," Larry said.

"Everybody says that they wish they knew what they know when they were eighteen," Billy said.

"They were know-it-all teenagers then and they would still be know-it-all teenagers now. What's the difference?"

"You joined the navy when you were eighteen?" Howard asked.

"I was still seventeen when I joined."

"Why did you choose the navy?"

"Actually I wanted the army. When I got to the National Guard armory I went to the army recruiter and talked to him and took the test. Then he ignored me and started talking to two guys who went over to the navy table then he talked to another guy for twenty minutes. I got fed up with being ignored so I went over to the navy table and signed up," Larry explained.

"You didn't like being snubbed. That's understandable," Billy said.

"I don't know why you would want the army anyway," Howard opined.

"When I was a kid, me and my little friends would watch Combat. Saunders with his Thompson and Kirby with his BAR were so great, we thought."

"So it was Voyage to the Bottom of the Sea," Billy joked.

"They don't make series like that for TV anymore. The audience is too small and the cost is too great. At least that's what my father told me," Howard said.

"Wasn't there a sitcom about this place? A small airline called AeroMass?" Larry asked.

"Wings. It was crappy. It was made in California. They only used a few outside shots and aerial shots of here," Billy said.

The Barmaid brought their beer and Larry gave her thirty dollars and she left.

"Three bucks isn't much of a tip for this place," Howard informed him.

You want a good tip, Baby? Come over to my place after work," Larry joked.

"That'll get you slapped." Howard said.

"Chasing women is fun...then you catch them," Larry said ruefully.

"The band is here," Howard said.

"Mister Show. I never heard of them," Billy said.

"They're from Ohio. I saw them in Alexander Bay."

"Where is Alexander Bay?" Billy asked.

"In the Thousand Islands area. That's the St. Lawrence river just east of Lake Ontario," Larry explained.

"What do people do over there?"

"Tourism for a lot of people. They have numerous castles on the islands and the excursion boats. They have a lot of charter fishing, duck, bear and moose hunting. Hotel and Cabin owners are very friendly. Sailing and snowmobiling in season. Since it's on the river, they get good wind with no waves for boaters and canoeists. The local humor is delightful," Larry explained.

"You had some trouble there?" Howard asked.

"I was involved in salvage operations in which people died. That put some of the locals off their humor."

"Did you kill anyone?"

Larry explained how he and Joe Cole had been attacked by men in scuba gear and how he killed both of them in the water. He also explained about Tim Lesher and the other people who had been killed, wounded or involved in that fiasco.

"And this is the same Joe Cole that was in that Piper Arrow?" Billy asked.

"Yes, my old shipmate."

"Incredible, just absolutely incredible," Howard remarked.

"For some of us, it just sucks," Larry said.

"Losing an old friend like that. I bet it does," Billy said.

"I know a couple guys who signed up to be Seals but they didn't make it. They got out of their enlistment because of that."

"If you tell them that you want to be a seal or a diver, you will never be one," Larry said.

"How did you get in?"

"After Boot camp, I qualified for submarines. I went to Torpedo School, that's where divers were trained. It just seemed to be the fun thing to do."

"I've seen those programs on the History Channel where they only accept the top two percent. I wouldn't want it," Billy said.

"In our outfit, if you met the criteria, you qualified. I would not tolerate making the guys fight each other. You mentioned that Seal team in Afghanistan. The only survivor was rescued by an Afghani. So much for the super men," Larry said. Three young women came to their table. The tallest one, a blonde, looked at him. She was the only one wearing a wedding band. They stood up.

"Good evening, I have seen you here before," she said with an obvious Nordic accent.

"You probably want to talk to these guys," Larry said, indicating Howard and Billy.

"You are Mister Mayer, zeh diver who found zeh airplane. Gentlemen, Yvette and Susanne want to buy you a drink at zeh bar," she said.

"Certainly," Howard said and they went with the other two women.

"That was slick, but I'm being rude. Would you please join me?" Larry asked as he pulled out the chair next to him. They both sat down.

"I'm Larry. You already know that I've done some diving."

"I am Lovisa Lutjens. I am also a diver."

"You sound like a Lithuanian."

"I am from Finland. I was here at Zhanksgiving time when you hit a man over zhere."

"Do you know why?"

"I did not care zhen or now, you see," she replied.

"That is a good answer. What's on your mind?"

"I wish to dive where you had dived."

"Is that right?" Larry asked rhetorically.

He took a napkin and wrote the longitude and latitude to the one hundredth second then handed it to her.

"There you go. Have fun. You'll have to retrieve your friends on your own," Larry said as he saw the backside of Billy as he went out the door.

"Zhey will take care of zhemselves," she said, adding-"Have you dived on zeh U-boat?"

"No, who wants a fricking U-boat?"

"It is too deep for zeh sport divers. I have been zhere twice with our group," she said then she pulled a business card out of her pocket and handed it to him. He looked at it for a moment. It was an outfit that he had never heard of.

"It's like climbing a mountain. It's all fine and good, but it's spending a lot of money and there's nothing tangible to bring back."

"I am sure zeh owners of our group have considered zhat."

"Is your husband also a diver?" Larry asked.

"He was. He died in an accident a year ago."

"Oh, bad break. Where was that?"

"Trondheim," she replied.

"Last year I dived with a Brigitte Svenson who is from Trondheim."

"I know Brigitte."

"I dived with her in the thousand Islands. A place called Alexander Bay."

"Zhat is freshwater. Zhere should be nothing zhere."

"It turns out that there was a brig, the Madamoiselle de Loire. It was full of goodies, but it belonged to the French so that was a bust," Larry explained.

"I did not hear of zhat," she said.

Her phone beeped and she took it out and looked at it.

"I must be going soon," she said.

"I'm staying with Shirley Douglas. If you have any questions, look me up."

"Perhaps it would be possible for you to join us?"

Larry knew that it was a question. He thought about what happened in Alexander Bay and what Shirley would say.

"No, I'm afraid not at this time."

They both stood up.

"It has been a pleasure, Larry," she said.

"Also a pleasure for me, Lovisa, good evening," Larry said.

Larry watched her to see if she was leaving the bar. After she left, Larry waited a few minutes to see if the young guys would return. When they didn't, he took his beer glass and sat at the bar. He thought about Joe. He remembered that last August he had told Joe that he was looking for a well off woman with a twin engine aircraft. He figured that Joe thought he was talking about Melissa. Be careful what you wish for because you have to take the whole package. Desire is the cause of all unhappiness, he recalled. He didn't feel like drinking, he was just angry at being reminded of losing an old shipmate. Eight or nine younger people came in. Off islanders by the look of them. Behind them came a man in a suit. He looked like a Ken doll, having a plastic face and plastic suit, Larry thought. When the band started, Larry planned to leave. Mister Plastic tried to wedge himself between the two guys to the left of him. They were wearing flannel shirts and looked like construction workers.

"We're all brothers in Christ. That's something you can't get with alcohol and casual companionship," he announced.

"Keep it down over there. You wanna' preach, do it in church," Larry snapped.

The two guys laughed.

"What are you up to, young man?" the plastic preacher asked.

"Staying out of other peoples' business."

"You're not doing a very good job of it," the preacher opined, adding- "What if I told you that Jesus could take the pain out of your life?"

"I'm doing just fine. The Magic Negro is president so why the hell do we need Jesus?"

"It doesn't work that way…"

"Sure it does. Jesus and the swamp crackers just don't get the joke and neither do you," Larry said as the preacher came over to him.

The flannel shirts were getting another laugh outta' that.

"Not everybody is deserving of Christ's forgiveness…"

Larry slugged him in the stomach. The preacher doubled over because the wind was knocked out of him.

"There's some pain in your life," Larry said then he shoved him aside and walked out.

He was walking home when the Sheriff pulled up next to him.

"Hi there, Sheriff, nice weather."

"I heard there was some trouble at the Gull?"

"Some people don't understand the concept of 'get outta' my face'. Do you want to run me in?"

"How about if I take you home?"

"That'll work too," Larry said then he got in the Sheriff's car.

"This isn't the first time that the Reverend has made trouble. I'm sorry about your friend."

"Yeah, it was a bad deal."

"How long did you know him?"

"Forty years now," Larry replied.

"I suppose you know that the feds took possession of everything in this investigation?"

"You probably don't need another headache like that," Larry speculated.

"Shirley said that there wasn't two more guys like you two, in the Navy."

"Yeah, we were quite a pair sometimes," Larry agreed.

"Shirley is a good friend," the Sheriff stated.

"She always has been."

"My philosophy is 'don't make an enemy of someone that doesn't want to be your enemy'."

"That is a very sage philosophy," Larry said.

"Have a good evening," he said as he stopped by the driveway.

"Thank you and sorry for the trouble," Larry said as they shook hands.

"Think nothing of it, bye."

"Good-bye," Larry said as he closed the car door.

He heard the door open and Shirley came out. He smiled at her as he came up the steps.

"How was your afternoon?" he asked.

"I thought they were keeping you over night."

"It was just a little misunderstanding."

"Dillinger and Capone were just a little misunderstanding," she snapped.

"That's very funny. Your humor always catches me by surprise," he said as he gently took her by the arms and kissed her on the cheek.

"What did the Sheriff say?"

"I told him about Joe and he told me that you were a good friend like that."

Shirley looked at him doubtfully.

"Really, he did," Larry insisted.

"Come in and get something to eat."

Larry followed her into the dining room. Since the food was already on the table, they dished themselves up and sat down. They ate in silence for a minute.

"When my mother and Adam died, I was angry at everybody and everything for a week. I never liked losing family," Shirley explained.

"I told this jerk to save his preaching for church. He had this real disgusting southern accent. He sounded like George Wallace. I wonder if he'll try to press charges. I could leave the state before he sues, I suppose," Larry said.

"Don't worry about it. He thinks of himself as a martyr. He has been hit by people before," Shirley assured him.

"He likes to take one for Jesus, eh? If he lets it lay then he's more of a man than I give him credit for. By the by, I was approached by a tall, hot blonde named Lovisa Lutjens."

"What did she want?"

"She asked me if she could dive where I found the plane. I wrote down the location for her."

"Is that all?" Shirley asked.

"She asked me if I wanted to dive with them but I turned her down."

"You turned down a woman who you describe as a tall, hot blonde?" she asked.

"It's cold and murky water. Only a clam loves that."

"Too bad it wasn't the Keys," she quipped.

"Those Scandohoovian babes just like it cold, cold, cold," Larry countered.

CHAPTER SEVEN

The next morning he had missed a phone call from Frank so we went to his shop after breakfast. Howard was also there when he arrived.

"How's it going guy?"

"You were at the Gull with the hottest woman on the planet and you're asking me!" he exclaimed.

"Oh yes, Lovisa Lutjens. Is it true blondes have more fun?" Larry quipped.

"You tell us!"

"What did she want with a tough old piece of gristle like you?" Frank asked.

"That's the same thing Shirley asked. She wanted to dive where I found the plane."

"Why?"

"I didn't ask her. I just gave her the GPS numbers."

"Did she say anything else?"

"She told me that ideally she likes to dive all she can in the daytime and screw all she can at night. She also urged me to join their little group for this dive," Larry said.

"With that philosophy I'm sure that Shirley would not approve of that arrangement," Frank said.

"I would be living on a diving boat the rest of my life."

"I would be singing 'Anchors Aweigh'," Howard said.

"She assured me that Yvette and Susanne would keep you entertained. You had a foursome for bridge," Larry remarked.

"That wasn't the first thing we thought of."

"Imagine that," Frank said.

"You never heard of playing partners?"

"So where did they get off to? That is not a rhetorical question," Howard said.

"Didn't you get the 'where and when' before you parted company?"

"They split the Ship Ahoy about an hour after we got there. A car was waiting for them out front," Howard said.

"When I was your age, we didn't blow it on ladies' night," Frank wisecracked.

"Har har."

"Lovisa got a phone call and she had to leave. That's hitting the sack awful early. Did you find out about their dive boat?" Larry asked.

"Umm…"

"What the hell were you drinking?"

"I'll call Billy and see if he remembers."

"I'll call the Harbormaster," Frank said as he picked up his phone.

Larry handed him the business card that Lovisa had given him. It took a minute to connect.

"Hello Wilson, what's the good word?…You don't say? It sounds like a demolition derby…Oh well, more business for me. I was looking for a diving boat. Venture Co. II…Okay, good…Well the weather's good. Thanks old buddy, bye," Frank said.

"They left Coffin's Wharf at sunrise. No specified return time," Frank said as he put his phone down.

"It sure sounds like they went hunting," Larry remarked as Frank handed him the business card.

"Billy's dad will let us use his boat. Let's cruise out there and check it out," Howard said.

"Were you invited?" Larry asked.

"No, but you were."

"I turned her down. It would be poor practice to show up out there now," Larry said.

"Make some excuse. Tell them you left a piece of gear out there," Howard suggested.

"Nobody would be fooled by that ruse."

In truth, finding a dead friend had given Larry a distaste for diving at that location.

"You can catch them when they come in," Larry said.

"It has already leaked out that you were looking for the Samosett and the newspapers gave the general location of the airplane. It may be getting crowded out there," Frank said.

"They may be heading for the Andrea Doria. Who knows," Howard said.

"There's already two big boats anchored out there now," Frank said.

"If they have the equipment, they would probably do a side-scan sonar survey, using the location that I gave Lovisa as a starting point."

"Sure as hell they have that capability."

"What was in that wreck?" Howard asked.

Since that information was easily obtainable, Larry decided it wouldn't hurt to tell him.

"Five thousand gold coins in a safe in the captain's quarters."

"Small wonder she went down. She was top heavy," Franky quipped

"All we would have to do is get a steel hawser around that safe and winch it onto the deck," Howard said.

"The bottom is more than two hundred feet. Have you ever been that deep?"

"Well, half that anyway," he replied.

"Meaning no offense, but it's no place for enthusiastic amateurs. It takes professional deep divers with a lot of bottom time and it's still a chancy venture at that."

"Finding the son of a bitch on an island surrounded by hundreds of shipwrecks is the first problem," Frank said.

"How is it laying? If it rolled over, a safe that heavy would have torn loose from the floor and probably went through the wooden bulkheads. Even at that depth, it would be moving in excess of sixty miles an hour when it hit the sandy bottom," Larry explained.

"Are there metal detectors for that depth?"

"The diver takes the probe down and they keep in touch with him by the telephone."

"You think that this is definitely a supplied air, dry suit proposition?" Frank asked.

"I wouldn't do it any other way."

"I'll bet anybody that Hank and Petey are already taking more divers out there," Howard said.

"What makes you think that?"

"I saw two guys, mid thirties, bleached out hair, great tans, walking to the wooden dock with Hank."

A bell went off in Larry's head.

"They have good looking bodies?" Frank quipped.

"These were serious looking guys and no mistake," Howard insisted.

"How long ago was this?" Larry asked.

"Five minutes before you got here."

"You got time to take a walk?"

"Yeah, sure," Howard replied.

"You mind if I come along?" Frank asked.

"Not at all," Larry replied.

Frank left the door unlocked and put on the ten minute sign then they left. When they turned the corner, they could see the long wooden dock. Hank's boat was tied up near the end. No one was on the dock.

"There was a lot of activity here during the prohibition. No Capone types, all family then. Sometimes the Feds catch tourists with drugs," Frank said.

"Drugs here!, Aargh," Larry quipped.

When they got to Hank's boat, they could hear somebody talking below. Larry saw the compressor, helium cylinders, high pressure regulators and the hoses on the deck.

"Ahoy, Sweet Pea," Larry called out.

They heard some moving about below then Hank came out of the hatchway.

"Good morning there, sea dog," Larry said.

The two men that Howard had described, came out a few moments later. Larry recognized them immediately.

"Oh, you have company? I can come back later."

"I wouldn't think of it. Do you know Brian and Steve?"

"Murray and Coakley. How's it going guys?" Larry said, smiling at them.

"This is Frank Folger. He knows everything there is to know about boats. And young Howard Hillier," Hank introduced them.

Since they stayed on the boat, there was none of the customary handshaking.

"Taking on another diving job?" Larry asked Hank.

"Something like that."

He looked at the other two.

"We ran into a couple of the crew from Venture Co. II. Have you been diving the Andrea Doria?"

"We may get over there this summer," Coakley replied.

"They talked like it's a pretty sharp outfit. No sweat when someone else is paying, I guess."

"Yeah, I suppose," Coakley said.

"You guys still surfing?"

"Not too much anymore."

"You remember, Smoky Mann, that retread Marine that dived on oil rigs?" Larry asked.

"I heard he was a diver for the cops somewhere," Murray said.

"That could be. I heard that he died while making a dive for a sheriff's department in upstate New York. Well, catch you on the flip side, guys," Larry said then they turned and headed back up the dock.

"They seem like real friendly fuckers," Howard said quietly.

"They always have been," Larry said.

"You know a lot of divers," Frank remarked.

"There probably aren't four hundred deep-diving pros in the world. Names get mentioned when jobs are discussed."

"Did you know that Lovisa?" Howard asked.

"No, she knew me. Funny you should mention that. We had both dived with a young lady, Brigitte Svenson. The first name I brought up," Larry replied.

"It was the same thing with those two guys," Frank observed.

"Mann and another diver named Truett, died on the bottom. They were diving at the same place where I recovered an SUV. They were using air. I like trimix at that depth. Any stupid little thing can get you killed. Another diver, named Tony Raymer, also died there."

"So you found treasure in the Thousand Islands when you were diving there with Brigette. This Brigitte knows this Lovisa you met last night. I wouldn't be surprised if Brigitte is here or on the way here," Frank said.

"Sammy Pike and Jans Trelleborg were also there. I wouldn't be surprised at anything."

"A million and a half in gold sure beats the hell outta' plates and silverware from the Doria. I've heard people say that you found it or you were real close."

All I found was somebody's watery grave, Larry thought.

"It's a free country. I can't stop people from diving," Larry said.

"Everybody says you're one hundred percent balls-out in the splash," Howard said.

"A couple little sharks aren't that impressive," Larry remarked.

"Are you kidding? You dive like there's no limitations. Other divers have died trying to do what you did!"

"Good luck to them anyway."

"Good luck is right. Last I heard there's a mass of cold air coming in from the mainland. It sounds like a fog coming in," Frank said.

"That will stop their diving," Howard said.

"That won't stop Murray and Coakley."

"Hank and Petey won't like it," Howard insisted.

For a couple hours, Murray and Coakley worked at setting up their equipment then they filled their tanks with a low grade mixture known as heliair. By one o'clock they were clearing the harbor. Hank steered to port and headed west until they had cleared the western end of the island then he steered to port again and passed between Nantucket and Tuckernuck islands. By this time it had gotten cooler and the sky began clouding over and a fog rolled in from the southwest. Hank had no radar but he kept track of his position on the chart by using the longitude and latitude numbers on his GPS. The location that Murray and Coakley had given him was nearly a quarter mile southeast of where Larry had dived. By the time they had arrived at the designated location and anchored, the visibility was zero. Murray and Coakley helped each other with their gear. They both went in at the same time. They left no instructions or time limit with Hank and Pete.

Because of the fog, they soon lost sight of the diver's bubbles. Forty minutes later, Hank was below deck when a Liberian flagged cargo ship collided with the Sweet Pea. Pete was thrown into the water as their boat heaved violently then broke up in a couple seconds. The freighter continued westward. Pete found a portion of the bow that was still afloat and he clung to that. From what he could see, that was the only thing left of their boat. He looked around and called out but he saw no trace of his father. He hung on and continued to hope that his father or the divers would appear, but no one came. As darkness came on, he saw a half full water bottle drift by. He swam the thirty feet to retrieve it. When he got back to his 'raft', his thirst made him forget about rationing and he gulped down the water in a couple seconds. With the coming of darkness the fog lifted and he could see the lights of airplanes flying overhead. Unfortunately he had no flare gun to signal them. He thought about the Coast Guard rescuing him. His father had told everybody that they would be out overnight so it was a cinch that nobody was missing them yet. The current was eastward, so it was taking him toward Martha's Vineyard or south of there. If he missed the Vineyard, the next place was Block Island. Without food or water or sleep, he figured his only chance was the search that would be started tomorrow night. He dared not sleep because he had to hang onto the wreckage or be washed off into the ocean. It seemed like it took forever for the sun to rise. As he watched it, he thought he heard a sail flap behind him. In the gray dawn he saw the white sail and white hull of a fairly large sailboat. Observing it for a minute, it seemed to be coming nearly straight at him. He unsteadily stood on the wreckage and began to holler and wave at the boat as it approached. As the boat got closer he saw that the Genoa sail was furled. This probably meant that it was being singlehanded by the guy at the wheel. Pete could see that it would pass about forty or fifty feet away from him and it showed no sign of slowing down or changing course toward him. As it was passing, he picked up the water bottle, which now contained salt water, and threw it like a football at the man at the wheel. The water bottle struck the wheel and hit the man's arm. He jumped up and looked to the starboard and saw a young man standing on the water and waving at him. He took off his earphones and heard the verbal tirade as he lowered the mainsail and brought it around on the 'iron genoa'. When he stopped, Pete climbed onto his boat and immediately requested water. He had never felt so thirsty and he didn't know if he had enough water in him to cry.

CHAPTER EIGHT

At noon, Larry received a call from Frank. He told Larry about how the Sweet Pea was run down by a large freighter in the fog. They were going to the hospital to see Pete. Larry left a message on Shirley's phone then took her Vespa scooter to the hospital. There was quite a crowd there already. It took him a few minutes to find Frank.

"Have you seen him?" Larry asked.

"I talked to Doctor Harmon. He said that he's not too bad physically but he's suffering from some sort of traumatic stress which was made worse by having to cling to a piece of wreckage all night. His mother is the only one allowed in there with him now."

They saw a young man in a Coast Guard uniform trying to leave the area.

"Albert," Frank called out.

The man turned and looked at him.

"Any more news?"

"Hank was definitely below deck at the time so there's not much hope there. Pete confirmed that there were two guys diving at the time of the collision and as far as he knows, they never came up. We're searching the area. I gotta' go," he said.

"Sure, thanks," Frank said.

They turned to leave also.

"It's like you said. It's a god damned cursed place. I see why you want to stay away from there."

"I already found two old friends while diving there. Why make it worse," Larry said.

"It's like that old Spencer Tracy movie where he says that the mountain doesn't want him climbing anymore."

"I'm not a bloody Mystic. I just don't have a diving outfit to support such a venture. It takes money," Larry said as they got to the door, which was open.

"There's my bike," he quipped.

"It's a bad machine," Frank agreed.

Larry got on and started it up then waved at Frank then pulled away.

When Shirley got home at six, she had two women with her.

"Larry, I don't think you have met Amy Westover and Jean Gardner."

"Hello, nice meeting you," Larry said.

"Jean is Hank's wife."

"I'm very sorry. Me and Frank tried to see Pete but they wouldn't let anybody in except family."

"Before they brought him ashore, Pete took the Coast Guard to the place where he thought they were anchored. They're not sending any divers down. It's supposed to be the county's job and they're not sending any divers down either," Jean explained.

"If Hank's body is trapped in the wreckage, it will never come up. They said to allow seven days," Amy added.

"I can't let Hank stay down there. The sea creatures will eat him. Please Mister Mayer, will you bring him up for me?"

"Well, what do you think, Shirley?" Larry asked.

"Can it be done safely?" Shirley asked.

"Even under the best conditions, there's always an inherent risk at that depth."

"There's insurance. I can pay you," Jean blurted out.

"For a job like this, I'll take no money, but there are boat owners, fuel costs, breathing gas costs to pay."

"Our friends have already offered all those things. You can have everything by tomorrow morning."

"Alright, you call Frank Folger and tell him to handle getting everything to Coffin's Wharf by tomorrow morning. Is there any problem with that, Shirley?"

"None whatsoever."

"One more thing, this isn't a walk in the park. Don't tell the Coast Guard or anybody else about the dive. I don't need anybody else getting in my way," Larry said.

"Yes, I can do that," Jean said.

"Okay, if all goes well, we'll shove off around 0800."

"We'll be there to see you off," Jean said.

"Very good. See you then," Larry said.

After they left, Larry called Frank and asked him to fill his escape bottle with air. He took both of his hundred cubic feet tanks to the dive shop and had them filled with 15/50 trimix for this dive. He got the loan of a larger light and two coils of nylon line, 250 feet long.

After he left the dive shop he drove to Frank's shop to drop off the gear. There were a couple guys there that he didn't know.

"Larry, this is Gil Macy. That's his boat out there," Frank said. The man looked to be about his age.

"Hello. That's a good looking boat. Do you dive?" Larry asked as they shook hands.

"Not so much anymore. My heart ain't what it used to be."

"This is Curly, Howard's father. They will tend for us," Frank said as they shook hands.

"Good deal. Good to have experienced guys," Larry said.

"Are we still using standard signals," Frank asked.

"Yes, those should work."

"Okay, we'll go over them again tomorrow," Frank said, adding-"Let's check out the lay of her."

After they looked at the diving boat, Larry went home. Shirley, at her computer, seemed quieter than usual.

"Everything looks ship-shape," Larry said as he looked at a diving magazine.

"Thanks for not telling me last time," she remarked.

"Are you gonna' worry about it all night?"

"And tomorrow, until you walk through that door," she said.

"I did it before with no problems."

"There's five dead men between then and now."

"I have seen dead men in this business before," Larry said.

She came up behind him and began rubbing his shoulders.

"So much weight on these shoulders," she said as she squeezed gently.

Larry thought about her having fits about diving before. If it had been his idea to make this dive, would she have so readily agreed, he wondered.

"Just finding the wreck will be the hard part," Larry reflected.

At six o'clock he got up and packed his clothes in a gear bag and put on his diving underwear and booties. Shirley drove him down to the dock.

"I don't mean to tell you how to dive, but if the slightest thing goes wrong, get the hell outta' there."

"That's very good advice," Larry said then he kissed her.

He got out with his gear bag and headed down the dock. When he got to the boat, he turned around and saw that Shirley's car was still there so he waved then boarded the boat. Frank, Gil and Curly were there to greet him.

"Howard, Tommy and Amy will be here shortly," Frank said.

"That coffee smells good," Larry said.

"I'll be wearing my ten millimeter and my exposure suit. I have my full face mask," Frank said

"Heaven help you if you have to pee," Larry joked.

"I'm not some old man suffering from incontinence," he joked.

"Let's go check the gear," Larry said.

"I'll let you know when the others get here," Gil said.

Everything looked good with the gear. The dive shop had filled his tanks from the same storage tank as before so Larry knew the gas was good. He laid out the accessories in the order that he would take them. When the others arrived, they got underway. There wasn't much boat traffic even though the sky was clearing and the waves weren't bad. As they approached the search area, he posted Howard and Tommy as lookouts. They were to look for debris or bubbles. It wasn't long before they saw bubbles ahead and to the port. They stopped the boat and looked at the bubbles with their binoculars.

"We're nearly a quarter mile from where Pete believes they anchored," Gil said.

"Those two were seldom above the board about anything," Larry said as he looked through the binoculars.

"What do you think, Chief?"

"Let's anchor here."

"Oui mon Kapiten," Gil said.

Since the current would drag them eastward, they backed up and dropped both anchors off the stern. It didn't take long for the anchors to catch hold.

"Alright, for those of you that don't know, the white Styrofoam cup means that I found something. The red diving buoy means that I have marked something and the yellow cup means I'm coming up," Larry said.

Gil and Curly helped them suit up while Howard and Tommy acted as lookouts. After they were suited up, Larry insisted on anther gear check. When everything checked out, Curly handed Larry his knife then his tool bag containing the diving buoys, the coils of nylon line, cutting pliers and a purse net. Larry put on his full face mask and checked the seal then turned on his escape bottle and inserted the regulator. The air made a gentle hiss as he signaled OK to Curly. He stepped into the water from the stern so he could follow the anchor line to the bottom. When he got to one hundred feet, he put more air in his suit and switched to his big tank. When he got to the bottom he checked his compass then swam about twenty feet when he noticed another anchor line. He swam until he found the anchor. Of course, the Sweet Pea had been at anchor when the freighter hit it. The violence of the collision tore the anchor loose, he thought. He continued swimming and found Brian lying on his back. His face mask and regulator were off. Larry removed one of the coils of line and tied it under his arms. He attached the buoy to the other end of the line and inflated it with the sparklet bulb. He let the buoy ascend slowly at first then he let it slide through the fingers of his glove until it stopped. He continued to move away from the diving boat. The big light was a great help in seeing on the bottom. He came to the compressor, which had obviously sank straight down when it was thrown from the boat. About thirty yards beyond that he came to the shattered hull of the Sweet Pea. Looking into the wreckage, he saw the body of Hank wedged upside down in the companionway. He released a Styrofoam cup then swam around to the after end of the hull. He found Steve laying on the bottom in the fetal position. His mask and regulator were still in place. He tied a line around him and fastened a buoy and inflated it as he had with Brian. He went to the shattered mess that had been the deck and released another cup. He went to the mashed in companionway leading below and grabbed Hank by his head and pulled in order to dislodge him but he didn't move. Setting his light down, he grabbed an arm and his head and pulled again and Hank came free from the wreck. He carefully backed out and retrieved his light while holding Hank with one arm. When he was out 'on deck', he released the yellow cup, put more air in his BCD and kicked hard to start himself and Hank to the surface. As he rose he had to vent air from his BCD and constantly check his depth gauge or he would shoot to the surface. After ten minutes he was at a hundred feet. He switched to his escape bottle and rose to the surface in a couple minutes. When he got to the surface, he could see everyone was at the stern a pointing at him. He found it difficult to swim with the lifeless body of Hank. He put him across his back, navy style, so he could use his arms and legs to swim. When he got to the boat, all the guys were reaching for Hank. Once relieved of the weight, Larry reached up and Frank and Curly pulled him up. On deck, Frank pulled out his regulator and removed his full face mask.

"Phew, that swim tired me out!" Larry exclaimed.

"Here, sit down and rest. Here's some water," Frank said.

As he drank the water, he noticed Tommy holding Amy as she sobbed.

Howard and Gil laid Hank on a tote bin canvas and closed it up by 'sewing' through the eyes. Larry saw that Hank had Pete's Mk1knife on his belt.

"Maybe you should take her inside. Those buoy lines are tied to Coakley and Murray," Larry said after a minute.

"Saints preserve us," Frank said.

"You're in Graves Registration now, I'm afraid."

Amy suddenly regained her composure and took out her phone.

"I must call people," she insisted.

"Certainly, would you like to go inside," Tommy asked.

"No, I must call, "she said as she pressed buttons.

Larry looked around to see if any other boats were nearby. All the sailboats were staying closer to the islands. The westerly breeze was holding.

"Hello, Jean. Mister Mayer brought Hank up…No, he looks good… You can see the surprised look on his face…They wrapped him up in canvas… Excuse me, Mister Mayer, are you alright?"

Larry nodded his head.

"Yes, he's alright…The other men? I'll ask.."

"Mayer got a line around them. We'll pull them up here directly," Frank said while pointing at the diving buoys.

"They'll be pulling them up as soon as Hank is secure…Yes, we'll be bringing them in…Don't let them know until I call…Yes…Yes, I will. Call you later, bye."

"This could be unpleasant, Aunt Amy," Tommy said.

"Oh, I must witness this. I don't want any trouble to fall on you guys after all you've done," Amy insisted.

Gil started the engine and slowly backed the boat to the first diving buoy. Frank pulled it up with the boat hook and Gil, Curly, Howard and Tommy grabbed the line and began pulling. When Brian broke the surface he was much heavier and Frank went in the water in his wetsuit and helped get him aboard. They laid him on deck and took off his gear but left him in his drysuit and wrapped him in canvas like Hank and took him below to the cold storage hold. They did the same thing with Coakley then headed home. Larry changed into his work clothes and Frank changed out of his wetsuit. Gil and Curly helped secure their gear. When Larry came out of the crew's room, Howard handed him a cup of coffee.

"That was some good work," he said.

"You did good spotting those bubbles."

"Whoever said that you are one hundred percent Balls-Out was not over stating the case at all."

"It was a day's work for a diver."

"Could you dive again today?"

"Not wise at that depth. Blood and tissues have to be given a chance to outgas completely," Larry explained.

"What do you think happened to the divers?"

"Hard telling if they were alive at the time of the collision," Larry said.

"I can't imagine being deep like that and a broken up boat comes down on you. What a fucking bitch that would be," Howard said.

"Yeah, I'm sure it was."

"You talked about things going to shit on you in Alexander Bay. You don't have to worry about that here. Amy's husband is a judge and their father is a selectman. Aunt Jean will be happy to see Hank in such good shape. That's what she wanted," Howard said.

"Yeah, he wasn't in the water that long."

"Was he in the hull?"

"What was left of it. The bow was torn off and the hull was smashed all to hell on the starboard side. Hank was lodged upside down in the companionway."

"Doubtless the Coast Guard will ask you to make a report. Too bad you didn't have the time to photograph the wreck. Pictures like that would be a big help."

He's gotta' be kidding, Larry thought as he looked at the island off the starboard side.

"Another guy would be required to take the pictures. I had enough to do as it was. If the Coast Guard wants pictures, let them go down there."

"They'll probably ask you to draw a picture or something."

"I have had to diagram wrecks before. I'll do it if they request it," Larry said.

Frank came over to them.

"How are you feeling?"

"Fine," Larry replied.

"That Trimix works pretty well for you at that depth?"

"Yeah, I like to keep the partial pressure of nitrogen below thirty five psi when I'm on the bottom. It was a good dive. It probably couldn't have gone any better."

"That's being objective about it. There will be some long faces when we dock," Frank said.

"True, but it's closure. People can get on with their lives now," Larry said.

"Jean and Pete will appreciate it. Do you know anything about the other guys?"

"The last I knew, neither of them were married. I gave their names to the authorities."

"Where are they from?"

"They lived in California when I ran into them last," Larry said.

"They were working divers out there?"

"Pro surfers. Among the best on the mainland," Larry said.

"You can make a living doing that?" Howard asked.

"Most of them are instructors and /or have a shop."

"How much do divers get paid?"

"Oil rig divers make out okay, but the requirements are pretty hefty. Salvage diving is a little more chancy. Some cities like New York have full time divers with decent pay and benefits. Outfits like Venture Co. usually pay expenses but the disposable pay is pretty low," Larry explained.

"Paying expenses means that they live on the boat and eat the mess garbage," Frank added.

"It is still the only way for many of the younger folk to get their foot in the door and get the bottom time and acquire the equipment they need."

"That doesn't sound too bad. Unlike the Navy, I could always jump ship for a better proposition," Howard said.

"Yeah, sometimes they do."

Larry didn't bother to tell him that due to the competitive nature of the business there frequently are inter-ship and intra-ship problems to deal with.

"If we hit the town tonight, we could have people buying us drinks."

"I'm getting my beauty sleep," Larry said.

"Good idea," Frank agreed.

When they docked, the Coroners van was there to pick up the bodies. Jean had the canvas opened so she could see Hank before he was placed in the van. Amy held her as she sobbed. After the Coroner's van left, Jean thanked Larry for recovering Hank's body then she and Amy left together.

"That's pretty rough," Gil said.

"Yeah, pretty rough for everybody," Frank agreed.

"I've seen it worse."

They looked at Larry.

"I recovered an eighteen year old guy in Bremerton, Washington. There were about ten thousand people there. His parents kept asking me How? Why? I just wanted to get outta' there," Larry explained.

"Shirley is here. We'll help you carry your gear," Frank said.

"Much obliged."

Gil grabbed the carrier with his two tanks. Frank got the gear bags with his suit, BCD and regulators. Larry picked up the gear bag with his diving underclothes and they walked landward. Shirley had parked her SUV at the head of the pier. She opened the hatch and waited for them.

"I heard that it went well," she said.

"All things considered, it was a good dive," Larry replied.

They put his gear in the back and closed the hatch.

"If you change your mind, give us a call," Gil said.

"Sure," Larry said.

They shook hands without saying a word then Frank and Gil headed toward the boat shop. Larry and Shirley got in the SUV.

"Jean had to see him before the Coroner took him," Shirley said as she turned the key.

"He wasn't bad. Still had his color. Still had that shocked look on his face."

She put it into gear and pulled out into the street.

"It is great the way you guys pitched in and made it happen and nobody asked for a cent. On an island where everything has a price tag, that is remarkable. You can bet it will be in the newspapers."

"Just so they don't ask me," Larry said.

"With wireless technology it will be all over the island in an hour."

"No visitors, no interviews. As the song says, this is just an ordinary day."

An hour after they got home, Shirley told him that a Coast Guard Lieutenant wanted to talk to him on the phone.

"Tell him I'm suffering from the bends."

"You tell him," Shirley insisted.

Larry took the receiver.

"Yes?"

"You are Lawrence Mayer?"

"Yes."

"You dived on the wreck of the Sweet Pea at or about 10:20 this morning?"

"Yes."

"The bodies of Henry Gardner, Brian Murray and Steven Coakley were recovered?"

"Yes."

"Can you come to the Coast Guard station and make a report?"

"No."

"Mister Mayer, I'm just trying to do my job."

"I wasn't doing any 'job'. I was helping out a poor woman who wasn't getting any help from you. You want a report, send your own diver down," Larry snapped then he hung up the phone.

"You want to shake him and slap him?"

"That was the good old days. I've mellowed out since then, don't you agree?"

"Hard telling. Jean didn't call the Coroner until she saw you guys coming in. She didn't want the county or the Coast Guard bringing Hank in like they had something to do with it."

"Just as well, it was rough enough without a crowd there," Larry said.

"If you had just brought in Hank, it would have still been tremendous."

"I tied buoy lines to Coakley and Murray. I brought Hank up in my arms."

"Amy told Jean that you did. The stock in Boston Mills just went up."

"Sell, sell!" Larry quipped.

CHAPTER NINE

The next day was warm and sunny. Shortly before noon, Larry was walking across the square. He didn't see the young woman coming from his right.

"Excuse me. I'm Kate Ferrare of the Mirror Enquirer. Are you Larry Mayer?"

Larry looked at her for a moment.

"Yes."

"I have to be sure. That man over there said that he was Larry Mayer."

When Larry looked that way he saw a man about forty years old. The man quickly turned and walked away.

"Clown," Larry said as pulled out his wallet. He showed her his Ohio driver's license.

"Alright, I want to ask you a few questions about the incident."

"No incident. It was just a dive."

"Do you know Jean Gardner?"

"Of course, she asked me to make the dive."

"How did you locate the wreck?"

"A lot of luck and some air bubbles," Larry replied.

"What was it like on the bottom?"

"Cold and dark."

"Did you see any marine life?"

"I don't recall seeing any but I wasn't looking for that."

"Were you ever apprehensive before or during the dive?"

"No."

"Never?"

"Only when I'm doing my taxes."

"You don't seem to any find glory in this?"

"Glory? Is that what this is?"

"What would you call it?"

"Pretty much just a job that needed done."

"Have you ever been the toast of the town?"

"No, I've been run out of town."

"Where?"

"The last time, Alexander Bay, New York."

"Why?"

"It's a long story which I don't have time to tell."

"Nobody can accuse you of any wrongdoing here."

"Yeah, nobody," Larry said as he thought of Harry Brown and company.

"How old are you?"

"Fifty six."

"Do you date?"

"Is this off the record?"

"Definitely."

"I am currently in a relationship with Shirley Douglas, so no."

"Very good. Thank you for your time, Mister Mayer. Maybe I'll see you again."

"It's a small island. Good –bye.

Larry continued across the town square and went to the library. People never bother you at the library. The house rule is no talking. As he walked by the desk he ran into Mrs. Frantz. Peggy Frantz was even taller than Larry. A wonderful person in every respect.

"Mr. Mayer, two television stations and a newspaper have called. They were inquiring if you were here," she said.

"If they missed once then they probably won't call back. Tell them I'm at the Spouter and I'll sneak out the back," he suggested.

"Your name has been in four major news stories. That is not the way that people will forget you. I managed to get copies of those charts you requested. Since they are copies of material from another library, you can keep them," she said. She reached under the desk and pulled out rolls of paper about two feet long and handed them to him. She had written the chart numbers on the rolls.

"Great, thanks. I can sneak home now."

"If you ever come out with a book, make sure I get one," Peggy said.

"The great diver becomes the great self-publisher," Larry quipped, adding-"Good-bye."

"Good-bye."

News does travel fast on this island, he thought. The media has already gotten the poop on him. They know where he hangs out and what he looks like. In the Navy it was easy, he thought. You were always at sea and always protected by the secrecy of the operations. By the time you got ashore it was old news anyway. At the time of the Ray Ronson affair they were docked. When a reporter said that Ronson's manager denied that the fight ever occurred, Larry called him a liar. When the reporter asked if he would fight him again, Larry suggested that next time the son of a bitch might get really hurt. The president requested that Larry refrain from talking to reporters and that was fine with Larry.

When he got home, the cook told him that Shirley had went to see her tax accountant. If he married Shirley it would be at least another six months of work for that guy, he thought. He told Rosa that he was going out to look for his diving buddies. He got on her Scooter and headed for the harbor.

When he arrived, the ferry had just docked and there was a large crowd. He parked his scooter and started walking toward the main street. He had managed to get around the mob and had a clear sidewalk in front of him when he ran into a familiar face.

"Good afternoon, Mister Mayer. I see you have not been idle," Lovisa said.

"That was a favor for a friend. Did you dive the Doria?"

"Two boats were zhere when we arrived."

"The more the merrier," Larry quipped.

"Unfortunately zhat was not the case."

"You probably have enough dinnerware as it is."

"Not much success on our dives, you see," she said.

"That happens."

"Would you like to see our boat?"

"Sure," Larry said.

They headed for the Coffin dock.

"We got in early zhis morning. We had already heard about your diving yesterday."

"News definitely travels fast on this island. It's not easy to hold down anything big. What's your fall back plan?" he asked.

"I have no idea. Zhis is something not shared with zeh divers."

"Howard and Billy have been doing their best to find you people," Larry informed her.

"Howard is not a deep diver," she said.

"Never too young to learn."

"Has he any other qualifications?" she asked.

"Two eyes, two hands, two lungs."

"Yes, I seem to remember zhat his eyes were very active."

"At his age, not surprising," Larry said as they started up the gangway.

"It looks Russian," Larry said as they went up.

"It was a Russian recovery ship. Zeh owners did not pay much money for it. Zhey have paid to modernize it."

"Boats are so expensive. Coedding it was a problem, I'm sure," Larry said when they were on deck.

"What is zhis coedding?" she asked as they walked forward.

"Having Quarters for men and women," Larry said as they started up the stairs to the bridge.

"I cannot say. I was not involved in zeh fitting-out. Zhat is the term?"

"Yes, that is correct," Larry said as they crossed the landing and started up another set of steps.

At the top, Lovisa opened the hatch and motioned for Larry to enter.

Larry stopped in the hatchway when he saw a man in an officer's uniform.

"Lawrence Mayer requesting permission to come on the bridge."

"Enter, Mayer," he replied.

Larry and Lovisa came in.

"I'm Edwin Thomas. I see that you have been taught the proper procedure," he said as they shook hands.

"Nice meeting you. Do you dive?" Larry asked.

"I did, but since taking command of this vessel I've been told to leave the diving to others. We heard about your diving when we were still out, yesterday."

"I had to make only one dive. I got buoy lines around Coakley and Murray and I brought Gardner up in my arms," Larry explained.

"I'm surprised that you could find them."

"Yes, Howard spotted the bubbles from Coakley's regulator. A great piece of work," Larry said.

"By the Coast Guard radio, we heard that Young Gardner was found with a piece of wreckage. Then we heard that you dived the next day and bought up the bodies."

"A yachtsman found Pete Gardner. Misses Gardner wanted us to bring in the bodies so the coast Guard wouldn't get any credit."

"You were diving in the Thousand Islands last November?" Edwin asked.

"How did you know that?"

"I got a letter of recommendation for Brigitte Svenson of Trondheim. She states that she dived with you on that occasion," he replied.

"Yes she did. She did a good job. I believe she made four dives at two hundred feet. Have you heard from Sammy Pike or Jans Trelleborg?"

"I know them. I've heard nothing from them since I took over here, six months ago. Are you looking for a job?"

"No, yesterday was just a favor for Jean Gardner."

"I dived with Sy Lampert a couple years ago. I heard he ended up in jail."

"He hired me for two thousand a day. I found the wreck for them and established that it was the Madamoiselle de Loire. The owners fired me and Sy jumped ship with some of the loot in the middle of the night. According to a treaty the ship still belonged to France," Larry explained.

"You're looking for the Samosett?"

"I was, yes," Larry replied.

We were looking for the City of Bristol."

"Without much success I take it. I've been out there. The movement of sand on the bottom is phenomenal. If there's anything left of her, it could be buried in twenty feet of sand," Larry opined.

"That may be the case," Edwin agreed.

"I was going to show Larry zeh lay of her," Lovisa said.

"Very good, I have to go ashore. We'll be at the Fog Island this evening if you want to stop by."

"Thank you, I might do that. Good-bye," Larry said then he left with Lovisa.

They went below and checked out the diving gear and the gas equipment. They went to the galley and the mess. Everything was ship-shape and it was twice the size of the Venturer 2 in Alexander Bay.

"I'm impressed, "Larry said as they headed to the crew's quarters.

"Zhis is zeh best boat I have worked on. Two quarters share an adjoining shower. Right now I am in single quarters. Some divers have double quarters. I was lucky zhis time, you see," she said as she opened the door and went in.

Larry hesitated to enter. He saw a bunk and a small table and a chair.

"Come in. I will show you pictures of Erik."

Larry came in and she took a large album out of the drawer under her bunk.

"You can take zeh chair if you like," she said.

As he sat down he remembered that Lovisa had told him, last November, that her husband died a year ago.

"Erik was much more zeh camera bug zhan I was. He was quite good I zhink."

She showed him some pictures of their later dives.

"Erik did not put zhese in order by time. He put his favorite ones first."

There were a couple pages that had pictures of both of them in various stages of undress.

"Erik called zhese our fun pictures," she said then she turned the page.

"That is good. When you get older like me, you can look at those pictures and remember how it was in happier times."

"Erik said it was for zeh times when we were not on zeh dive boat together. I thought zhat was silly because we were always on zeh boat together."

"Darla was very modest. She would never wear a bathing suit. She was never photographed in anything less than shorts and a t-shirt," Larry explained.

After she showed him the album, she put it back in the drawer under the bunk.

"Erik was much like you. He believed zeh water was not a barrier. He succeeded where others had failed."

He wasn't an ugly old man either, Larry thought.

"I'm sure he loved diving like I do," Larry said.

"I'll show you ashore," she said.

"Thank you for showing me the boat," he said as they left her quarters.

"You are quite welcome."

"Are you going back out soon?" he asked.

"I'm sure we are. We cannot remain idle for long."

"Good luck to you," Larry said.

"Has Misses Douglas ever dived?"

"Not to my knowledge."

"Would it be better for you with a diver?"

"It hasn't been a problem yet," Larry said when they got to the gangway.

"You have my card?"

"Yes I do," Larry said.

"If you, how do you say, crack up wizh Mrs. Douglas, please give me a call."

"I certainly will, good-bye," Larry said as they shook hands.

He turned and walked down the gangway. As he was walking landward, he met Howard and Billy.

"Hi guys. Getting some sea air?" Larry quipped as he fell into step with them.

"We were delivering some fishing gear and just happened to be in the area," Billy said.

"Did you ever hear the one about the alcoholic that happened to run into the whiskey wagon?" he joked.

"Like you happened to run into Lovisa?" Howard said.

"Yes, like that."

"What were you doing on that boat with her?"

"Funny you should ask that. We were in her quarters and looking at naked pictures of her and her former husband."

"You're shittin' me!" Howard exclaimed.

"Absolutely not, that's what we were doing, among other things."

"Yeah, I'll bet!" Billy exclaimed.

"We were talking about you," Larry said, looking at Howard.

"I heard those foreign babes have some weird ideas about foreplay," Billy quipped.

"I told her that by locating those bubbles, you did ninety percent of the work for us. I also told her that you're ready to be wrung out for deep diving."

"Telling jokes during sex. Why didn't I think of that...Oww," Billy said as Howard punched him on the arm.

"They're considering taking on Brigitte Svenson. Remember I told you about diving with her in Alexander Bay."

"I could handle working on a dive boat," Howard declared.

"Take five seconds of your valuable time and tell us what you know about pro diving," Billy said.

"Could you go diving with me like before?" Howard asked.

"I'm not sure that would be wise. It's a matter of PR. If I lost a diver that I was instructing, things could turn sour on me here."

"The viewing for Gardner is tomorrow. You wouldn't dare bring up that subject with mommy and daddy," Billy declared.

They ended up at the Claw and Tail. The lunch crowd was thinned out so they didn't have to wait. The waitress came over. A pleasant looking young lady in her early twenties

"Hi Howie."

"Hi Eadie, do you know Larry Mayer?" Howard asked.

"By reputation,of course. How are you?"

"Not too shabby," Larry said, smiling.

"Edith went to school with me."

"There's one School on this island. Everybody went to school together," Eadie said.

"What do you have that's fit for a hero?" Howard quipped.

"How about the house special, crab and scallop casserole?" she asked.

"That sounds good," Larry said.

"We'll have your chowdah for an appetizer," Howard said.

"Very good, I'll have the chowder out in a few minutes," Edith said before leaving.

"I'll get it on the house. Watch this," Billy declared.

"Forget it. I got all kinds of money," Larry said.

"Here's your buddy, Frog," Howard said.

"Precious. Where's my precious," Billy hissed.

Larry saw a smallish guy with dark hair and 'bug eyes', coming their way.

"How's it going frog?" Billy asked.

Since they had to be introduced, Larry stood up.

"Larry Mayer, this is Michael Poole," Howard said.

"Hello Mike," Larry said as they shook hands.

"Have a seat if you're staying," Billy said.

"Just a few minutes. I understand that you're a diver."

"Yes, I am."

"God, you would have to be deaf and blind if you haven't heard more than that, Mikey!" Billy exclaimed.

"My father and grandfather have fished around this island for sixty years. They have snagged their nets on a lot of wrecks in that time. They located them pretty accurately so they wouldn't damage the nets again. Stop by and see my father. He'll be happy to help you out," Mike said.

"Thank you, I may well do that," Larry said.

"Have you ever heard of the Farrallon Islands?" Mike asked.

"Yes I have."

"There's a lot of good wrecks around there."

"Yes there are," Larry replied.

"Have you ever thought of diving there?"

"No, it's federal waters. In the first place, the government will take everything. In the second place, it's the Department of the Interior and nobody can dive anywhere near there," Larry replied.

"What's the limit?"

"Twelve miles."

"Tough break, Frog," Billy said.

"My uncle is in the Navy. He can get over there," Mikey said confidently.

"Good luck with his diving," Larry said.

"Have you done a lot of diving on the west coast?"

"Oh yeah, a lot," Larry said casually.

"I gotta' run. Catch you guys later," Mike said as he stood up. Since the others didn't stand, Larry didn't.

"Nice meeting you."

"Same here," Mike said then he left.

"What a dweeb. What a bozo. He can't say anything without sounding stupid," Billy remarked.

Larry thought about how he would deal with him if he were in the Navy. He would probably have him sent to another outfit. He could deliver mail. Some job like that where he wouldn't be too unhappy and he couldn't do too much harm.

"He's not your favorite classmate I take it."

"Definitely on the bottom of the list," Billy said.

"Does he go out with his father and grandfather?" Larry asked.

"I don't think they let him near the boat. I know he gets sick on an airplane."

"His eyes aren't set back. He would have to wear the old style mask."

"In his kiddy pool! I'll never dive with him!" Howard declared.

Eadie brought the Chowder and cornbread.

"I'll be right out with the casserole," she said.

"Super," Larry replied.

He noticed Howard looking at Eadie as she walked away. At his age it's perfectly normal and acceptable. If he looked at a young woman like that, he would be labeled a pervert, Larry thought. Howard looked at him.

"So, are you going to pay Lovisa another visit?"

"No, there's no reason to now."

"Did you see Yvette or Suzanne?" Billy asked.

"No, I didn't see any other women. They must be ashore," Larry replied.

"Now clarify this for me. She showed you pictures of her completely nude?" Howard asked.

"With nothing but what God gave her."

Howard looked at him for a moment.

"It didn't occur to you that you could have rode her!"

"In fact it did, but that would have made things a little awkward with Mrs. Douglas."

"Howie, you're just not thinking with the right head," Billy quipped.

"She suggested that a diver might be a more suitable mate for me. Her deceased husband was a diver. She's looking for a guy to keep her wetsuit clean and her bunk warm. How's that suit ya'?" Larry asked.

"She sounds like a woman who's starting to go through husbands. Have you ever known a woman like that?" Billy asked.

"I've known a lot of women like that, unfortunately," Larry replied.

"I just have to get my foot in the door," Howard said.

"Take note, Howie, she's looking for a real stud not a chipmunk."

"That leaves me out," Larry said.

Eadie brought their food on a cart. She cleared their dishes and set the casserole pan on the table and gave them clean plates.

"Anything else?"

"An opinion please. Does Howie look like a deep sea diver?" Billy asked.

"No he doesn't," she said after a moment.

"How about Mister Mayer?" he asked.

"Yes, he looks hard. Hard enough to take anything life throws at him," she opined then she left.

"Oh he's hard, real hard," Howard said in a feminine voice.

"All the women say that about me," Larry said.

Billy nearly choked on his food.

The owner came to their table and took a picture of him. Before they left, Larry signed and dated it. Studs Terkel said that there's no such thing as a free lunch, Larry thought as they left.

"Larry Mayer slept here' signs will begin springing up all over the island," Billy joked as they started walking down the sidewalk.

"Are you gonna' check out the info that Frog was talking about?" Howard asked.

"Probably not. If I had a dollar for every time someone said that they could locate a wreck for me, I wouldn't lack for money."

"Just when it was getting fun," Billy quipped.

"I was there this time. Nobody was having a good time, I assure you," Howard said.

"What's your plans, Larry?"

"I'll probably be returning to Ohio to bury Joe Cole."

"You said he lived in the Virgin Islands. Why not bury him there? The virgins can weep at his grave," Billy quipped.

"No virgins with Joe there," Larry countered.

"No such luck on this island either."

"Oh Eadie!" Billy quipped.

"They'll be at Fog Island tonight. Check it out if you like," Larry said.

All the guys who were on Gill's boat were given a chit for a free dinner at Fog island. At eight o'clock, Howard and Curly arrived. They were taken to the table where Frank and Gil were. The waitress came right over and gave them menus.

"Would you like anything to drink?" she asked.

"I'll have coffee," Curly said.

"Whale's Tail Pale Ale," Howard said.

His father looked at him but said nothing.

"Very good, I'll be right out with that," she said then she left.

"Larry said he can't make it," Frank informed them.

Howard felt let down.

"You look unhappy," Frank observed.

"No, I'm fine," Howard said.

"Larry gave you top billing. He tells everybody that we couldn't have done it without you," Frank said.

"He's being too kind, as always."

"We know that but the rest of the island doesn't," his father quipped as he punched him on the arm.

Several people stopped by to say a word or two before their steak arrived. The waitress picked up their glasses and brought their steaks and steak sauce. Howard looked at his steak for a minute. He didn't notice three people going by on the right. One of them stopped and looked at them. Frank, Gil and Curly set down their silverware and stood up. Howard looked to his right and saw Lovisa looking at him. He jumped up and knocked over his Pale Ale.

"Hello again, Howard," she said.

"Hi, uhh...this is my father, Harold Hillier, Frank Folger and Gil Macy. Gentlemen, Lovisa Lutjens."

"Hello, Good evening," they said in turn as they shook hands in turn.

"I'm afraid zhat zhis is rather inopportune for you. We may be leaving tomorrow so if you wish to see zeh ship it must be now."

"Uh...can you get me a box?" Howard asked.

Curly figured that it was Howard's way of asking if he could go with her.

"Yes, certainly," he said after a moment.

"I'll give you a call," Howard said then he left with her.

The waitress came to the table and tried to wipe up the beer.

"What was that all about?" Curly asked after she left.

"Lovisa is a diver on the Venture Co. II. She is usually looking for Larry. Howard and Billy are always talking about her at the shop," Frank explained.

"Some foreign cradle robber, I suppose," Curly remarked.

"Howie will be twenty one in November," Gil said.

"Lovisa is a professional diver. Howard wanted Larry to put in a good word for him. It looks like he did after all," Frank speculated.

"I have to go home and explain to his mother why he isn't with me. Oh joy."

"Well, it had to happen sometime, Curly," Gil said.

"What's the deal with this deep diving? How long does that take to learn?" Curly asked.

"If he doesn't wash-out anywhere along the line, at least two years," Frank said.

"Could Larry teach him?"

"He really doesn't want to. Howie should be taught in a real diving outfit that has the gear and the facilities for doing that," Frank explained.

Outside, there was a big Cadillac parked on the street. Lovisa introduced Howard to the other two divers, an Italian and a Russian, who were waiting for them. They drove to the airport and picked up two more people.

"Four crew have decided to leave, you see," Lovisa said, adding-"Zhis is Brigitte Svenson and Gunnar Vissten," when they got in the car.

"Hello Brigitte. Larry Mayer mentioned that he dived with you in Alexander Bay in November," Howard said.

"Pardon us, Howard. Brigitte knows very little English. I translate for her. I am the tender for Brigitte. You are a friend of Herr Mayer?" Gunnar asked.

"Yes, I have dived with him. Simple stuff, nothing below a hundred and ten feet," Howard replied.

"He is on this island still?" Gunnar asked.

"Yes, I think he is at home. I'll give him a call," Howard said as he took out his phone.

He dialed and waited.

"Douglas residence, Mayer speaking."

"Hey Larry, Howard, I'm in a car with Lovisa and some other divers. There's a Gunnar Vissten and a Brigitte Svenson here."

"Well if that don't beat all," Larry remarked.

"We're headed for their boat. Can you meet us there?"

"Roger that," Larry replied.

"See you there," Howard said then he disconnected.

The Cadillac arrived at the Coffin Wharf a minute later. The other two divers helped unload their bags then they left in the car. The ship was lighted up and a red light was flashing.

"Zeh ship is being refueled, you see," Lovisa explained when they got out of the car. Howard helped them with their bags.

They walked down the dock and stopped at the gangway. Howard was feeling apprehensive. There was something surreal about the lighting and the men in the fire suits.

"We must wait here a few minutes. The transfer will be complete soon," Lovisa said.

"Very good," Gunnar said, adding-"Howard, how long have you known Herr Mayer?"

"Oh, six or seven months now," Howard exaggerated.

"He is a very reliable fellow, is he not?"

"He is the most balls-out diver I have ever seen. He took out a seventeen foot shark like it was a goldfish. He facilitated bringing up three dead men in one half hour dive. He is 'can do' all the way!" Howard declared.

"Yes, he certainly, how you say, brought home the bacon in Alexander Bay," Gunnar said.

"I heard that two armed men in scuba gear knocked him into the water in the darkness and he killed them both in a minute," Howard said.

"Yes, I understand that is what happened in August of last year," Gunnar said.

Brigitte said something in Norwegian. Gunnar talked to her for a minute.

"Brigitte is tired. I told her it won't be long now," Gunnar said.

"Will she be bunking with Yvette and Suzanne?" Howard asked.

"Both of zem could not extend zheir contract to zeh end of zeh year. Zhey wanted to leave zhis month," Lovisa explained.

"I couldn't learn much from them. How long had they been diving?"

"Both have been diving for five years now," Lovisa replied.

They saw a single light of motor bike in the parking area.

"Larry has Shirley's Vespa. It's a bad machine," Howard quipped.

Gunnar said something in Norwegian while pointing landward. Brigitte said something and Gunnar nodded his head.

"Herr Mayer has had much good luck. Is this not so?" Gunnar asked.

"Not always. Last winter he lost the job he had for fifteen years," Howard said.

"That is indeed unfortunate."

"Please don't mention it," Howard requested.

"Of course," Gunnar said.

They could see Larry on the dock. They heard a loudspeaker on the ship.

"Zeh fuelling is completed. Zhey are purging zeh hoses now," Lovisa said.

After a minute, Gunnar called out, "A scurvy lot, not so, Herr Mayer?"

"I'm never too quick to judge a crew, Herr Vissten," Larry replied.

"I regret that we did not say good-bye," Gunnar said as he held out his hand.

"I heard that things didn't go too well."

"We never heard what happened to you." Gunnar said as they shook hands.

"Lampert set up a teleconference. A German named Strauss says-nice to meet you Herr Mayer and you're fired. I told him that I wanted paid and he tried to give me some shit about their accountants so I told him that I wanted paid right now. Sy went to the bank and got me a cashier's check for six thousand," Larry explained.

"When the boat docked, we were told to get off. We were told to leave Schooner Bay hotel. Seven of us rode in an old van to Montreal. We got paid about a month later but it was just a couple hundred dollars. We had a couple harbor jobs over the winter. Things have been rough but this boat is going back to Europe so that is good."

"Did Pike and Trelleborg come with you?"

"No, we did not see them when we left the boat. I talked to Jans a month ago. A friend paid for them to return to Denmark. They said nothing to any of us, of course. We also worked with Honore and Mark earlier this year. We have been living out of the suitcase as you say."

"That doesn't sound like much fun," Larry remarked.

"We have to carry the gear with us," Gunnar said, indicating the large gear bags.

"If there is anything I can do to help you on your way, let me know," Larry said.

"Thank you, Herr Mayer," Gunnar said.

They heard the Bosun's whistle.

"We can go aboard now," Lovisa said.

"I'll help with the gear," Larry said as he picked up two of the gear bags. Howard picked up two more and they went up the gangway.

"Well Howard, it looks like they'll be leaving soon," Larry said when they got up on deck.

"Yes, it looks like quite an outfit."

"Zhis way," Lovisa said, as she went through a hatchway on the left and down a narrow steps.

When they got down to the next deck, the passageway was painted a light gray and they could hear the hum of machinery.

"You will be forward. It is quieter zhere."

Howard was trying to take it all in as they went forward.

"Zeh women's quarters have a white bar. Always knock when entering other quarters," Lovisa explained.

She stopped at an open hatchway.

"Zhese are your quarters, Herr Vissten. You can leave your zhings in zhere if you like."

Gunnar took his bags in and came out after a minute.

"You have no room mate yet. It is a good bunk," Lovisa said then they headed forward again.

A couple 'doors' down they came to a hatch with a two inch, horizontal white line. Lovisa opened it.

"Zhis is zeh quarters recently vacated by Yvette and Suzanne. It has been cleaned and a new pad and sheets used," Lovisa said as gestured for Brigitte to enter. Brigitte went in and she said something to Gunnar and he went in as well. They talked in Norwegian for a minute then Gunnar looked at Lovisa.

"Will she have the quarters to herself?"

"For now, yes. She is zeh only woman diver except for me," Lovisa replied.

Gunnar said something to her and she nodded her head.

"She likes the quarters," Gunnar said.

"Good. Gentlemen if you will," Lovisa said.

Larry and Howard brought her bags into the quarters and set them next to the bunk.

"Good deal. They got you all set up here," Larry said.

"Let us see zeh captain," Lovisa said.

They went back the way they came and took the outside steps to the bridge. Edwin and another man were there. He looked at them.

"Come in people. Sorry you had to wait. The regulations allow for only the people necessary for the fuelling."

"Ed, zhis is Brigitte Svenson."

"Hello. Are you secure below?" he asked as they shook hands.

Brigitte looked at him quizzically.

"All her gear is aboard," Lovisa said.

"Very good," he said.

"Her tender, Gunnar Vissten."

"Nice meeting you," Edwin said as they shook hands.

"Thank you for expediting our travel, Herr Thomas," Gunnar said.

"Thank Larry here. He couldn't say enough about you," Edwin said.

Gunnar looked at him.

"For the short time we worked with him, he was absolutely correct in everything," Gunnar said.

"Zhis is Howard Hillier."

"Nice meeting you, Howard," Ed said as they shook hands.

"Nice meeting you."

"You have done some diving?"

"I have been diving since I was sixteen. Air only. Down to one hundred and twenty five feet," Howard replied.

"How old are you?"

"I'll be twenty one in November."

"Ooh, not good. The corporate regulation is twenty two years old, I'm afraid," Edwin said.

"You know Larry, of course"

"Great seeing you again. I heard about the diving you did a couple days ago. You were using a gas mixture I take it."

"Fifteen/fifty trimix. I had a hundred feet tank and an escape bottle with air for going down and coming up," Larry replied.

"I'm sure that you have seen that we can achieve any gas mixture we might need. We also have the capability to mix Argon, but we haven't used that yet," Edwin explained.

"Yes, you certainly have one of the better equipped boats that I have seen," Larry said.

"Another diver should be showing up here. A Bill Cowler. Do you know him?"

"Yes I do."

"What do you think of him?" Ed asked.

"He's not that good of a diver and he'll be trying to tell you how to run this boat," Larry said.

Edwin just looked at him for a moment.

"I talked to him on the phone. He seemed knowledgable and experienced."

"Yeah, he can make a good first impression but he's been trouble in every outfit he's been in. Talk to Harry Smythe at Sunset Trips and Ron Groves at Diving The Deep. They'll tell you about him," Larry assured him.

"That won't be necessary. I'll trust your judgement," Edwin replied.

"We'll let you get back to your fun. Any idea when you'll be shoving off?"

"The owners would definitely like us to be on our way by sometime tomorrow."

"Well, it's been great seeing you again and good luck out there," Larry said as they shook hands.

"Thanks mate. You take it easy now," Edwin said.

"If only it were that kind of a world."

"Nice meeting you, Howard," Ed said as he shook his hand.

"Thank you. I really enjoyed seeing the boat," he said then they left the bridge.

"I will see you ashore," Lovisa said as they started down the steps.

"I would have liked to dive with you," she said when they got down on deck.

"Too much of this cold water and I will wrinkle up like a prune. Every winter I try to dive in Florida or the tropics. I would like to dive with you down there. Let me know if you are available," Larry said.

"Zhis sounds like something I would like," Lovisa said.

When they got to the gangway, she gave Larry the customary embrace and a kiss on the cheek. She did the same with Howard then she remained on deck while they went down the gangway. When they were on the wharf they turned and waved again then they walked landward. They had nearly reached the parking area when they saw a man carrying a seabag. He turned to get a better look at them. Larry glanced at him briefly. Even in the dock lights he recognized him immediately, but he went on like he didn't know him.

"Is that the guy you were talking about?" Howard asked after a minute.

"Old Mr. Bill! Mr. Bill!"

"I'd like to see his face when the Captain Thomas shoots him down," Howard said, chuckling.

"You took it pretty well. I was impressed," Larry stated.

Howard felt elated by that.

"You win some, you lose some. I was looking forward to do some more diving this summer. Maybe find some stuff worth keeping."

"Yeah, we gotta' find us something more than sharks and starfish," Larry said.

"It must be possible to dive in a wetsuit and an exposure suit. Frank was backing you up in that gear."

"Possible, but it's not the best gear for that. Hypothermia can be the greatest danger of all. The greater the depth, the greater the chance that some stupid little thing can get you killed," Larry explained.

"Brigitte must have been able to take it."

"On her first dive she started breathing like she was cold so I had her brought up immediately. You could be Arnold Schwarznegger, but you're no less subject to the problems than anybody else," Larry explained.

"What's the initial wash-out rate in the Navy?"

"By the time they get to the submarine tank, eighty percent or greater."

"Pheeew! Why is it so high?" Howard asked.

"Claustrophobia and not being able to see the surface usually causes them to panic. We would tell them what to expect so they would know, but most of them would become more anxious than if they didn't know. Fortunately this usually manifested itself right away so we were able to get them up without decompression problems."

"When I took Scuba lessons we started out with more than a dozen in the class, but only seven of us were there for the open water," Howard said.

"I can get in touch with some diving outfits I know of. Maybe we can find one that will give you a lot of bottom time," Larry said.

The next morning Larry was awakened by Shirley handing him the telephone.

"It's Howard," she said as he took the phone from her.

"Calling me this early! I hope the ocean is going to dry up in the next ten minutes," Larry said.

"Have you seen todays Mirror?" he asked.

"It's probably still a tree," Larry quipped.

"They did a follow-up article on the front page. Your picture was supposed to be top center but somebody put in a picture of Doreen Frobert, the cooking lady."

"Dumb bastards! They can't even do that right," Larry said.

"I know. Dad gave them four pictures of you. Let's sue them off the planet," Howard suggested.

"Let's call them dumbasses and let them try to sue us," Larry countered.

"I'll see you at the memorial service."

"Yeah, we'll see you there. Bye," Larry said then he disconnected and handed the phone to Shirley.

"FUBAR?" Shirley asked.

"Even for this place."

Larry picked up the neighbors newspaper and looked at it for a moment before setting it on their porch. Since he was dressed, he decided to take a little ride. When he got downtown, he parked Shirley's scooter in front of the library. As he took off his helmet, he saw a young man approaching him.

"Hello, I'm Ed Holt from the Morning Journal."

"So, we have the Morning Journal and the Morning Joke," Larry quipped.

"Oh good, you've seen the Mirror Enquirer," he said.

"I'm prettier than Doreen Frobert, but I can't cook for shit."

"I'm sure that their editor will print an apology for putting her picture in the follow-up article," he said

"He can apologize for being a stupid dip shit," Larry suggested.

"Would you like us to print that?"

"Sure, go ahead," Larry said.

"I understand that you refused a request by the Coast Guard to write a report of your activities during the dive."

"Yes."

"why?"

"I was there to dive, not write fricking reports," Larry replied.

"Do you always give people a hard time?"

"No, I usually just ignore them."

"Who did you talk to from Mirror?" Ed asked.

"A woman named Ferrare."

"Oh, Kate. Were you just as uncooperative?"

"No, less."

"Why?"

"I didn't feel like talking."

"Did she ask the same questions?"

No." "What did she ask?"

"If she could buy me lunch."

"What did you tell her?"

"No."

"I think we're just about done here."

"Good," Larry replied.

The reporter left and he went on his way.

Later that morning, Larry and Shirley attended the memorial service and the funeral for Hank. In the afternoon, he had previously arranged to meet Harry Brown in the same place as before.

"Welcome to our local hero."

"A genuine good Samaritan," Larry said.

My Aide, Tyrone McLeod, is here to take notes," he said as Larry entered.

A black man, about 6'4" and five or ten years younger than Larry, stood up when they entered.

"Tyrone, Larry," Brown said.

"Hello," Larry said as they shook hands then they sat down.

"I have familiarized Tyrone with our last conversation."

"Then I see no more reason to be here. I withheld nothing and I have nothing to add."

"I have received quite a bit of material from the Navy and from a couple police departments...."

"There is no reasons for me to go over any of that. I'm sure the documentation is complete. I did not withhold any information then either," Larry stated.

"Now let me finish, Chief. I have been doing these investigations for years and I have seldom run into a guy like you. I think I can trust you when you say that you are telling the truth. I saw the look of surprise when I mentioned that Joe and Luis were in that airplane. By your reaction, I think you didn't believe me, but I can forgive you for that. When Ellington showed you the FAA report, the names had been deleted, isn't that so?"

"Yes they were," Larry replied.

"I'm afraid that we have been withholding information from you. There was a third man and his luggage in that Arrow according to witnesses and the flight plan, but there was only Joe Cole and Luis in the airplane when it came up. Now you said that you did not remove anything from the aircraft. Do you still stick by that story?"

"Absolutely. Except for attaching the diving buoy to the propeller, I touched no other part of that aircraft," Larry insisted.

"That is very interesting. You are the most unlikely 'likely suspect' I have ever seen. Do you recall Joe Cole mentioning an association with anybody else?" Brown asked.

Larry thought about Melissa Macklin but he saw no reason to involve her and if the CIA already knew about his and Joe's activities in Alexander Bay then there was no reason to mention her.

"When the three of us were sitting on Luis' verandah, Joe left for a few minutes to use the head. Luis said 'Joe is a good friend of your intelligence chief Jones, no?' That is the only time he mentioned a name. I told him that I didn't know anything about that. In fact I don't know any intelligence chief, Jones or otherwise," Larry stated.

"Do you know what this was in reference to?" Brown asked.

"I thought he was talking about Joe being a mole for the treasury department in the Art smuggling operation in Florida and the casino skimming racket in Alexander Bay," Larry explained.

"Who, What?" Brown asked.

"According to Joe, he got a big payout for helping bust an art smuggling racket in Florida. He used that money to pay his debts. Then he got a big payout for the casino skimming racket in Alexander Bay. He used that money to buy a house in the Virgin Islands. I killed the bad guys for him and I only got the three thousand bucks that I already had," Larry said.

"Nothing about these operations was included in the material we received," Brown said.

"Well, the FBI was also in Alexander Bay if you wanna' touch base with them."

"Do you remember the agents you dealt with?"

"Tony Smith in the treasury and Paul Shaffner in the FBI," Larry replied.

Brown and McLeod wrote down some things.

"Is there anything else you can tell us?"

"I got the impression that after Joe had bought the house, he didn't have much money left. That had happened to him before so I wasn't really surprised by it," Larry added.

"Okay, good, that gives us some more people we can talk to," Harry said after a minute, adding-"I guess we're done here."

"One more thing," Larry said.

"What's that?" Brown asked

"I don't know what kind of man Luis was but Joe was a great shipmate and a genuine hero in the service. I want him to be buried as such and not dumped in some landfill," Larry said.

"I'll see that you get a notice of the funeral," Brown said.

"Have a productive day," Larry said as he shook hands with McLeod then he left.

Larry saw Tyrone in a diner a couple days later. He was surprised that he and Brown were still on the island. He was also surprised when he sat next to him.

"Hi guy, what's the good word?" Larry greeted him.

"I was doing some interesting reading about you," McLeod said.

"Pay no attention to that credit report," Larry quipped.

"Most people quit killing when they leave the service."

"Were you a cop in another life?" Larry asked without caring.

"I was a marine for twenty five years."

"How did you end up with the Spooks? Uh, no pun intended."

"I always stopped at the first place that doesn't say 'whites only'," he replied.

Larry wanted to ask him why he was on the island then.

"When my father enlisted in January of 1942, you wouldn't have been allowed in the Marines. Whites only in those days," Larry informed him.

"Marines are the greatest fighting men in the world," he declared.

"Yes indeed, you have Oswald, Whitman, Greenwood, all kinds of great marines here."

"All white boys. How about Ira Hayes?" You wanna' spit on him too?"

"He drank until he passed out and fell in a ditch and drowned in two inches of water. Typical behavior for a marine."

"I was in Beirut, at the aiport. I was decorated for that."

"For what, picking up bodies? I hate to disillusion you, Marine, but you were a target and not a hero."

"What do you mean by that?"

"Your commanders told you that you were heroes to cover the fact that they were negligent in barricading the airport so that a truck couldn't get through. It was the same attack they had used three times previously and your general couldn't pull his heads outta' his ass to see that. Because of that, I had to target them. I had to give it back to them tit for tat. I always operated on the principle of targeting them before they could target us. In the second place, Obama and the democrats are not only spitting on veterans, they're spitting on the whole damn country. Our constitution, our laws and our way of life, everything," Larry declared.

"I can see you're not color blind," Tyrone remarked.

"In grade school we had those milk cartons with the presidents on them. If you learned nothing else, you picked up that every one of them had an Anglo-Saxon or Gaelic name. You were supposed to learn to vote for the guy who sounded like a president. No Hunkies, no Polaks, no Wops. This jerk has a name that befits somebody in Gitmo."

"Oh yeah, the chief is always right," McLeod replied.

"I didn't need anybody fucking up when I was in the water. Joe Cole was one of the few guys I could depend on. He always came back for me and I always came back for him. Don't expect that in your outfit."

CHAPTER TEN

Later that afternoon, on a cabin cruiser, Tyrone checked in with his boss.

"The FAA report shows nothing unusual. Nothing wrong with the plane except its fuel tanks were nearly empty," Brown said as he handed the report to him.

McLeod looked at it for a few minutes.

"Their last radio transmission was a Willco with November1129 Charlie for landing at silver Lake," Tyrone observed.

"Not unusual. Eighty percent of airports have no ATC."

"With all these cellphones, the pilots get chatty with each other and stay off the air. Has anybody checked out Miss Susan McDonald? Tyrone asked.

"Her story is good. According to her, she knows no Larry Mayer."

"I can't believe that anyone who ever met him could forget him. I just talked to him at Fog Island."

"McDonald accounted for all the places she has been since birth. It doesn't look like she and Mayer have ever been at the same location at the same time. She claims that Mister Cole was a casual meeting. We may have to give her a poly."

"I would like to give Mayer a poly. I still don't believe his coincidence story."

"There's 51,000 people on this island. How did you end up sitting next to him," Brown asked rhetorically.

"It's just my lucky day, I guess."

"I'll fax these to Durwood. Do you know that he is being considered for Deputy Director?" Brown asked as he collected the paperwork.

Tyrone shook his head.

"Did you ever have any political aspirations?"

"In eleventh grade I was appointed Student Body President when the elected one moved. I never took so much abuse and was called so many names as I got in that job."

"Getting appointed is good. It saves you from doing all that campaigning. Smiling at some asshole that you would rather beat the shit out of," Brown said.

"They can keep their elected offices. I was reading in Mayer's service record that he knocked Ray Ronson right out of the ring while aboard the USS Ranger. Later on Ronson and his manager claimed that the fight never took place," McLeod said.

"I got a confirmation on that. Mayer knocked him over the ropes in twenty seconds. That part about rifle butting the army general is also accurate. That turned out to be a very successful operation so the president backed Mayer on that," Brown informed him.

"So, our Mr. Mayer is a heavy-handed old bird," McLeod remarked as he picked up a binder.

"Have you heard of the Honesto Court martial case?"

"Can't say that I have," McLeod replied.

"This Mexican Seaman Second Class gunned down three of his shipmates. He refuses to say anything until they get to Norfolk, then all he says is that he'll talk to Larry Mayer only. Mayer drives up from Jacksonville and talks to him. At the hearing, Mayer tells the JAG that the three were gang members, extortionists, drug dealers. He claims that Honesto did the government and the Navy a big favor. Honesto gets to finish his enlistment and gets an honorable discharge. Mayer really stuck his neck out for him. He hardly knew him," Brown explained.

"The only person he trusted in this world, Larry Mayer," McLeod remarked.

"According to the information he gave the FBI and the Secret Service in November, while he was in the Thousand Islands, he had a relationship with Karen Schachtler(twenty), Cynthia Morrow(twenty) and Jackie Dunlap(thirty two). Dunlap is the pilot for Melissa Macklin, who was the mole for the FBI. Melissa is also a hotel and casino owner and the richest person in Alexander Bay."

"Mister Mayer can ingratiate himself to the sweet and innocent and the well heeled, it seems," McLeod remarked.

"None of them would seem to be of interest except that Cynthia Morrow accompanied him to Florida where they hooked up with Cole, then in Puerto Rico where they may have crossed paths with Macklin and Dunlap then to the Virgin Islands where the three of them ran into Luis Valero," Brown concluded.

"Susan McDonald claims that she knew none of these people. She had only known Cole for two days and met Luis on the airplane, you concluded."

"That's correct. That's what I'm sending to the office."

"It's all happenstance. Just one big coincidence," McLeod said.

"If they don't like it, they can send another team," Brown said.

The next day Larry received a telegram informing him of the time and date of Joe's funeral. Since it was a military honor guard, he and Shirley would wear their old uniforms when they got there. He would be buried in Glendale Cemetery in Akron. Joe had a mother, who Larry had met and a brother, Eddy, that he hadn't met. Larry knew of no other family members. Brother Eddy called him the day before they left, two days before the funeral. There would be a showing and a memorial service in the morning then a military funeral in the afternoon. Normally Joe would be buried in dress blues with his medals. The flag given to Corinne,his mother, would also have his medals. Bonnie and Sunny had been contacted but Eddy hadn't heard if they were coming. He had no problem with them coming if they wanted to.

The day before the funeral, Larry and Shirley flew into Boston then took a commercial airline to Akron/Canton. Since Meghan was staying on the Cape, Beth picked them up at the airport and took them to Boston Mills. She met Beth's three children. Larry noticed that she looked happy to see children. Many of the women that he had known became upset to some degree when they saw his relationship with his children and grandchildren. Many of them had been the only child and they couldn't handle being part of a 'large' family. They all had supper there then his daughter and grandchildren left.

"The grandkiddies trashed the house," Larry said as he started cleaning up the mess.

"They're so darling. You let them run around the yard, squirt water on each other and wrestle on the floor. When I would stay with my grandparents, I had to wear a dress, say 'yes sir and yes mam. I couldn't play with other children. It was a bummer."

"They have to be children so when the time comes, they can be adults."

"You weren't kidding about calling them 'little bastards'. They don't seem to take any offense at that."

"It's boot camp all over again. They have to know when I'm talking to them," Larry said.

She handed him a stuffed toy and he tossed it in the toy box. She took him by the hand.

"I've been a bad girl," she said.

"You're telling me!" Larry exclaimed.

"I'm not doing anything to not get pregnant."

"That's okay, Meghan and Beth can take care of it," he quipped.

"I don't know if I can give daddy the three grandchildren he wants."

"Four at least."

"How do you get that number?"

"Two are just as easy to take care of as one. Then you gotta' have another one to get some use out of all that baby stuff you bought. As they grow up, two of them will try to gang up on the third so you have to have another one to put a stop to that," Larry explained.

"Is that the way it is?"

"Absolutely."

"You got this all figured out?"

"Yes, you'll have one. Women always follow their mother. Darla was one of five children so she had four. My mother was one of nine children so she had ten," Larry explained.

"This woman in Chile has fifty four children. Explain that?"

"With having all those children, she obviously didn't have time to go to school. Ignorance of basic math," he said.

That evening they met up Corinne and Eddy and Eddy's wife, Judy, at the funeral home.

"Larry, it's been such a long time," Corinne said as they hugged.

"I wish it could have been better circumstances," Larry said.

"This is Eddy and Eddy's wife, Judy," Corinne said.

"Hello, nice meeting you. This is Shirley Douglas from Nantucket."

"Did you know Joe?" Corinne asked.

"Yes, I was on ships with him several times," Shirley replied.

"You seem very nice. Poor Joe never had much luck with women I'm afraid."

"Have you heard anything from Bonnie or Sunny?" Larry asked.

"I'm afraid not. I got several letters from a lawyer that has been trying to contact him since last November. Since he has been found, his property will have to be settled, I suppose," Corinne said.

"If you and Eddy need help, let me know."

"I got my lawyer in contact with his lawyer. We'll decide the best way to handle this," Corinne said.

"Very wise," Larry said, adding-"Has anyone contacted you about expenses?"

"Yes, a fellow from the Veterans Administration said that he'll be buried with an honor guard. Joe's wish was that you perform the burial at sea ceremony. They're covering all expenses. He'll be kept under the canvas at all times. I'm afraid that his body was somewhat deteriorated," Eddy replied.

"Very good. Well, we'll see you tomorrow at eight," Larry said then they left. After they left the funeral home, they weren't aware that a Lincoln Towncar was following them. Larry drove to the Mall so Shirley could buy some make-up that she needed. Since she might take a while, he went to the bookstore. He was looking at an Ann Coulter book when he noticed two men in suits walking toward him. Automatically he fixed his sight on their hands and grabbed for his pepper spray with his left hand.

"Larry Mayer?" one of them asked.

"Who are you?" Larry asked since they obviously knew him.

"We are friends of Joe Cole," the other man said.

Larry knew they should have said "The late Joe Cole."

"You are here for the funeral?"

"In fact we are," the first one said.

"Well Mister Anonymous, you can get the fuck outta' here and stay the fuck away from me," Larry snapped.

They looked at each other then turned and walked away without saying a word. Larry knew that only ignorant street gangs will open fire in a mall. These guys were some sort of cops, he figured. A few minutes later Shirley came in and they left.

The next day there was a short memorial service for Joe before the viewing. There were at least five hundred people there. After Eddy and

Judy left with Shirley, Larry stood by the casket and looked at Joe wrapped up in sailcloth, through the glass panel.

"How did you fuck this up, old buddy?" he said softly.

"I wish I had known him when he was alive," Brown said, surprising him.

When Larry turned around, he saw Brown in a black three piece suit and an older man, similarly dressed. Larry thought that he should know him.

"You know Judge Advocate Marshall Lewis, of course."

They shook hands.

"Oh yes. That was quite a while ago," Larry said while smiling at him.

Actually that was a generic answer. He had to wing it until he could ascertain who he was.

"I haven't forgotten you. I busted you in that West Point prank," Marshall said.

"Unsuccessfully, because you got it wrong. The army guys were the pranksters. We caught them in the act and gave them an appropriate punishment. There have been no pranks at the football games since then," Larry stated.

"You stripped them of their uniforms and tied them up in sexual positions in a public place."

"The four plebes got the doggy style. The two upperclassmen got the sixty nine because they should have known better," Larry said.

"You and Cole were a disgrace to the uniform," Lewis snapped.

"I'm sure that Joe is laughing as much as I am," Larry replied.

Lewis just looked daggers at him and walked away.

"He's still a dip shit," Larry said.

"Nobody is perfect, I suppose."

"Have you come up with any answers?" Larry asked.

"I was going to ask you that."

"How about the other guy in the plane?"

"That guy was really a woman, Susan McDonald, twenty four, five-six, brunette, from Philadelphia. Does that ring a bell?"

Larry thought for a moment.

"Those are common names but I don't seem to remember her."

"She claims that she never heard of you either. She claims that she just met Joe the day before the flight. Everything she told us checks out"

"What's the forensics?"

"No carbon monoxide or anything else in the blood samples. The fuel tanks were nearly empty which indicates to the FAA that they ditched. They're ready to put it down as pilot error."

"No radio transmissions?"

"Only a Willco to another plane that landed at Silver Lake before they took off," Brown replied.

"That doesn't mean that it was working at the time of the crash."

"I was there when the FAA investigators put another battery in the plane and checked out the systems. The radio worked. Surprisingly a lot of things still functioned normally," Brown informed him.

Larry thought that with the deterioration of the bodies, any blood analysis would prove useless. Any carbon monoxide would have been reduced to carbon dioxide before now. In fact their blood would probably be unrecognizable.

"So the FAA hasn't found anything wrong with the airplane. So much for product liability insurance."

"We use the example of Japanese golfers having to buy hole-in -one insurance."

"That would be totally unnecessary for me, I assure you," Larry said.

"They also pay off for a double eagle."

"I've double bogeyed. Does that count?"

"Hmm, probably not."

"Punishing people for doing the best that they could possibly do. Those Japanese are inscrutable folk," Larry said.

"Chief Complaint!" A voice declared.

"Willy, you old son of a sea cook."

Willy was wearing a tailored three piece suit. Larry didn't remember him as a clothes horse.

"I always said that uniform went clear through you," Willy said as they shook hands.

"It's so my friends will recognize me," Larry quipped.

"You have friends?" Willy said.

"This may be the last one," Larry said, putting his hand on the coffin.

"Oh yeah...so his friends will recognize him. Yeah, Cole pulled that gag on me."

"I'm surprised you heard about this," Larry said before Willy could say anything else.

"I work in the Pentagon. I ran into the Defense Intelligence Chief at the coffee pot. He told me that Joe had died in an airplane accident."

"Oh yes, Joe mentioned Jones. That's his name, right?" Larry asked.

"Uh, I think so…"

"You don't use names in the Pentagon? You just say-Hi Chief, Hi General, Hi Admiral?" Larry quipped.

"It has been nice seeing you," Willy said then he turned and walked away.

"There's a person of interest for you, Harold McWilliam," Larry remarked.

"What's his big trick?" Brown asked.

"He'll spend a week trying to find a reason to not do a task that would take him five minutes to do," Larry said.

"It sounds like he didn't want to talk about the Defense Intelligence Chief."

"You can bet your ass that he's his boss and that he sent him here to look around. He's no intelligence gatherer though. You see how he ran when I acted like I was on to him."

"I can get in to see his boss if I want," Brown said.

"Good luck with that. Well looky here, it's Old Briny and Spiny. How's it going guy?"

"I'm surprised that you remembered me."

"You certainly have changed. Brandon Caldwell this is Harold Brown," Larry said and they shook hands.

"Briny here used to tend for me and Joe."

"I heard that Joe got divorced."

"He was married and divorced twice after he left the service," Larry informed him.

"Are you still married?"

"No, Darla died three years ago," Larry said.

"Where are you living now?"

"I'm back and forth between Boston Mills and Nantucket," Larry replied.

"I haven't been there since we were at the research station in Newport. Remember that?"

"Oh yeah, that was some fun times," Larry said, smiling.

"It was like Pearl. If you weren't careful, all your pay could be gone in a night."

"You were always careful, which is why you were my tender."

"You scared the hell outta' me. When I came on board in Lebanon, you were slapping the hell outta' out of Zimmer. You were pissed because Bernhart had him doing some other crap while you were down."

"I don't remember ever having to correct you," Larry said.

"Yeah, I got the idea right off. So, what's the philosophy for today?"

"Never take another man's lie into your mouth. Ninety five percent of the trouble in the world is because men are willing to do that."

"Example?"

"You see that Edwards guy got his aide to claim that he was the father of Reilly Hunter's baby. If you take a paycheck from somebody, you don't turn on them but you don't lie for them either," Larry stated.

"I found out that Joe lived next door to Scott Peterson in Modesto," Briny said.

"He golfed with him for a couple months. He claimed that Peterson would frequently try to cheat when adding up the score, so he quit playing with him."

"That sounds very wise. I heard that you're doing the burial service."

"Yes, that was Joe's idea."

"I heard that you found him. If you hadn't he would have already been buried at sea," Briny said.

"That is correct," Larry said.

"I think I'll skedaddle before somebody tries to sell me insurance," he quipped as he shook hands with Larry then he shook hands with Brown and left.

"So what's the joke about recognizing you?" Brown asked.

"You tell some seaman recruit that Rock Hudson was laid face down in his coffin. When they asked why, you tell them it is so his friends will recognize him. Some of those youngsters were pretty naïve."

"He was talking about Lebanon. I remember reading that you had a dozen Phalangist rebels on the run. They tried to grab Civilians for human shields, but you shot them anyway," Brown said.

"I shot three right off and they saw that the human shield thing wasn't working so they released the civilians and started running again. I shot all of them anyway."

"Nice guy! That was a police action."

"I never arrested anybody, I just killed them."

"The difference between a military and a police operation is that a military operation has an acceptable casualty rate while a police operation doesn't," Harry informed him.

"I must have been sleeping during that briefing. I carried out operations so they were successful. Getting your command shot up all to hell is usually not a successful operation."

"You obviously never saw 'King of the Kyber Rifles'. It doesn't bother the generals if the casualties are colonials."

"I say, good show! We don't have to pay them now," Larry quipped.

Larry saw Sunny with a tall unshaven, shaggy headed guy in blue jeans and a sweatshirt with cutoff sleeves. When she approached, he stayed behind.

"Hello there," Larry said.

She put out her arms and embraced him.

"Harold Brown, this is Suni Mei Zhou."

They shook hands.

"Sunny was Joe's second wife. Harold here was investigating the accident," Larry explained.

"I understand that Joe had some property in the Virgin Islands," Sunny said.

"I think he did. I'm sure he had an attorney. You can probably find out from Corinne or Eddy."

"I received a letter from an attorney around thanksgiving time. He was asking if I had seen Joe. I telephoned him and I told him that Joe may have died. He told me that a person has to be missing for a year before they can be declared legally dead."

"I'm sure that Harry here can get you a copy of the death certificate."

"Certainly Misses.."

"Cole."

"If you give me a mailing address and a phone number, I'll get that to you immediately."

Sunny pulled out a business card and handed it to him.

"This is very important. When we were married, I was the beneficiary of a life insurance policy on Joe," she said.

"Certainly, I can overnight it to you," Brown said.

"Yes, that will be acceptable, good-bye," she said then she turned and walked away.

"She didn't look too aggrieved. She didn't even look at him," Brown said.

"They were married for only two months. She left him two and a half years ago. If Joe could do it, he will have stopped that life insurance," Larry informed him.

"Larry Mayer, you've gotten even uglier," a voice declared.

Larry looked that way and saw a thin man in casual clothes. He was his height, had brown hair and he noticed that he was missing his four upper front teeth. Larry looked at him for a moment.

"Do I know you?" Larry asked.

"Randy Grier. I cooked at the Fry House."

"I'm sorry, I don't remember hardly anybody from those days. Did you know Joe Cole?"

"No, I don't," he said then he turned and walked away.

"He got put off awful fast," Brown observed.

"Probably one of those guys always mooching," Larry speculated.

At the grave, Larry and the other pall bearers placed the open bottomed casket on the framework. The people gathered around. Larry realized that it looked obtuse to be using the burial at sea ceremony.

"All hands, bury the dead," he called out.

The bugler blew the assembly while they stood at attention. After the assembly, he called out 'Parade rest'.

"Lord God, by the power of your word you stilled the chaos of the primeval seas. You made the raging waters of the flood subside and calmed the storm on the sea of Galilee. As we commit the body of our brother, Joseph Lauren Cole, to the deep, grant him peace and tranquility until that day when he and all that believe in you will be raised to the glory of a new life promised in the waters of baptism. We ask this through Christ, our lord. Amen."

"Attention," Larry called out as the body, wrapped in sail cloth, was lowered on the straps, into the vault below. All servicemen saluted. When the body was in the vault and the straps pulled up, Larry called out-

"Firing party, attention." The seven man firing party stood at attention.

"Ready." They shouldered their rifles.

"Fire."

"Fire."

"Fire."

The bugler played taps.

"Order arms," Larry called out.

A sailor handed him the encased flag and he handed it to Corinne.

"Please accept this flag on behalf of a grateful nation."

Instead of taking the flag, she embraced him.

"That was beautiful....I know he is happy now," she said softly.

Eddy took the flag from him.

"Joe had faith in one man in this world and that was you," his mother said.

"You are being too kind," Larry said.

"When I heard it was you, I knew that his faith was not wrong."

"Mom, we must see the other people," Eddy said.

"You have my phone number and address in Boston Mills. Let me know if I can do anything for you."

"Yes, I will," Corinne said before they turned to the other people waiting for them.

Shirley came over and joined him. Larry was glad because people like Brown wouldn't bother him with Shirley around. The graveyard workers were already there to remove the casket.

"That was a good job, Master Chief."

"Thank you, Flight Lieutenant. Let's try to sneak out," Larry suggested.

As they tried to walk around the crowd paying their respects, a man called to them.

A man about forty years old with a boy about nine or ten years old, looked at them.

"I'm Kevin Hartmann. I'm the son of Chief Chris Hartmann, a shipmate of yours." They shook hands.

"Oh my goodness, yes. He and I were both instructors at Jacksonville. How is he doing?" Larry asked.

"A couple years ago he was crippled in a diving accident. He has difficulty walking now."

"Oh, I'm sorry to hear that. This is Shirley Douglas."

"You were a flight Lieutenant?" he asked as they shook hands also.

"I flew Helos," Shirley replied.

"This my son, Doug."

"Glad to meet you, Doug," Larry said as they shook hands.

"My grandpa always says that you know everything," Douglas said.

"If I don't know it then Shirley here will probably know it," Larry said while smiling at him.

"Some people say that the world will end this year. Is that true?" he asked.

"No, the world will go on as it always has," Larry replied

"When will the world end?" he asked.

"In one billion years," Larry replied.

Doug looked at him quizzically.

"That's about twice as long as there has been life on this planet," Larry said, adding-"One thousand years times one thousand years times one thousand years."

"Oh, we're good then."

"Yes, the only thing you have to worry about is Obama and the democrats," Larry quipped.

"Mister Mayer is joking. It will be eight years before you can vote for president," Kevin said.

"Where does your father live?" Larry asked.

"Right now he is living in a trailer park outside of Las Vegas."

"Wait a moment," Larry said. He took out one of his former work business cards and wrote a phone number on it and handed it to Hartmann.

"Please let your father know that I'll be here for a couple days."

"Yes, certainly I will. It's nice meeting you," he said as they shook hands.

"Nice meeting you...and nice meeting you, Doug," Larry said as he shook hands with him.

"This Hartmann was a good friend of yours?" Shirley asked when they left.

"He was a great guy. One of those guys that was so good in everything he did that I felt I had to be better every day. I'm sure that you have met guys like that when flying."

"There was this instructor named Parker. He always wrote good reports about me. It would have killed me if I disappointed him in the slightest," Shirley said.

"I would say 'If all else fails' and he would say 'Naturally all else will fail. Ninety percent of people will fail you if you give them half a chance." He didn't like those kind of people diving with him. He chose me for the deep saturation dives and I wouldn't have done it with anybody else."

"How about Joe?"

"He said I was crazy to do those dives."

Eddy ran over to them before they could make it to their car.

"I'm sorry! Mother is feeling sick. Could one of you drive her home in my car?" he asked as he took out his keys.

"I have to return these flower holders. Could you take her, Shirley?" Larry asked.

"Certainly," Shirley said.

"I'll pick you up at Corinne's," Larry said.

"My car's over here," Eddy said as they waved good-bye to each other.

Larry placed the flower holders in the rack behind the old stone crypt. The man who called himself Randy Grier, came around the corner.

"I was telling you the truth. I was a cook at the Fry House."

"I don't doubt that you were. It's not something to lie about," Larry said.

"How's Darla?"

"She died three years ago."

"Oh, I'm sorry. She was always civil to me...Umm, my veterans benefits ran out six months ago. I had a bypass and a bowel section. You know that people won't hire you when you have surgical incisions from your neck down to your navel."

"The shit hit the fan, eh?" Larry remarked.

"I can't stand on the corner and hold a cardboard sign. I can't do that."

"Standing out in the weather is no good for you anyway." Larry said.

He took the one hundred and two dollars out of his shirt pocket and handed it to him.

"Thank you so much. I always knew that you were a great guy...Uh, I was in the parking lot looking for cigarettes and there was this guy in a red Mercedes. One of those convertible sports cars. He was talking about you on his cellphone. He was telling the guy at the other end, who you were talking to. I forgot to get the license number. I crawled away. I was afraid that he would see me."

"Okay, it's probably nothing. Just a bored cop," Larry said, adding-"You take it easy."

"I can eat tonight. Good-bye," he said and they shook hands.

CHAPTER ELEVEN

One week later

A woman and her twelve year old son and fifteen year old daughter came home to their Georgetown four bedroom colonial. When they came into the living room they found their husband/father in the recliner chair. There was a two inch hole in the top of his head and blood splattered all over the wall behind him. The woman called 911. It was 11:45 AM.

Larry was coming up the walkway when the phone rang. Somebody has to have a pressure activated switch hidden out here somewhere, he thought as he ran to the cottage. He opened the door and left it open as he ran to the phone.

"Hello."

"Chief, this is Harry Brown. Whatcha' been up to?"

"Staying out of trouble, Harry. What you been up to?"

"Oh, you know, saving humanity from death and destruction"

"That sounds like a big job. It's a good thing that you got Tyrone helping you," Larry quipped.

"Yes, that man is going places. I got some information for you. Are you alone?"

"Yes."

"No bugs on your phone except the ones we put there?"

"Check."

"We got some answers in the Joe Cole case. A man who works for another 'company' was found in his Georgetown home with a big hole in his head. Yep, he stuck the muzzle of his Gold Cup under his chin and pulled the trigger. Quite a sight for mama and the kiddies when they got home. Anyway, he sent a collection of 122 emails to the FBI. It seems that he didn't trust us"

"Imagine that?" Larry said.

"What I can tell you is that it was a 'false flag' operation. They were trying to wiggle out of it and cover their tracks when somebody in the 'company' pulled a high tech hit on Joe and Luis. It was totally unnecessary but somebody went ahead and did it. They thought that since the airplane went down way out in the ocean it would never be found. That's where you came in. You should see some of the emails about you. They thought that you had them pegged from the get-go. Bucko thought the whole thing was going to blow up in his face at any minute so he sent the emails and cashed his own chips."

"I don't remember any Bucko."

"I can't use his real name, of course. He was at Joe's funeral."

"There were five hundred people at Joe's funeral. At least three hundred were men," Larry stated.

"That's the way to narrow it down," he quipped, adding-"You'll hear about it eventually. Somebody blowing their brains out in their Georgetown mansion will always get out. It will just be made to look like it has no significance. Just a sad ending to a life that held so much promise."

"Hallmark can always use you," Larry quipped.

"You talk! I quote-'Joe always said to have food so people would come'. I never heard that in a eulogy."

"His unedited original draft said nooky. I can send you one if you like. So how about Bucko? Did he get a good send off?"

"I'm sure he did. He was a faithful servant of the people. He just fucked up."

"It seems to happen a lot since the Magic Negro came to town," Larry observed.

"Yes, quite. I have to be shoving off here. Keep doing those good deeds and pay those taxes."

"Will do, good-bye."

"Good-bye Chief."

Larry hung up the phone.

After supper, Shirley told him that she had things to do. Larry turned down he sound on the TV, reclined the chair and closed his eyes. A few minutes later he heard Shirley come into the room.

"I have your baby, Larry," she said.

"How did you get that?"

"The same way a woman always does!" she exclaimed.

"Oh yeah, what was I thinking. What do we do now?"

"Get married!"

"Good idea, let's get married. Where?"

"I'll make the arrangements. You just get yourself into a suit, guy," Shirley declared.

"A suit, I can do that. Where do I meet you?"